RISK IT ALL

risqué two

SCARLETT FINN

<u>Also by Scarlett Finn</u>

<u>GO NOVELS</u>
GO WITH IT
GO IT ALONE
GO ALL OUT
GO ALL IN
GO FULL CIRCLE

<u>MCDADE BROTHERS NOVELS</u>
ALL. ONLY.
ONLY YOURS

<u>WRECK & RUIN</u>
RUIN ME
RUIN HIM

<u>THE BRANDED SERIES</u>
BRANDED
SCARRED
MARKED

<u>EXILE</u>
HIDE & SEEK
KISS CHASE

<u>TO DIE FOR...</u>
TO DIE FOR TRUTH
TO DIE FOR HONOR
TO DIE FOR VIRTUE
TO DIE FOR DUTY
TO DIE FOR LOVE

<u>LOVE AGAINST THE ODDS STANDALONE COLLECTION</u>
SWEET SEAS
HEIR'S AFFAIR
RESCUED
MAESTRO'S MUSE
GETTING TRICKY
THIRTEEN
REMEMBER WHEN...
RELUCTANT SUSPICION
XY FACTOR

<u>NOTHING TO...</u>
NOTHING TO HIDE
NOTHING TO LOSE
NOTHING TO DECLARE
NOTHING TO US
NOTHING TO SAY
NOTHING TO YOU

<u>KINDRED SERIES</u>
RAVEN
SWALLOW
CUCKOO
SWIFT
FALCON
FINCH

<u>THE EXPLICIT SERIES</u>
EXPLICIT INSTRUCTION
EXPLICIT DETAIL
EXPLICIT MEMORY

<u>MISTAKE DUET</u>
MISTAKE ME NOT
SLEIGHT MISTAKE

<u>RISQUÉ & HARROW INTERTWINED</u>
TAKE A RISK
FIGHTING FATE
RISK IT ALL
FIGHTING BACK
GAME OF RISK

<u>LOST & FOUND</u>
LOST
FOUND

<u>THE FORBIDDEN NOVELS</u>
FORBIDDEN DESIRE
FORBIDDEN WANT
FORBIDDEN WISH
FORBIDDEN NEED

PROLOGUE

AS A KID, Brianna Wilcox struggled to make good choices. Perhaps because, back then, she left so many decisions up to her brother and now-ex-boyfriend. Their actions frequently got her embroiled in some mess that was nothing to do with her. That was supposed to change when she freed herself from both of them.

Growing up with junkie parents had been tough. Her brother, Gary, got her through the difficult times until at high school, Gary met Blaser Warner, and her life had changed forever.

After Blaser made his interest in her known, she hadn't put up much of a fight. Why would she? Hot in all the right ways; bad in all the others. For a teenager, the prize didn't get any more enticing. For months, they snuck around grabbing clandestine moments, worried what Gary would do when he found out they were together.

As luck would have it, they'd been discovered on a dark night when the rain was pouring, and the wind was howling. The weather, and rush of their own raging hormones, hid the sound of Gary's approach. He'd ripped open the back door of Blaser's truck and caught them semi-naked. Denying it was impossible.

The men fought, physically fought, which left her in tears and Gary needing stitches. Watching the two men she loved fighting tore her apart. In the months that followed, the feuding increased as had her internal conflict. She had really believed it would come down to a choice between the two men and she didn't want to make that choice.

Everything came to a head when Blaser discovered her secret. To get by after her parents took off, she'd started dancing in clubs for money. She loved the dancing but didn't always love the patrons, especially those who tried to touch or loitered with intent outside the club.

It didn't help that the only places willing to take her were the ones who turned a blind eye to her age. If management was happy to ignore the fact that she was only seventeen, they were also happy to feign ignorance when the men paid the dancers for intimate services.

Blaser caught her coming home from work one night. The second he registered her outfit, or lack of it, he flew off the handle, blaming Gary for their family's need. Once again, the men were at each other's throats.

A few days after, they'd called a truce and held a meeting… without her. The first she knew about them getting along was Blaser pulling up outside to drop Gary off. The men talked for a few minutes, then her brother came inside. That's when she got the story: Gary was boosting the cars, Blaser was chopping them. They were going to look after her and she would never have to work again.

It was horrifying. After that she did everything in her power to talk the two out of their illegal business venture. Nothing would stop them; the alliance remained. Eventually, the men became the best of friends again and they settled into life together. Blaser and Gary did what they needed to support their trio. But it was more than that. Both of them seemed to like the money and the street cred that came with their success.

Everything had muddled along for almost a decade until Blaser was arrested. She hadn't been present for the crime, but she had been present when the cops took him from her bed, cuffed him, and took him in. From there, he pled guilty and was sent to prison. She promised to wait for him until, a few weeks into his sentence, he called her into visiting and ended their relationship.

At the time, devastated, she tried to talk him out of it. He was adamant and went so far as to demand she get out of town, away from her brother and everyone in their lives. He told her to start over. And, not long later, that's exactly what she did.

Picking Jersey, she'd packed and left without telling a soul. She got a job and an apartment and for a long time, lived like any other Josie on the street, nothing special. Only she knew a part of her was missing.

Five years after the relationship was over, she did the unthinkable and emailed Blaser. Much to her surprise, he emailed back, and communication began to flow. They moved onto phone calls, and she was delighted to hear he had straightened himself out and owned two legitimate businesses.

After almost six months of emails and phone calls, they'd agreed to meet. Blaser was actually going to travel up to take her out for dinner. Bri was beyond caring if it was smart for them to open the can of worms again. The idea of seeing Blaser delighted her too much.

So there she was, in the restaurant where they'd agreed to meet. She had spent hours getting ready. Despite buying a new dress for the occasion, she tried on at least five others before settling on the new blue one that she'd spent too much money on.

Although she'd arrived at the restaurant early, it hadn't been her intention to be so premature. Their meeting place was in Atlantic City, which wasn't her neighborhood. To be sure of finding it in time, she'd chosen to leave her apartment earlier than was probably necessary. She didn't know how long the journey would take and didn't want to leave her date waiting.

Twenty minutes after the meeting time, he still hadn't appeared. Worry that maybe he had changed his mind was quickly shaken off, Blaser wasn't the type to leave her sitting there all night without any explanation.

Maybe something terrible had happened. She slid out

of the booth the maître d' had put her in and made her way outside into the cool evening air. Her jacket was still at the table, so if Blaser went into the restaurant another way he would assume she was just in the ladies' room or something.

Her clutch was just big enough for the essentials, so she found her phone quickly. Striding away from the traffic on the street, she walked down a service alley to get away from the noise and passing foot traffic. Bowing her head close to the phone, reading her contacts, she scrolled through looking for Blaser's number. She had just pressed send when something hot and moist closed over her mouth.

Confused terror fired adrenaline through her system when another two thick arms circled her waist and she was hoisted off the ground. Her phone skittered out of her grasp as she tried to wrench the hand away from her mouth and punch back. Flailing her legs did nothing because the man holding her waist lifted her off the ground and clamped her knees together against him. Before she could count how many assailants there were in total, she was tossed into a van. Metal grated on metal signaling the door had been closed, and screeching tires heralded movement.

Although she tried to get up from the cold metal floor, so dirty that grime smudged across her cheek, it was no good. A heavy foot landed on her ribcage and something that felt like rope was wound around her ankles and wrists. The man with his foot on her chest leaned down and stuck a strip of duct tape over her mouth.

Widening her eyes, she tried to scream at the sight of the mask concealing his face. Another masked man sat toward the back of the van; he must have been the one to bind her. Two of them were in the back with her, but with the top of her head squashed against the back base of the front seats, she couldn't see how many there were in total.

The man standing on her chest increased his pressure then moved his foot away to sit on a seat that folded down from the van wall. He whipped off his mask to show ice-blue eyes glistening above a confident smile.

"Don't you worry yourself, beautiful," he said. "I'm John, and I bet you're wondering what the fuck this is about."

She mumbled, unable to do more. Her attempts to force out a scream were burning the back of her throat. Makeup blurred in her eyes, streams of it ran in hot rivers down her temples, some dripping into the shells of her ears.

"You did nothing wrong, but a lot of girls I pick up for the boss done nothing wrong."

She couldn't ask questions, but a million of them zinged through her. This wasn't a standard street attack. The men hadn't mugged her; they hadn't groped her. They had grabbed her, bound her, and now she lay there in the back of this van helpless, on the road to God knew where.

"I work for a guy called Victor, does that mean anything to you?" She managed to shake her head, freeing more tears. "Doesn't surprise me, but see, someone you know did something to piss Victor off. And when people do that, he sends me out to pick up something valuable of theirs. You're valuable… you're valuable to a guy who is valuable to Victor."

How could she be associated with anyone connected to something like this? Her mind came up blank. Gary and Blaser were the only two people from her life involved in anything illegal. It had been years since she'd been a part of that world. Unless… could the fact she was talking to Blaser make her valuable to him in a way that might upset this Victor guy. She couldn't believe it. Blaser had promised he was legitimate. He was a business owner mending bridges with his brothers, a real respectable guy.

"What you come up with?" The guy bent lower. His grin made her recoil, she couldn't believe he was grinning. It wasn't like he enjoyed the moment, he seemed indifferent to his own words, yet his grin was smug. "I'll give you a clue," he said. She held her breath in anticipation, hoping she could put all this down to a misunderstanding. "Does the name Warner mean anything to you?" Her hope sank. "Ruger Warner?"

Shock struck her immobile. Ruger was Blaser's younger brother. He'd always been the secretive type, but not in an illegal activity type way. Yet there she was, bound and gagged because Blaser's little brother pissed off a crime boss. No misunderstanding. She knew Ruger, and he'd delivered her into something far more sinister than anything she, Blaser, or Gary had ever been a part of. How the hell would this end?

ONE

"YOU REALLY DON'T have to be nervous," Lyssa said to Bri, the patient on her couch. "I know that it's easy for me, as the therapist, to say that, but I promise you won't be judged here."

"Blaser seemed to think it was a good idea for me to talk to you," Bri said. "He keeps mentioning you in conversation and well, I want to get him off my back, that's why I came."

"It's a start," Lyssa said with a smile and put her pen on the table next to her armchair. "Why don't you tell me about your relationship with Blaser?"

"How much time do you have?" Bri asked, examining the rug on the floor between them.

The brunette doctor was confident and gregarious. Although her intrigue was subdued, Bri could feel Doctor Cutler's genuine desire to get to the root of the problem. Being in the unfamiliar space of the immaculate doctor's office, Bri wasn't sure what to expect, which made her nervous. One thing she could talk about without any fear was

Blaser Warner, the ex-boyfriend she'd once been in a relationship with for more than ten years.

"Blaser and my brother went to high school together, that's how we met," Bri said. "We started dating and kept on dating until Blaser went to prison."

"When he was twenty-eight?"

Bri nodded. "That was six and a half years ago. Almost as soon as he got there, he broke up with me. He called me into visiting and told me that was it, we were over."

"Had you ever broken up before?"

"Here and there, you know, for a few weeks, just over stupid things. But we were never with other people," Bri said, rubbing her pinkie finger while she tried to think of a way to even up the playing field in the intimidating situation. "You're going to marry Blaser's brother? Colt never liked me. But I guess he told you that."

"Colt doesn't know anything about my patients," Lyssa said. "And there's no reason to assume he needs to."

Blaser only knew Doctor Lyssa Cutler, the sex therapist, because she was engaged to Colt, Blaser's twin brother. Apparently, he had mentioned her trauma and Lyssa had offered to help. At first Bri was mad he'd brought up her shame with a stranger, but eventually had to admit Blaser only ever acted in her best interest. Offering up free therapy sessions with the woman soon to be his sister-in-law was his way of telling her it was okay to need help.

"Colt always thought Gary and I were the ones getting Blaser into trouble; that we were the reason for Blaser going to jail," Bri said. "I guess he was right. They ran a chop shop together, Blaser and Gary, they stole cars and sold them for parts. It all started when we were teenagers because Blaser wanted to support me. My parents had gone, leaving Gary and me alone."

"That must have been difficult for you."

"Gary looked after me, and Blaser did too. I was seventeen when my parents left town. After that it was just the three of us. Their crew grew over the years and then Mattie started to dabble in his own endeavors."

"Mattie Warner?" Lyssa asked, sitting back.

Bri looked up to see the doctor's narrowed eyes and she couldn't help but feel like a science project. "Yeah, Blaser's older cousin."

"I have never met him."

"You won't," Bri said, shaking her head. "Colt hates him. Colt was the hotshot cop with the criminal cousin, he hated to admit to anyone, but everyone in the precinct knew it."

"Let's keep our focus on you," Lyssa said, returning her clipboard from the side table to her lap. "You said that you and Blaser broke up six and a half years ago? How did you come to be in his life again now?"

"After he broke up with me, I moved to New Jersey to start a new life there. It was what he told me to do. Well not Jersey exactly, he said I deserved better and told me to get out there into the world to find it. So I went to Jersey and for the next five and a half years I tried to move on."

"But you didn't?"

"Blaser…" Bri said. Smiling, she squeezed her thighs together. "He's not a usual type of guy. He's powerful without being domineering and he's sweet though he'd never show anyone but me. He's not the type of guy a woman can just get over."

"You pined for him?"

"I did try to move on," Bri said, lifting her eyes to the doctor's. "I really did, I promise, I dated other guys, but… But I was too curious about where he was and if he'd moved on… so I emailed him."

"A year ago."

"About that, yes," Bri said. "We started talking on the phone and agreed to meet up."

"What happened on the night of that date is what brings you here to me, isn't it?"

"It didn't go to plan. I went to the restaurant, I was waiting in there, but Blaser was late. I went outside to call him and find out where he was."

"Can you tell me what happened?" Lyssa asked in an ever-patient voice.

"I'd rather not, you know… I'd rather not get into

that in our first session."

"Okay," Lyssa said. "That's completely fine and I'm glad that you were honest with me. It's important that you are honest. You can always tell me if you're uncomfortable with any subject, don't ever feel under pressure."

"Thanks. I mean, I'm sure I'll maybe get there… though I can't be sure, can I? But it is why I'm here, what happened that night is why I'm here."

"I told Blaser that I would help you process that trauma and move on, that's why he wanted you to come to me," Lyssa said to Bri. "But we can't expect it all to happen in one session."

"No, I suppose not. I've been carrying my experience from last year with me since then. After it, I… I didn't get in touch with Blaser. I shut myself off and stayed in Jersey. I didn't want anything to do with anyone."

"That's understandable."

"But my brother, Gary, was so worried about me, it was him that… He persuaded me to come home. He thought it was a good idea that I try to build a life for myself here, closer to home and family."

"That's a very good suggestion. Gary must care for you a great deal."

"He does."

Her brother wasn't always the best at showing his emotions and they often manifested themselves in the wrong way. But Gary was her brother and the only family that she had left. Other than knowing her father was in prison, she had no other connection to relatives. Her mother had been AWOL ever since her father went inside.

"So you came back here?"

"Three months ago," Bri said. "So many things have changed… but some things are just the same."

"You mean Blaser?"

"Yeah," Bri said. "I'm staying with a friend, at least I was until she took off ten days ago. But I'm still living in her apartment. I didn't want to stay with Gary and get sucked into his world again. I wanted to still be independent. It would be too easy to rely on him to do everything for me."

"That's very sensible."

"A few weeks ago, Blaser showed up at Erika's door," Bri said. Her faded smile returned when she replayed that night. After Erika answered the door and called her over, the vision of Blaser's concerned scowl poured a warmth of familiarity into her. "We talked."

"And you've been seeing each other since?"

"Not like that, not like seeing each other," Bri said, certain she didn't want Lyssa to get the wrong idea and pass those ideas on to her fiancé. "He's come over a couple of times and we've talked. We talk on the phone. When Gary was arrested a couple of weeks ago, Blaser came straight to me, you know? He didn't even care that I whaled on him for what happened between the two of them. He just… held me… You're probably one of the few people who can understand what it's like to be held by a man like Blaser. You're marrying his twin."

"When things are going wrong in my life, if I panic or I'm scared, there's only one place that makes me feel better."

"Right," Bri agreed, thrilled that someone else could understand it. "They just make you feel like no matter what it's going to be okay. That as long as they are there, and they can hold you…"

Her elation began to drain.

She didn't notice the silence between her and Lyssa at first and couldn't have verbalized the visions playing through her mind if she wanted to. All she could comprehend were the darts of ice meeting her skin as she considered the last time she'd thought like that.

"Maybe we should call time for today," Lyssa said. "We just met this evening, and you weren't expecting a full session. Would you like to call it quits or carry-on, Brianna?"

Snapping out of her enveloping trance, she shook her head. "No, I should probably go. I have some errands to run anyway."

Lyssa stood up and reached for her hand. Bri bounced up off the couch.

"I'm really grateful that you chose to come here," Lyssa said.

"I'm not sure you could say I chose it," Bri said, trying to keep things light. "Since Gary went to jail, since you and Colt got engaged… Well, Blaser raves about you. It was very generous of you to offer your services."

"Did you tell him that you were coming?"

"Blaser? No," Bri said. "I wasn't sure I was coming myself. I just… I felt awkward using the phone and I wanted to check you out for myself I guess."

"I'm glad you did," Lyssa said. "I know this is off the books, but would you like to make a follow-up appointment? I would like to continue working with you… there's no harm in making the appointment, you can always cancel."

Although reluctant to formalize the arrangement, she didn't find it easy to say no. She'd never been the most assertive person. Perhaps that flaw stemmed from her history with Blaser and Gary. If there was a situation in which someone had to be told no, one of them always stepped in. It wasn't a skill she had ever learned.

Still, she made an official appointment believing she could cancel it if necessary. She didn't want to chicken out. Dealing with her trauma, processing it, was the only way to move forward.

The idea had been to come get a lay of the land, check out the doctor, and make an appointment in person. Given it was later in the day, she expected the doctor to be finished with patients. Except as soon as Lyssa answered the large front door of her townhouse, and Bri identified herself, the doctor had brought her inside, which was how they got talking.

After saying goodbye to Lyssa and getting out onto the street, she felt strangely liberated. Therapy, she'd assumed, would leave her feeling exposed and used. Instead, she was pleased to have taken another step toward recovery.

Other than picking up something for dinner, she didn't really have any errands to run. As part of her own personal therapy plan, she bought a sandwich and went to the park to eat it. Throughout the last year, teaching herself to enjoy being outside again was tough. At first, every shadow and concealed corner seemed sinister. She had been jumpy and unwilling to turn her back to any open spaces.

A year after the event, she was much better at being outside in the open. She didn't want to be complacent about that ease and was always careful about maintaining her schedule. So she ate her sandwich and watched a couple of squirrels in a tree before starting the long walk home.

Erika's apartment, where she was staying, was more than an hour's walk from Lyssa's house. Not that she minded the exercise. With evening encroaching, getting home meant getting to bed. All she had to do was get there and then she could relax.

The moment she got to her floor, that dream evaporated. The apartment door was open. Creeping forward, she peeked in at the disaster area that was supposed to be her home. The whole place had been trashed.

Picking her way through the mess, she was standing dumbfounded when the door flew further open and banged off the wall. Startled, she pounced back and almost fell into the chaos before registering the sight of Mr. Lieberman, the apartment landlord.

"You're gonna get your shit and get the hell out, today!"

"No. No! I'm sorry, Mr. Lieberman. I'll have it all fixed and cleaned up. I promise that—"

"No, no more of your promises, Brianna Wilcox! You are trouble! I want you out!"

Brianna watched the short, stocky landlord pivot and steam out of the apartment she'd been sharing with Erika for three months. For all the drama swirling around her at the moment, the only mistake that she'd made herself was believing Erika had cleaned up her act.

Erika's boyfriend had taken off six weeks ago, leaving a great big mess of trouble trying to find him; one that she and Erika had been left to deal with. Trouble, Brianna thought looking around the trashed two-bedroom apartment. Clothes were scattered everywhere, furniture was turned over, crockery broken. Yes, the place looked like trouble had rocked up, flashed its dashing smile, and strolled straight back into her life.

She used to court trouble, to seek it out. Her brother worked on the fringes of legality, so she was no stranger to cops. And Blaser… he was a bad boy straight out of every girl's wet dream.

Bending to pick up a chair, she scanned the riot of objects scattered all over. Tidying up was likely to take the rest of the night. She could get it done but doubted it would change Mr. Lieberman's mind about letting her stay. Erika had taken off ten days ago to get away from her boyfriend's trouble. Being that Erika was the only one on the lease, Brianna shouldn't have stayed after that.

The landlord had turned a blind eye to her staying in the first place. Bri had used her Bambi act and persuaded him she was really in dire straits. She hated to act pathetic and hated to ask for favors, but she hadn't expected to stay for long. Since Erika had left ten days ago neither Bri nor the landlord had voiced the obvious fact that she was living there alone and illegally.

Glancing at the door, she speculated as to how long it would take Rafe and his cronies to show up again. Rafe was the dealer looking for Erika and her boyfriend. His squad would delight in doing this kind of work. She couldn't even kid herself that staying there would be safe. Whoever had done this job for Rafe kicked in the door to gain entry. Her only choice was to get her stuff and get out.

As much as she hated running away from responsibility, and the mess technically was her responsibility, she was the last man standing on one side of a war she hadn't been around to start. The abode was hardly the Ritz. Erika and her boyfriend had long ago destroyed or sold anything decent in the apartment. Upkeep had been neglected too, so it struggled to call itself watertight. The state of the apartment hadn't bothered her, she'd only come back to town on the pleadings of her brother.

Gary had told her to stay with him, he'd practically begged. But being sucked back into living like her brother, paycheck to paycheck or dabbling in illegality, wasn't a positive forward step. Staying with Erika in the hope of maintaining her independence hadn't exactly worked out.

Being back home had its disadvantages and advantages, the biggest example of both presented itself when Blaser came knocking on her door. Erika had warned off Bri's ex when he showed up unannounced. But it didn't matter what Erika said. Very little would sway Blaser Warner once he'd made up his mind about something.

Gathering up some clothes, and what she could find of her other possessions, Brianna tidied as she went along. The suitcase that she'd originally brought was broken, but she managed with a duffel bag and large tote. Erika and her boyfriend were gone. They weren't coming back to chase old luggage.

She was just about ready to leave but slowed in her collecting. What was the plan? Where would she go? Her brother was the only person she'd relied on growing up. Any so-called friends in the area wouldn't be any safer than Erika.

Gary wasn't an option anyway. He was doing his own time in jail, awaiting trial because they couldn't afford bail and no bondsman would stand up for him. Hooking the strap of the tote over her shoulder, she let her eyes drift to the window. Only one other person in the world loved her as much as Gary did. One person whom, from everything she'd heard, had gotten his act together.

Just like her, Blaser wasn't a part of that world they came from anymore. He would never get her involved in anything criminal or abandon her if things got rough. None of that meant Blaser wasn't trouble. Blaser was the kind of trouble a girl could never tell her mother about, at least he used to be.

She could still remember hearing the words as he broke up with her in that cavernous prison space. The moment the syllables hit her ears she'd gone numb, her ears rang. In truth, they were still ringing six and a half years later.

Except she was stuck, with little money and little choice, she had to risk opening that door again. She would just have to figure out how to keep him on the other side of her threshold because if he came inside… all hell would break loose.

TWO

"WANT ME TO LOCK UP?"

"No," Blaser said, straightening a Risqué emblazoned glass on the shelf behind the bar. "You get home to that gorgeous wife of yours."

"She's pissed about some shit," Dax said, resting a fist on the other side of the bar. "She'll have waited up just to give me earache when I get home."

"Way I hear it, the fight is sorta foreplay for you two."

Dax's usually clear expression became smug. "That's definitely the truth. She's a minx, everything is foreplay to her. I'm never sure if she's going to jump me or kill me."

"Sounds perfect."

"As close as you'll get," Dax said, opening his hand to push away from the bar. "See you tomorrow."

Blaser listened to his newest security man exit through the front of the building then went through his usual checks. Everything was where it was supposed to be. Lights were off. Check. Check.

Two weeks ago, Dax showed up shouting the odds, making sure every guy knew Ivy was off-limits. His new desk girl at Warner Autos, Ivy, was hot, maybe under other circumstances he would've made a play. But that kind of casual encounter held no interest for him.

Womanizing wasn't his way, never had been. He'd spent most of his life with one woman. The woman he set free when he went to prison. That was the final straw. Breaking up with her, breaking her heart, was the most difficult thing he'd ever done in his life. He didn't doubt being crazy in love with her, even as he said the words that severed her from his life. Selfishly, he'd wanted to keep her, but the truth was, he'd made her cry too many times. Back then, at twenty-eight, he was supposed to be getting his act together, not losing his shit. So he'd called her into visiting and ended it. Six and a half years later, and he still thought about her every day.

Shaking off his fleeting thoughts of Brianna, he swept up his leather jacket, stuck his arms in the sleeves and went around all the exits to ensure they were locked.

Risqué was a strip club. A place he'd dreamed of owning since he was a kid. When they were an item, Brianna went along with his dream. Together, they'd fantasize about what building their own business would be like. They even went so far as to name it and talk décor.

She liked the idea of having a high-class place where men could enjoy beautiful women. Her own experience with strip clubs was those of the lowest sort, so they'd always promised to stick to the rules when they owned their own place. It was that decision that prompted his rule of not hiring anyone under the age of twenty-five.

Risqué was legit. The dancers could hold their own, no one was taken advantage of or exploited. The patrons were happy with the display of flesh; at the end of the day that was all that mattered to them.

At one time, Brianna had dreams of Julliard and greatness, but he hadn't been able to deliver those dreams for her. After her parents took off and she started stripping, Blaser had sought out Gary, Bri's brother, blaming him for Bri needing to go out there and sell her body to support herself. Turned out Gary had been in the dark too. They ended up talking and making a plan to look after her. It wasn't long after that he stole his first car, then it became habit.

He knew it was illegal and knew that his parents would be disappointed if they found out about the chop shop he ran with Gary. Back then, he hadn't cared. It was about keeping Bri safe and making sure she never had to sell any part of herself to anyone just to get by.

Prison put a stop to his criminal ways. He had broken up with Bri before coming to the conclusion he could do better. Once he did, he cut all ties with his previous associates and decided to go straight. On leaving prison, he bought Risqué with the financial help of his brothers, who backed him on the proviso he kept his nose clean. It had taken a lot of hard work to get himself to where he was, and he had no intention of putting all that to waste by sliding back into what so many considered an easier life.

Buying Warner Autos happened at the same time he left prison. He got it at a discount from his cousin because he promised to manage Mattie's apartment block right next door. So with two businesses of his own, and shared responsibility of managing Mattie's apartment block, Blaser was a busy guy. Gus, Mattie's brother and another Warner cousin, managed the lion's share of the work at the apartment complex. Blaser just picked up the slack.

Risqué had become his life. He hired men to take care of things at Warner Autos and with Ivy answering phones, ordering parts, and doing paperwork, he had less to do with the garage, meaning he could devote his time to Risqué.

Content the club was secure, he exited through the rear employee door and locked it up too. He zipped his leather jacket, dug his hands into his pockets and began to mentally prepare the following day's to-do list as he trudged down the alley. Two paces beyond the dumpster, he heard a sharp inhale that made him pause.

"Quiet, you fucking 'ho," a low male voice grumbled.

Blaser glimpsed the movement of a shadow further down the alley to his left. Peering closer, all he could make out was the shape of a large guy, dressed in dark clothes. The shadowy guy raised his arm, there was a slap and then a female exclamation of pain before a body collapsed to the ground between the shadowy guy and the club wall.

"Rafe wants you taught about disrespect," the shadow snarled and dropped down out of view behind another dumpster.

Striding over to see what was going on, the scuffling sounds got louder the nearer he got and were soon joined by muffled female objections. More definition grew in the shadow man who was sprawled on top of someone, all he could make out were naked female arms and legs beneath.

"Hey!" Blaser said, storming over to haul the shadow up from the ground by the back of his neck.

The guy swore and lashed out to free himself, then he spun around to take a swing. Blocking the sloppy move was easy, as was landing a punch of his own. The shadow staggered back, giving him his first real chance of getting a physical description. Blond hair, angry eyes, and a scar intersecting the perpetrator's brow. Bloody scratches on his neck and face joined the blood now seeping from his lip. Obviously, the punch did its job.

Widening his stance, ready to brawl, if necessary, the blond male shadow spun around and bolted off. Giving chase briefly entered his mind as an option, but in that area, there was no guarantees who might be connected to who. Drugs were rife, prostitution and gangs too, it was a shady part of town. Even if he caught up with the guy, he wouldn't call the cops, that just wasn't how things went down and he wouldn't risk trouble visiting the club.

When the attacker vanished out the end of the alley, he turned his attention to the woman on the ground and immediately wished he'd done more than just split the perp's lip. At five-five, with streaks of blonde in mousy brown hair, Blaser knew the woman sitting on the cold asphalt outside his club. She kept her face down, giving him a view of the jagged parting in her hair. Her reluctance to lift her attention only betrayed she recognized him too.

"What I should do is ask if you're okay and take you to hospital," he said, putting his hands on his hips, still fixated on the woman sprawled on the asphalt. "What I'm actually going to do is ask if you're fucking insane."

She twisted her legs to look at a scrape on her calf

then lifted her rear from the ground to wriggle her skirt down. Her hand rose, indicating she wanted help up, so he took it and pulled her to her feet.

"Thanks," she said, smoothing the skirt that barely covered her ass.

After enjoying the flash of her midriff, his focus carried on up to her breasts, covered by a red halter top. Man, she was always hot. Every damn minute.

"What are you doing here, Bri?" he asked while reminding himself she was no longer his to scoop up off the ground and into his arms.

"I need your help," she said.

Tossing her hair back, she revealed the bruising on her cheek, the blood on her chin and the fullest, softest lips he'd ever known. She still didn't look at him, she twisted her body to examine a cut on the back of her upper arm: doing everything she could to put off meeting his eyes.

"You don't need my help," he said. Being near her again was surreal. He still hadn't figured out how to act around her now their relationship wasn't sexual, as it always had been before. "You never need my help. Does Gary know you're here?"

That question changed her mood, and she chose that moment to blink her long-lashed eyes at him. "Blaser," she said. "You know my brother is in jail, exactly where you put him."

"I didn't put anyone in jail," Blaser said. "Your brother mouthed off to an undercover cop, that's how he got himself in the slammer this time. Let's not kid ourselves that Gary is an upstanding member of society. He had this coming."

"You don't know everything, Love. You don't know what's going on or why I'm here."

"Don't call me that," he said, backing away, taking his hand out of hers. If she opened those floodgates and got him thinking this was just like the old days, he didn't trust himself to act like an ex without full privileges should. "And don't do that…" He lifted his hand toward her face then thought better of touching her again. "Thing."

Her step in his direction only made him take another backwards. "What thing?"

He ignored the question because she knew the answer; she knew exactly what she could do to him with a flutter of those lashes.

"What are you doing behind my club at three in the morning?" he asked. "Who was that fucker? What did he want?"

Bri took in a short breath and panted it out. "It's a long story, I was waiting. I didn't want to come in because… I didn't know if Colt would be there. I thought I would catch you out here, and we could talk."

"What do you want to talk about at three in the morning?"

"I need a job."

"You need a job?"

"I need money," she said. "So yeah, I need a job."

"What kind of job do you think I've got for you?" he asked, sorry his first thought took his eyes to her legs.

"I don't screw people for money," she said, folding her arms under those pert little tits that he remembered too well. "That's your department."

And the spite in her tone was enough to cool his desire. "Oh, ho," he said, exhaling his own frustration and turning on his heels to begin walking away. "I'm not having this fight with you, Dollface. It's late and I've had a long day."

"You've always had a long day," she said, snatching something from the ground then scurrying along at his side. "You've always been a workaholic, even since before you actually had a legit job."

Brianna and he had a history that was Shakespeare meets Tarantino. As many tragic episodes as there were comedic ones, they'd seen bloodshed together, been at drug crazed parties, had wild sex in crazy locations, and been arrested together.

The criminal underworld was his stomping ground when he hung with his own team. At the head of that team, at Blase's side, was Brianna's older brother Gary, his once upon a time best friend. All that changed when Blaser went to prison.

"That's a different fight," Blaser said, striding out of the alley to head towards home. "Can you pick one fight and stick with it? I'm not in the mood to flip back and forth between them. I'm not sure I'd be able to keep up."

"You saw what that guy did to me, Blase, what he was going to do to me. You stopped to help me because you didn't want him to hurt me."

"I didn't know it was you."

"Are you saying if you had, you wouldn't have helped me?"

He stopped, struck at the core by that implication. "If I had known it was you, I would've gone back into the club for my gun."

Protecting her was the first goal he'd ever set himself.

"That's because you love me."

Her smile begat his. As much as she was teasing, trying to win him over, her declaration just might be true. "How much money do you need?"

"No," she said, losing her smile and shaking her head.

The bag slung over her body shifted. She pushed it away from her hip to rest it on her back. It was then he noticed she was carrying another bag over her shoulder. Two bags might not be much, but he took the larger of the two from across her body and lengthened the strap to fling it over his own torso.

"No?" he asked.

"I will only let you give me money if I earn it. You know how I feel about something for nothing."

As far as he knew, Bri had never owed anyone a real debt in her life. "I'll call it in later when I need something," he said, knowing it was unlikely he ever would.

"By which time, I might be married with kids. I don't think my husband will like the idea of an ex-boyfriend calling me up and demanding sex."

"Since when do you make me pay for sex," he said. "I thought all I had to do was ask."

"Those days are long gone, and you know it," she said, then lowered her lashes. "I don't do sex anymore."

Brushing a finger down her cheek, he thought about all the times they'd been together, and how they'd been torn apart. "I know," he said, with a half-smile.

"I heard that Ruger left town."

Changing the subject was her way of retreating from an awkward topic. No matter how many times he tried to bring up the incident from a year ago, she always closed the door in his face.

"Again," Blaser said, continuing his walk with her at his side. "He'll be back eventually, he always is."

"I heard he moved a woman into his apartment."

"Yeah," Blaser said. "Sort of."

"Ruger the cohabiter, who would've thought… I never figured out what I did to that guy to make him hate me so much."

"He doesn't hate you," Blaser said. His younger brother didn't trust Bri and made no secret about it. Colt, Blaser's twin, didn't trust her either. At least he made his reasons clear; Colt thought Bri was trouble. Full stop. "And Suzette isn't his girlfriend, she's Lyssa's best friend."

"Lyssa? Doctor Cutler?"

"Yeah, you know, Colt's fiancée? Suzette needed a place to stay, and Ruger was leaving town, so he said she could use his place."

"I thought he had a trillion secrets."

"He does," Blaser said. "But I don't think he keeps them all in his apartment."

"I can't believe Colt is really getting hitched."

"He says so, he just moved into her townhouse this week," Blaser said. "Lyssa's nice, she's a doctor, a therapist, you know that… I've told you that already, a bunch of times. She said if you ever wanted to talk or, you know, or we wanted to talk together that—"

Brianna stopped. "You never told me why you told her, about what happened to me."

Turning to see the curious vulnerability spread across her face, guilt seeped into him. When he first brought up Bri talking to a doctor, she'd been horrified that he'd shared her secret. Now she seemed more accepting. He hoped that was a sign she was ready to move on from the trauma.

"I didn't give her the details, just… Don't you think it's time you talk about what happened to you?"

"I talked," she said. He recognized defensive hackles firing from her eyes. "I talked to cops and lawyers and doctors. I talked to them all. I talked and I talked. This is something that happened to me, and I don't like the idea you think I'm broken because of it. Why can't you just forget it? Forget you know and think of me like you used to."

"You haven't forgotten it. You said it yourself, you haven't had sex since it happened, have you?"

"I get along just fine without sex, Blaser… Sex isn't everything. A person can live a long and happy life without ever—oh to hell with you, I don't even know why I came here. I should've listened to Gary."

She spun around, but he snagged her arm and brought her back to him. Bri wasn't usually so short tempered. The strong reaction betrayed she hadn't dealt with issues from her past that desperately needed to be dealt with.

"I'm sorry," he said. "I shouldn't have brought it up, not out here like this."

"You didn't say you shouldn't have brought it up at all, which means you're not finished harassing me about it."

"I don't think I'll ever be finished harassing you about anything," he said, managing a smile, silently praying she would relax and forgive him.

Fingering a rip on the strap of her top, she moved her eyes away from his. She was practically naked in the revealing outfit. He couldn't handle seeing that much of her skin without his body reacting. Unzipping his jacket, he wrangled it from under the bag strap and draped it around her. She stumbled back, blinking up at him with round eyes.

He held his hands up to show he had no intention of hurting her. "You shouldn't be out like that. You'll give guys ideas."

"Guys like you?"

Being up close to her again, he wished he didn't have a rule against messing around with subordinates. But he was brought back to considering her original request because he couldn't act on the impulses he had around her, not anymore.

"I'll let you wait tables."

"If you let me dance, I'll make more money," she said, but he shook his head. "I can work in the garage for you too, just like I used to. I can answer phones and do your inventory and—"

"I've got a new girl," he said.

Back in the day, Bri would come to Warner's Autos when it was a chop shop and do their admin. Things were different now that he was legitimate.

"You replaced me?" she asked.

Her mock indignation was enough to make him smile. Something she'd always had a knack for, making him smile even when others failed.

"I've replaced you a couple of times, but the girls never seem to stick around for long. They're intimidated by the guys, or they date them, and things get awkward."

"So if I hang around long enough, your new girl will quit, and I can take over again."

"I don't think Ivy is the type to be easily intimidated," Blaser said.

"Sounds like you like her. Is she pretty?"

"Jealousy?" he said and had to laugh because Bri had never been the jealous type.

Never in all the years they were together did she even accuse him of so much as looking at another woman. That might have been because he never did. Bri kept him enraptured; he'd been besotted since they were teenagers. Looking at her, he didn't think that enchantment had ever gone away.

"I can be jealous of other women sharing your bed," she said, toying with his pinkie finger at his side.

She always fiddled with his digits when flirting with him or playing coy. He had never seen her do it with another soul, but she was entitled to his body in a unique way.

"You could be, but she's not sharing my bed. Her husband works security for me at the club."

"She's married? What's her husband like?"

"I haven't figured him out yet," Blaser said,

narrowing his eyes as he once again considered Dax Harrow's story. "So far he's doing his job and that's all that I care about, the rest isn't my business."

"You're too trusting," she said. "You hire people that no one else would touch."

She still wouldn't look at him, so he took the opportunity to scope out the figure he still dreamed about at night. "It doesn't mean I trust them. I know how to handle things if they go wrong."

"I know you do," she whispered and clicked her nail under his.

She was stronger than she gave herself credit for, which was good because Risqué didn't employ many wallflowers, meaning he was used to being around women with gumption in spades. Risqué women had to be tough enough to deal with wandering hands and savvy enough to retort to mouthy patrons without causing an altercation.

"Thank you for stopping in the alley and helping me out," she said, gratitude was another way of repaying debts.

Sometimes she wasn't strong enough to save herself. In the times he'd done it for her, she had always been generous with her appreciation afterwards.

When he resumed walking, he was happy she stayed at his side. "Who was the guy?"

"He works for a guy called Rafe. I didn't realize he was following me. I was coming to the club to ask you for a job, I thought it was best to talk to you outside, so I waited. Rafe will be pissed you stepped in, but he's not going to start a war with your family. I don't think that he's that dumb."

"We're not the mafia," he said. "My family can deal with shit. We've been dealing with lowlifes and scumbags for years. Do you need help with this Rafe guy?"

She exhaled what sounded like a laugh and slipped her arms into his jacket sleeves. "I wouldn't even know where to start."

"At the beginning," he said.

They kept walking and turned away from the main drag to head for his building.

"I saw Crystal last week," Brianna said. He didn't

think that was the beginning of an explanation for what was going on with Rafe. "She practically took my head off."

Crystal was the head dancer in Risqué and had worked there since day one. She had helped him design the uniforms and come up with the ground rules. She was probably his best friend in the world, after his two brothers. Though there had always been some distance there, his path through life hadn't been as kosher as theirs.

"What for?"

"She heard that we... that we'd been seeing each other."

"No one was happy about that," he said. "Ruger and Colt have been giving me shit for getting involved again. I still can't believe that Gary called in a raid at the club and showed up to cause shit with the girls. I think he'd be happier if I backed off quietly."

"I was surprised you showed up at Erika's like you did."

"I'm surprised that you let me in," he said.

Bri slid an arm through his and folded her arms, holding herself close to him. "I miss you sometimes. I mean I know we can never go back..."

"No," he said. Just talking to her again had both of his brothers raising the DEFCON level and Gary was on the offensive. If they ever thought about getting physical with each other, he dreaded to think how it would turn out. "Your family wouldn't appreciate it."

"Neither would yours," she said.

His family was huge and spread into most areas and vocations of life. Brianna's family consisted of her brother who was presently in jail.

"Crystal told me I would stay away if I knew what was good for me."

"But you're here."

"Gary's in jail and I've been kicked out of Erika's apartment. I need to get a job and to start supporting myself again. I need money, and the quickest way to get it is to dance for it. Your club is one of the few I'd trust to feel safe in."

"Tell me more about the guy," he said, needing to

know what trouble she brought with her.

Brianna usually brought trouble, but it was always someone else's, she rarely caused it herself. The unfortunate woman trailed her brother's messes everywhere she went. Though Blaser couldn't judge Gary too harshly because there was a time she'd trailed his messes with her everywhere too.

"He was an enforcer," she said on a sigh. "Erika and her boyfriend owe Rafe money, but they left town."

"So they're coming after you?"

"Guess so," Bri said, making them wait for a light before crossing the street despite there being no traffic. "Erika took off, then my landlord kicked me out."

"So where are you staying?"

"After I convince you to give me a job, I'll head over to Marshall's."

Marshall. A friend of Gary's he knew from back in the day.

"You're going to walk all that way?" he asked. "If you go to Marshall's, he'll expect gratitude."

"I don't have much choice," she said. "With Gary out of town, there's no one else around here I trust."

"With Gary inside, you have a chance to get your life together."

"That's what people told me about you," she said. "When you went to jail, they all told me it was my chance to break free."

"We broke up, didn't we?" he said. Setting her free was supposed to give her the chance to get herself a good, respectable life. "You moved to New Jersey."

"For all the good that did me," she muttered.

"You have a helluva story, Bri. All the crap you put up with from the men in your life…"

"Everyone has a story, Blase. You should hear the stories that follow your family around."

"I've heard them," he said.

She laughed, which intrigued him. "Not all of them."

"Okay, hold up," he said, taking her forearm to draw her to a halt. "I'm not going to let you walk all that way to Marshall's. You're scratched up and it's not safe."

"Let me?" she asked.

He ignored her surprise. "I've got a vacant apartment, Colt just moved out."

"You want to rent me an apartment?"

"You've lived in the building before, it's right next to the garage. You're not going to be isolated in the middle of nowhere."

She jerked her arm back. "And just what do you want in exchange for this generosity?"

"Three hundred a month for employees. It's a one bed, half bath, nothing fancy. You know the setup."

She began to shake her head. "I'm so disappointed. I really didn't think you would… What are we talking? Blowjobs once a day? Once a week? Once a month or do you want the full package?" Her index finger dug into his pec when she prodded at him. "I am not a hooker. I have never sold my body and I never will. I'd go hungry and homeless before I let a sleaze like you slobber on me again."

She spun to storm off, but he grabbed her arm again. "Hold on there, quick draw. I don't want sex." She frowned, reeking of suspicion. "I'm presenting a legitimate rental contract. Do you think I'm screwing all my tenants? That would open me up to all sorts of lawsuits and most of my tenants are guys. Even if I did swing that way, I don't know where I'd find the time to have all that sex. Between the club, the garage, and the apartment complex, I haven't had a girlfriend in a long time. But I guess if you're still that hot for me, I could shoehorn in an hour a week somewhere."

"You want to help me?" she asked after pondering him.

"Where I come from, family sticks together and you know damn well that I think of you as family. That's why you came to me, why you showed up at the club. You knew I'd never turn you away, Dollface. Come on, don't act surprised I want to help, you came here because you knew I'd insist on it."

"You always took care of me," she said.

"Let me prove that I always will."

"What about the strippers, the dancers, do you take

care of them?”

"You’re not really asking me that. You’ve never been jealous of me being around other women.”

“No, but I’ve always been able to stake a claim,” she said. “We haven’t been together in six years. I can’t do that anymore.”

“Do you want to?”

When her big eyes slunk up to his, he was worried she might say yes. Then as soon as that concern popped into his head, he got more worried she’d say no.

“Three hundred?” she asked, ignoring his question. “Month to month?” He nodded. “Okay, let’s check it out.”

With a shrug, they resumed their walk toward the apartments.

THREE

FOR MOST OF HIS TWENTIES, during their inseparable years, they'd lived together in the very apartment complex they were heading for. They'd moved in at the same time his cousin, Mattie, bought the building back when Blaser was twenty-one. It had been rife with the drugs that Mattie was selling and became a sort of base of operations for the Warner family's criminal element, of which Blaser was an integral member.

At the time, Blaser was careful to never let that wicked world into their cozy little apartment. Protecting Bri against all life's evils was naïve, she'd seen life. Throughout her childhood her parents openly used drugs. It wasn't like she didn't know their effects. But there was something comforting about playing house with the woman he loved. He'd wanted to believe they could keep the illusion of virtue going in their lives.

Things were different in the building nowadays. The two-story complex had five units on each floor, leading off an open-air, communal porch and balcony respectively. Blaser resided in one apartment and Gus lived next door to him. Ivy and Dax had a unit on the second floor, Ruger did too though his was currently occupied by Suzette.

The other five units were filled by employees of the garage and security men from Risqué, most of whom were ex-cons. None of them had a history of violence against women, Blaser was particular about that. His choice of tenants could prove serendipitous. If Bri was in trouble, it wouldn't visit her now; no one would want to mess with the characters who resided there. The apartment block bordered Warner Autos, and with a view over his garage, he'd be able to keep an eye on her.

"Tell me more about Erika," he said, trying to keep the conversation going on their trek to the apartment.

"Her boyfriend borrowed money for drugs, he had a serious problem. Erika worked off some of the debt for him. Then he took off and the debt kept visiting her."

"The dealer wanted her working for him?"

"Right."

"He's a pimp too?" Wrapping her arms further around herself, she nodded. "Then Erika disappeared. Now they want you to work it off? Do you know where Erika or her boyfriend are?"

"No," Bri said. "Rafe's guys trashed the apartment when I wasn't there. The landlord found the mess just after I did."

"So you got thrown out and that guy followed you to Risqué?"

"He works for Rafe, the dealer. I told Erica not to get involved…"

"Do you do drugs?"

She stopped in her tracks. "No," she said. "God, Blase, this is me. How can you ask me that?"

He started walking and she moved in time with him. The woman he knew Bri to be wouldn't use drugs, but after the year she'd had he would understand if stress had gotten the better of her. It was reassuring to hear she still stood by the pledge she and Gary made. After seeing what drugs did to their parents, the siblings promised never to travel that road themselves.

Passing a broken streetlight, he pointed to the

apartment building separated from the sidewalk by a wide strip of grass and a row of vertical parking spaces. "Here we are. Is it like you remember?"

"It looks exactly the same."

It might look the same, but it was completely different. Gone were the drugs and the fights and the graffiti. Blaser and Gus had worked hard to change the building's reputation. Other than the ex-cons who lived there, the place was squeaky clean. If tenants wanted to stay, keeping themselves legit was essential. The rental contract stated they had to refrain from illegal activities.

"I'm in unit one now," he said, pointing to the bottom corner unit behind the external stairway. "Gus is in two, and Ruger's in seven… when he's here."

"You've graduated through the ranks," she said.

Unit ten had been theirs when they lived together. That apartment still held special significance for him. He would never be able to live there again, not without her. Which was ridiculous because all the units were the same layout, identical to the naked eye. Dumb or not, number ten was different, he could still smell her there when he walked through the door.

"I'm surprised Mattie still has this place. He thinks of himself as a big shot now, doesn't he?"

Blaser smiled at the understatement. "Damn right he does, and he'll never let anyone forget it."

"The money in the family," she said as they crossed the grass and parking lot to head for his place. "He's always been proud of that."

"Even when no one in the family is," Blaser said.

They still saw Mattie at the occasional family function, but it was rare. Mattie liked to think it was all beneath him; that the Warner clan was beneath him. For the most part, the Warners were glad Mattie stayed away because of his vocation and superiority complex.

"Colt was in number six," Blaser said. "The first unit on the top floor, right above mine. You'll have a storage space in the basement. I'll have to check if Colt's cleared it out. I'll get you the keys tomorrow after I check it out. Rent is due on the first of the month."

"That's in four days."

"Yeah, we'll call these four days a free gift."

"You don't have to do that. When I get paid, I'll—"

"We can work out the details tomorrow," he said. "My keys are in my jacket."

She fished them out of his pocket and handed them over with a laugh. "You're like a janitor, how many keys are on that thing?"

"This isn't even my biggest bunch," he said, and her face lit in a smile. "Come inside, let's get you cleaned up before we do anything else."

Holding his door open, he let her enter first. To the left was a kitchen with a circular table in the center, the living room was to the right. The bedroom, bathroom and rear communal patio were accessed from the short hallway at the opposite side of the apartment. Warner Autos was located about forty feet from that patio, beyond the dividing chain link fence.

Cars were his first love. Growing up, whenever he got the chance, he tinkered. Being self-taught came in useful when pleading ignorance to the cops, he'd figured that out young.

On his release from prison, Mattie was the only one willing to give him a break. It helped that he hadn't ratted on his cousin's enterprises or associations. So when he asked for ownership of the garage they'd run the chop shop from, Mattie gave him the place at a major discount on the proviso he help Gus manage the apartments.

"Sit down," Blaser said, gesturing at the leather couch positioned in front of his widescreen TV.

When he dumped her bag by the door, Bri followed suit and dropped hers too. She took off her shoes and made herself comfortable on the couch while he gathered supplies.

Taking a seat at her side, he pressed an ice pack to her cheek.

"This isn't necessary," she said but held the pack in place while he cleaned blood from her chin and the scrape on her arm.

"The blood on your chin must've been his."

"I bit him," she said.

"You fought. I saw the scuffle. You'll be bruised up tomorrow."

"Do you think my new boss will ask questions?" she asked.

The glow of her eyes scorched through him. To prevent himself from leaning in and doing something stupid, he slid down to sit on the floor at her feet to tend the wound on her calf.

Brushing dirt from the edge of the abrasion, he tilted closer to blow dust from the center.

She shivered. "Don't you kiss me."

Sometimes it was like she lived in his head. "No kissing," he said, clasping her leg and cleaning out the injury.

After he'd done that, he covered and bandaged it.

"You're good at that," she said. "Have you played nursemaid recently?"

"I have four hundred cousins," he said, exaggerating… slightly. "We've got in plenty of scrapes over the years… that we didn't want our parents to know about."

"I remember," she said and hissed when he touched a sensitive spot. Her hand landed on his shoulder, and she squeezed. "I've never liked the sight of blood."

"I don't think anyone is supposed to," he said. Sitting on the floor beside her legs, he appreciated the view. Once upon a time it was normal, everyday behavior to toss her leg over his shoulder and bury his face between her thighs. To ensure nothing so intimate happened, he moved away from her gripping fingers. "Any others?"

Twisting her legs toward him, she showed him a scratch on the back of her opposite thigh. He switched sides and gave it a clean before covering it. While he worked, he tried not to notice how high her skirt rode or the smooth, clear skin on her back.

His desire became curiosity when he noted the scar on her ankle. About three inches the jagged mark was so silvery pale against her pure skin that he wouldn't have noticed it from further away.

"Where did you get this?" he asked, running his finger

over it.

"Nowhere," she said, snatching her legs back and averting her eyes.

The defensive anger told him not to push his luck. "Do you want to wear pantyhose tomorrow?"

"Isn't that against uniform policy at Risqué?"

"I'll make an exception," he said. "We have our weekly briefing tomorrow, it's Friday night. If anyone says anything, I'll deal with it, but I'll tell Crystal in advance."

In Risqué, what Crystal said went. Even the security guys bowed down to her, but that may be more to do with her kickass figure than her service record. If he told Crystal to accept Bri in pantyhose, all the girls would.

He wouldn't broadcast it, but Bri could get away with anything where he was concerned. Something about her snatched hold of him young, and it had never let go. His brothers warned him against getting too close to her because her family were known as no good.

They were only looking out for him, but he always believed he knew what he was doing. As it turned out, he'd fucked up the first half of his life. It took prison for him to get his shit together.

Colt always judged him and jumped to the worst conclusions. Part of that kneejerk response was embarrassment. At the time of his arrest, Colt was a vice cop. Their friction went deeper than that. Ruger, the youngest of the brothers, warned him too, those warnings felt more genuine.

As far as his siblings were concerned, getting involved with Bri meant getting involved with Gary and his crew again. After that, it would be a slippery slope back to his criminal practice. When his brothers found out Bri was in his life again, back in every part of his life, they'd remind him, as was their way, that she was bad news.

He didn't see things that way. In his mind, Bri was independent of Gary. She had to be a separate entity given all the naked time they'd spent together. What was between them was more than a basic sexual attraction; their spark had always been undeniable. This woman drew him in unlike others, and he was no stranger to pretty girls. But Bri acted like she could take on the world, even though no one stood at her back to help her out. For some reason, that really irked him.

"Wait here a second," he said and disappeared to the bedroom to fish out the keys for the apartment above his.

At the same time, he grabbed a sports bag and tossed a few items into it. With both in hand, he returned to her in the living room.

"I think this is okay," she said, putting the ice pack on the table and tentatively touching her bruised cheek.

"Let me see," he said, dropping the bag to the coffee table and slipping the apartment key into her hand. Sitting down beside her, he tipped her head toward the light. "I don't think you'll get a black eye."

"Good," she said, curling delicate fingers around his wrist to draw his hand away from her face. "Do you need me to sign something?"

"Don't you want to see the apartment first?"

"I've lived in this building before, I think we're okay… and no offense, but it's not like I have a lot of options right now."

"I haven't had the locks changed yet. But I'll get you new keys, okay?" he said with a strong urge to reassure her. "Unit six is free." He extended a forefinger. "It's the one directly above me. So if you need me, just stamp three times."

"Okay," she said, trying to lower her smile.

His concern seemed to amuse her, but he elevated her chin with a curled finger. "You're still not used to people being nice to you, are you?"

"Not without an ulterior motive," she said. "What is it you want from me?"

"To be a friend. Just be good. Stay clean and out of trouble."

"I've never been dirty."

Now it was his turn to grin. "I know for a fact that's not true."

She rolled her eyes. "Drugs, I've never used drugs. I've seen what addiction can do to people and families. It's not for me, no way. You know that."

"Then all you have to do is be good," he said. "Think you can handle that?"

"I guess we'll have to see," she said, rising from the couch to head for the exit. "Unit six?"

"Yeah, I'll take you up."

"No need," she said, slipping her shoes on. He took his sports bag to her. "What's this?"

"A few essentials, linen, towels, I put in a tee-shirt, soap, a new toothbrush. You can keep it all; I figure that's not what you're carrying in your bags."

Grabbing up her things, he let her absorb what he'd said.

"Thanks, I appreciate it."

When she opened the door, he followed after her. She paused to look at him over her shoulder, a question in her eyes.

"I'll see you to your door," he said. "Given what happened outside the club tonight, I think that's smart."

They went outside and up the stairs parallel to his front door. The external walkway extended the full length of the building. Hers was the very first apartment, she jiggled the key in the lock and opened the door to step inside.

"I can get bolts and chains put on the inside if it will make you feel safer."

"I'll be safe here... I should call Marshall. He's been sort of filling in for Gary as a surrogate brother. He calls me a couple of times a day. He called when I was on my way to Risqué. I didn't tell him I was going there, but I told him I'd been kicked out of Erika's, and he offered me somewhere to stay. I should let him know I won't be going over there tonight."

He figured that was supposed to be his cue to split, but he didn't. "Is your phone number the same?"

"As the one you used last week? Yes."

They'd only been back in contact with each other for a few weeks. When Gary found out they were spending time together and that she'd moved back into these apartments, he'd be in all sorts of trouble himself. Colt was just going to love that.

"My cellphone is in my jacket." She handed the phone to him. "Do you want me to call Marshall and explain?"

"Explain what?" she asked and smiled. "If you call Marshall, all hell will break loose, and you know it."

"I'm not scared of your brother, or any shit he might try to bring."

Her smile faded as her chin rose. "Don't go acting tough for me, don't show off. I hate that you and Gary can't get along, worrying about you both keeps me up nights."

"You still worry about me?"

As soon as he asked, he wished that he hadn't. She took her bags from him and tossed them into the dark apartment. Leaning on the door frame, she held the door behind her with her foot.

"I worry about you every day, Blase," she said. Curling her pinkie around his, he watched as she linked them. "You broke my heart, Warner."

"I was trying to—"

"I know what you were trying to do," she said, lifting her eyes to his. "You broke my heart and for five years, I lived without you. But I looked you up last year because… you never went away."

He hadn't expected her to confess that. Most of their chats in the past weeks had been superficial. Other than his nudges suggesting she talk to Lyssa. This was more profound, and he wasn't sure how to respond.

"We were together for ten years," he said. "I guess it's natural that we… care for each other."

They'd had bumps along the way and broken up for a month or two here and there in the early years. But he'd wanted her since first laying eyes on her. Without intending to, she'd snared him right then on that first day, and he'd never pulled out the hook, he never wanted to.

"When we agreed to meet last year… that date…"

"You never let me apologize for—"

"It wasn't your fault," she said with a flare of ire flashing in her eyes. "I know exactly whose fault it was. You're not the one who should apologize."

"If you ever want to talk…"

"I'll call up Colt's fiancée," she said. Whatever else she'd planned to reveal was gone. "I do appreciate this; you've helped me out of a bind. You have no reason to still be nice to me after… I know things have been tense with you and Gary."

"I didn't put him in jail, Bri. It's important to me that you know that."

"That's not what he says."

"And if you believed him, you wouldn't be here. At least you would've spent more time reading me the riot act."

Rolling on her arm, she swayed closer. "I know my brother well enough to know there are two sides to every story. He hated it when we started dating, do you remember?"

"Yeah," Blaser said, exhaling a laugh at the memory. "I thought he was going to murder me."

"It didn't help that he caught us doing it in the back of your truck."

"Probably not," he said and smiled.

They were kids, so full of potential. None of them could have foreseen the paths they'd end up on.

"I thought he'd never forgive us, but he did…" she said. "I think he actually sort of grew to like the idea of us getting together. But now…"

"Hey," he said, resting a hand on her shoulder. "Don't waste your time trying to figure out the dynamics of my relationship with your brother. I usually can't figure out my relationships with my own brothers. Gary and I want you to be safe, we have that in common. Focus on that."

"Okay," she said, accepting that for now, but he knew it wouldn't stick. "Thank you, Love."

"You're welcome, and you don't need to say that anymore."

He had meant the thank you, but the pet name stuck in his throat too. It had been a long time since he had been her love.

"Okay, I'll try, but I make no promises."

"You sleep well, Bri. If you need me…"

"Just stamp," she said with a nod and a smile. "Goodnight." Then she closed the door.

Running back down the stairs to his apartment, he reprioritized the following day's tasks. He'd have to fit in Bri's paperwork somewhere and figure out if she needed help to move. He would also have to figure out what to tell the guys.

It might be later in the night than he'd hoped, but when he eventually got to bed, he was loose and content. He'd done something good and productive with his day. Whether it made sense or not, knowing that Brianna was safe and asleep in the bedroom above his made him feel better.

FOUR

THE NIGHT'S SLEEP from which she'd just awoken was probably the best she'd had since last waking up in the building. Being back with Blaser, in proximity to him at least, was comforting… dangerous too. Seven years ago, she was with the man she was going to spend her life with, then he was arrested.

He pled guilty, so no trial, just straight to prison. Waiting for him was a no brainer, so she didn't think twice about his visitation request and liked that he wanted to see her.

Letters were exchanged after he broke up with her, but he refused to see her again. Then the letters stopped, so she tried to call, again nothing. Eventually accepting that he didn't want her anymore, she moved to get a clean break. Away from him; away from Gary.

In that new city, it didn't matter how good things were going, Blaser occupied her mind. Dreaming about their life, the time they lived together, got her through tough times. Whenever she felt scared or alone, she reminded herself what it was to be safe and loved.

Curiosity led to her reaching out to him. A year and a

half ago, she'd looked him up, and after a few flirty emails, they got to talking on the phone. Eventually, they agreed to a date.

Sitting at that restaurant, full of nerves and excitement, some part of her reverted to believing it could be the beginning of her future. Their future. Blaser was her first love, her only love. In truth, there was nothing horrible about the way they had broken up. Nothing except how little choice she had in the matter.

Still lying in the sheets Blaser had stuffed into the sports bag, Bri told herself to get up. She couldn't lie there all day, there was too much to get done. It was also only a matter of time before Rafe tracked her down.

Coffee was all she could think about during her shower. As soon as she was done in the bathroom, she darted along the hall to the open plan living-kitchen-dining space.

The sight of a person in the kitchen brought her up short, though it was a relief to see a woman rather than a familiar male, such as Rafe.

"Can I help you?" Bri asked.

The brunette whipped around, and her stunned expression quickly became a smile. Bri relaxed on recognizing the therapist, Lyssa Cutler.

"Sorry…" Lyssa said. "I had no idea Blaser had rented the apartment already and to a female no less," Lyssa said. "This confirms how special you are to him."

"To Blaser?" Brianna said. "I guess if you suck a guy's dick enough times, he starts to take a shine to you."

Instead of shocking Lyssa, Bri was surprised to see the doctor's smile widen and her eyes glitter. "Wow, take you off the therapy couch and you really open up."

"I'm sorry, I… I don't know why I said that," Bri said, ashamed by her urge to shock or scare the intruder away.

Lyssa's smile faded. "Don't be ashamed of honesty. It's fine to be sassy. I invaded your space… unknowingly, I'll admit. But you're allowed to be annoyed and to express that annoyance."

"I know that," Bri said. Swallowing, she moistened her lips to delay asking the question she wanted answered.

"Did you…? Have you spoken to Colt about what I said? Did you tell him that I came to you?"

"No." Lyssa shook her head. "Colt knows nothing about it. I don't discuss my patients with him."

"I'm not your patient, though, am I?" Bri said, tucking in her towel again to keep it secure. "I mean, I'm not paying you or anything."

"You are my patient, everything you say to me is confidential. My specialty is sexual therapy, I deal with abuse victims all the time. Trust takes time to be earned," Lyssa said, fishing in her purse and pulling out a business card. "My personal phone number is on this."

When Lyssa began to cross the room, Bri backed away, holding up her hands. "Please, don't," Bri said. Lyssa immediately stopped. Maybe it was because she was naked, or because this woman knew intimate things about her, but her proximity alarm manifested as a tickle of anxiety on the back of her neck. "I don't consider myself an abuse victim."

"How do you identify what happened to you?"

"It didn't happen to me, it—" Biting her bottom lip, she rolled her gaze to the side. The familiar scorch in her sinuses was a prelude to tears that she promised herself she'd never let come again. "I'm really not interested in talking about it here."

"Okay, we can leave it until our next appointment," Lyssa said, nodding, putting her card on the kitchen table. "It's been my experience that these things fester and seep into other areas of survivors lives. I tell my patients that letting their experience taint their other relationships, and the way they live their lives, only lets their attacker keep on winning."

"My attacker is dead," Brianna said. "The Sniveller isn't winning anything anymore."

"That's what you called him?"

Brianna nodded. "The others called him Skeeve. There was a gang of them, but… he had no power with his colleagues, I think he used women as a way to…"

"Feel powerful?"

Brianna nodded and let the weight of her head fall. "I really don't want to talk about this."

"Okay," Lyssa said. "I really hope you'll come back to see me. We can talk about whatever you want. There's no pressure to rush any particular discussion. You're important to Blaser and I'm marrying his brother, we should get to know each other."

Brianna frowned. "We should? Why? Colt hates me. Have you heard the way he talks about me?"

"No," Lyssa said, grinning, taking on a sarcastic air. "But if he so much as thinks about saying anything negative about you in my vicinity he'll find himself sleeping in the guest room."

Brianna didn't want to like this woman, but she did. She had never given much thought to Blaser's brothers' girlfriends in the past. Perhaps because he hadn't spent a lot of quality time with his brothers while they were together, Colt especially.

Colt had been a cop, married, respectable, everything that Blaser wasn't. The funniest part of it was, they were twins, yet the two brothers couldn't be more different.

"Colt is a good guy," Brianna said, feeling guilty for her outburst.

Her emotions were right on the surface these days. Being with Blaser and talking to the doctor brought a lot of things bubbling from the dark place she'd tried to repress.

"He's a great guy," Lyssa said. "That doesn't mean he always makes the best decisions. I've treated people he doesn't like before. What Colt thinks doesn't impact what I do, or who I do it with." She seemed to ponder for a moment then a smile quirked to her lips again. "Professionally at least."

"Karri would've said the same thing."

Karri was Colt's first wife; she'd cheated on him and broken his heart. It was odd to have this protective, defensive urge with his fiancée. Colt was known for giving his twin a hard time. As Blaser's girl, she got the brunt of the judgment. She and her family were blamed for every bad decision Blaser ever made.

Maybe she was to blame for him getting into so much trouble in his youth. After Gary accepted their relationship, his bond with Blaser grew. Blaser wanted to be with her, so he tolerated or complied with everything Gary wanted. Maybe if Blaser hadn't been so intent on keeping her happy, and keeping the peace with her brother, he wouldn't have done the things he did. Half of which she didn't know about at the time.

Lyssa must have registered the harshness in words, and the emotion behind them. "I would never cheat on Colt. I love him so much you wouldn't believe… Did you know Karri?"

"I was at the wedding."

"Sure! You were with Blaser then." She nodded. "Were you close with Karri?"

"No," Bri said with an involuntary bark of laughter. "Karri looked down her nose at everyone. The only person I ever saw her get along with was Ruger."

"Everybody loves Ruger," Lyssa said.

A chill tensed her. Bri kept her teeth together, fearful that if she let them separate, something might slip out.

"Ruger can go to hell," she said, managing not to move her lips.

"You don't like Ruger?"

"Oh, he's great if you're on his good side. But piss Ruger off and… let's just say he has friends in all the wrong places."

"The wrong places?"

"Did you come here for a reason?" Bri asked, suddenly very aware they were on her property and that Lyssa hadn't been invited.

"Yes. I came to get a bag that we forgot," she said, glancing at a fabric tote bag on the kitchen counter. "I was next door having coffee with Suzette, she's staying in Ruger's place while he's gone. I just picked this up in passing, like I said, I didn't realize that Blaser had rented the place."

"Well, he has," Bri said. "So I'd appreciate it if you and your fiancé stayed out of here."

"We will, of course," Lyssa said. "I'll go and… leave you to your day." She went and grabbed the bag and began to head for the door. "I'm looking forward to our next session, I really think I can help if you give me a chance. I promise everything you say will be confidential."

Sharing her deepest secrets with Colt's future wife would be difficult and not just because of her fiancé. "Sure, thanks."

Lyssa's half smile was comforted yet gave a dubious impression. "It was nice to see you again."

Bri didn't reciprocate the nicety while tracking Lyssa's exit with her gaze. Once the door was closed, she went straight over to double bolt it, ensuring there were no more uninvited guests.

First item on the agenda was getting new locks and a few slide bolts for both external doors, front and back. The Warners were adept at everything and knew people with all kinds of skills. She had come to Blaser for help with her problem. As each second passed, she was reminded that Blaser was her biggest problem, just like the old days.

FIVE

BLASER'S DAY WAS shaping up to be manic. At ten a.m. he was dashing away from the garage, through the gate in the chain link fence to cross the back yard of the apartment building. He had to tell Gus about putting Bri in Colt's place before he wandered in on her naked or rented it out to someone else.

The development with Bri took him on a detour from his usual routine. On a typical day, he would spend these hours getting through the half dozen jobs he had at the garage before running over to Risqué.

Ivy had been a godsend. She'd taken on the admin work of the garage without blinking, she never complained, just did what needed to be done to keep the place going. With that relief, Blaser managed to get his hands dirty again, a thing he often missed.

When he got to Gus' place, his cousin was sitting at his kitchen table drinking coffee, still bleary eyed from bed. In years gone by, Blaser had been just as lazy, doing the barest minimum in order to pay the bills, which usually meant selecting the easiest, often criminal, jobs. Nowadays he wondered how he'd ever existed that way. Of course, back then, he had great incentive to stay in bed. That incentive had just moved into his brother's old place.

Blaser stayed by Gus's front door after he closed it. He'd left the oil draining out of two vehicles at the garage, meaning he didn't have much time to hang around shooting the breeze.

"Glad to have it occupied," Gus said once Blaser had filled him in about their new tenant. So far, he had managed to avoid telling his cousin about Bri's trouble with Rafe. "Are you going to be okay having her around? Gary's in jail now, but he'll get out. He'll go crazy when he finds out you're screwing with his sister again."

"I'm not sleeping with her," Blaser said, sick of the accusation.

Much as he hated everyone jumping to conclusions, he didn't regret going to Erika's to find Bri or helping her with a place to stay.

"I didn't say you were," Gus said. "I'd guess if you were sleeping with her, you'd have moved her into your place instead of Colt's. Doesn't mean Gary is going to be happy she's over here."

"Bri makes her own decisions," Blaser said. "And she's not going to stay around here for long."

"You think?" Gus asked, swinging back in his chair. "Something happens when the two of you get together."

Blaser didn't want to address that. Everyone seemed to think it was their place to comment on his relationship with Bri. Nothing pissed him off more. But he didn't want to fly off the handle and reveal the strength of his feelings on the subject. That would raise questions he couldn't begin to answer for himself, let alone for others.

"We should go back to renting only to men," Gus said. "Less drama."

"Bri won't bring drama," Blaser said though he couldn't be sure of that.

The drama Bri had on her tail already got her flung out of one apartment.

"It's just Suzette and Ivy around here. Ruge will kick Suzie out when he gets back into town," Gus said. "Bri okay being one of two? Ivy has Dax mind. All the other guys know to keep their hands off, Bri will be the only single girl."

"She'll be safe here."

"Yeah, *we* know that, but she might not be so sure. We didn't have to worry about anyone being safe when we had the guy only rule."

"That was never a rule, it just worked out that way. Gender was never a factor in tenancy decisions."

"If you say so," Gus said, yawning and scrubbing his hands through his hair. "You know the guys can get rowdy. Most women would have trouble shacking up with so many ex-cons."

"Not every guy here is a felon," Blaser said.

Gus only had minor misdemeanors on his rap sheet. "Don't know about Dax, but with Colt gone… Ruger and I are the only two who have never seen the inside of a prison cell," Gus grumbled and slugged his coffee. "You're hardly Mr. Squeaky Clean over there."

Squeaky clean was a joke, Blaser wasn't even just mildly mucky, he'd waded in up to his neck and got himself good and filthy. But he was trying to clean up his act. Since leaving prison five years ago, he'd been completely legit.

A knock on the door interrupted the conversation. Because he was right next to it, Blaser swung it open. The guest obviously wasn't expecting such a quick response, she did a double take when he appeared in the frame.

"Oh," she said and smiled.

Man, in the light of day, she looked like the sweetest thing. It was an optical illusion: he'd seen her fight.

"Bri," he said. "We were just talking about you."

"Were you?"

Swinging the door further open, he swept his arm to gesture her inside, but she stayed outside and just looked at Gus. Smart girl, she didn't enter an apartment and block herself inside with two men, especially when, for all she knew, there were more of them. As soon as Gus was done checking her out, he was off his feet and at the door by his side.

"Gus," she said. "What happened to the army?"

"Navy," he said. "Gave it up. Got discharged."

"Oh yeah, why was that?" she asked, looking the tall, lean form of his cousin up and down. "You look good to me."

"Thanks, it's your eyes doing that to me, honey."

"Right," Blaser said. Brianna flirting with anyone would set his nose out of joint. But doing it with family was more than his sanity could handle. "It was mental reasons; the dude is a loose cannon. The military finally realized what we already knew."

Gus laughed and sloped back to retrieve his coffee from the table. "They say all geniuses end up insane."

"They say the same of fools," Blaser said, giving his cousin the evil eye.

"I wanted to return this," Brianna said, thrusting his jacket at him while changing the subject.

"Thanks."

"I tried your apartment, but you weren't there. I thought Gus might know where you were… I'm glad I found you. I wanted to say thanks for last night."

"No problem," he said. "Did you sleep okay?"

Curling a finger under her chin, he turned her face toward the light to see that her cheek was discolored. She'd covered the bruise with makeup. This close, he couldn't help thinking that she looked as great in jeans and a scoop neck tank as she had in last night's meager outfit.

"Yeah," she said. "The bedroom window wouldn't open but other than that it was great."

"You want me to come and look at it?" he said aware his hands were filthy.

"Oh, no, I'm heading out just now."

"Where are you going?"

"To meet a friend," she said. "He's going to help me—"

"He?" Blaser asked.

Although she'd said she got on fine without sex, men would still be sniffing around for it.

"Yes," she said. "Don't get jealous, Love. The color doesn't suit you."

Her teasing reminded him that his cousin was watching.

Clearing his throat, he adopted her changing the subject technique. "The briefing is at nine thirty tonight, that's switch over time," he said. "I could come over before, open up the bedroom window, and then give you a ride to the club."

"You would do that?"

"Sure," he said. "I'll text you when I'm on my way."

"Great." She smiled. "I've switched my SIM, so if you want the number... Do you have a pen?"

They both looked at Gus who took a while to remember they were in his place. That put it on him to retrieve the stationery. When Gus got back to them with the pen, Bri grabbed Blaser's elbow and lifted it to write her phone number on the inside of his forearm, beneath the folded-up sleeve of his coveralls.

"Thanks," she said and handed Gus his pen.

"No worries," Gus said.

Bri smiled, spun around and disappeared.

Blaser closed the door. Only then did he notice the grin on his cousin's face. "What?"

"You would do that?" Gus mimicked Bri. "Damn, she looks good. Maybe I'll fix her window and chase her down for the paperwork."

"I dare you to think about it," Blaser threatened, shoving his laughing cousin. Violence wasn't usually his first instinct, but the smile on Gus' face could drive him to it. "She's been screwed around enough without adding you and your shit to the mix."

"Where the fuck did you find her at three in the morning?"

Knowing it would come out eventually, Blaser gave a rundown of events with Rafe. As he went on with the story, all mischief left Gus. He became serious, folding his arms as he listened intently.

"So she's under your protection, that's what you're telling me?"

"Yeah," Blaser said, having not thought of it that way. "Yeah, that's exactly what I'm saying."

"Which means she's under our protection. Any woman claimed by a Warner gets full family and affiliate protection. You better be damn sure she's worth it before we wade into God knows what. Protecting her means we're willing to go to jail or die to protect this woman if that's what it takes."

He doubted, hoped, it would never come to that. "If that's what it takes, that's what I'll do."

"Then she's under Warner protection. Only a lunatic would approach her, especially here or at the club, but I'll put the word out."

"She doesn't have to know about this." Blaser said.

Gus' mischief returned. "Do you think half our women know what we do full stop? Let alone what we do to protect them and keep other men away?"

The question was rhetorical. Not even their mothers and sisters knew half the stuff Warner men did. Respect and protect was the number one rule when it came to women.

"Right."

"She's one of us again, cuz," Gus said, slapping his shoulder then returning to his coffee. "You've done well for yourself."

And just like that, Bri somehow became his woman again. Gus was already heading to the coffee machine for a refill like what he'd said was no big deal, but Blaser was stuck. After so long apart, Bri shouldn't still feel like his woman, yet she did.

Warners were tough and fair. They gave their steadfast focus to whatever they dedicated themselves to. Whatever Bri was mixed up in, he'd take care of it. He just hadn't realized his actions would involve asking the family to take care of it as well.

SIX

GOING TO RISQUÉ shouldn't make her apprehensive, so why was she so edgy? A sharp tapping on her apartment door beckoned her, but when she opened it, there was no one there. Stepping outside to seek out the source of the knocking, she saw Blaser at the top of the stairs.

"Come on," he said, sliding both hands down the metal railings on either side of the stairs. "Chop, chop."

Reaching into the apartment, she snagged her purse then locked the door as quickly as she could. "So much for fixing the window," she said, running down the stairs behind him toward the idling truck still blaring its headlights.

Driving highlighted how desperate he was to get back to the club.

"I'll do it another time," Blaser said. "I don't like to be away from the club."

"I can tell," she said. Hopping into the truck, she was still putting on her seatbelt when he rocketed out of the parking lot. "Have you had a chance to think about my request?"

"Your request?" he asked, flashing her a frown.

"To dance. I can make more money…"

He was already shaking his head. "Every girl starts waiting tables."

"It's not like I need an audition, you've seen me dance."

"In private," he said. "That wasn't a public show. Dancing in a club is different."

"I've done it before."

"When you were seventeen," he said. "There's no point fighting with me. I stick to the rules. Just like we always said we would."

"Yeah, but…"

"But the rules don't apply to you?" he asked. "They apply tenfold, Doll. I won't take advantage of you."

"It's not taking advantage if I ask."

"Argue all you want," he said. "But I'm the boss and my rules are law in Risqué."

She knew better than to believe him when he was so obviously lying. "The rules aren't why you're saying no to me. Do you remember when you used to love me?" she asked, twisting in the passenger seat to rest a hand on the center console.

"What do you want now?"

"No, I'm just saying, our relationship went for more than a decade. I know when you're bullshitting me, Warner."

"I'm not bullshitting you, it's true, ask Lyssa."

"Lyssa is in the club?" she asked.

He pulled into the parking spot at the back of the club and turned off the engine. "Yeah, why?"

"Why would a woman want to hang around at a strip club?"

"Lyssa…" he said, a smile decorating his face. "I can't get the damn woman out of the place. She loves it here, Suzette's in all the time too. She comes in to hang with Lyssa."

"And why does Lyssa like it so much? She's weird. She smiles too much and has no shame when it comes to sex."

"She's a sex therapist," he said. "You should hear some of the things she's said to Ruge." He frowned. "How do you know what Lyssa's like?"

"I went to her place yesterday and I saw her this

morning before I went out, she didn't tell you?"

He shook his head. "Lyssa's a secrets woman. She prefers to be the one asking for information. She doesn't offer much unless you ask directly." Meeting her eye, he made no attempt to get out of the truck. "You went to see her? Twice?"

"I went to her office yesterday and yes, we… I guess you could say that we had a session."

Relief flooded his expression before he smiled again. "Babe, that's… I'm proud of you."

Just hearing those words nipped her sinuses. Any doubts she had about returning to Doctor Cutler disappeared. Going to Lyssa and talking about her trauma meant so much to Blaser because he cared about her. It was as simple as that. He cared about her, and she wouldn't let him down.

"Thanks," Bri said, unclicking her seatbelt.

Blaser got out and around the hood to open her door for her. Her fingers automatically threaded themselves between his on their walk to the rear entrance of Risqué. Only when he shoved the door and held it open for her did she realize holding his hand wasn't natural… rather, it wasn't appropriate.

"Any girls I should look out for?" Bri asked, trying to be discreet about slipping her hand out of his.

Being subtle didn't work. He glanced down when her hand disappeared from his. Despite thinking how inappropriate it was, she could read his urge to grab hold of her again. Ignoring that, he cleared his throat, saying nothing about what had just happened.

"If you're looking for the inside scoop on the locker room," he said, "you'd have to talk to Crystal."

"Crystal doesn't like me," Bri said, walking at his side down the corridor of the backstage area, past a flight of stairs. "Which probably isn't the best start for me."

"You went to school with Crystal. You guys used to be friendly."

His tone suggested that he wanted more information, but he wasn't going to get it from her.

"Those days are gone," she said, passing him to move down the corridor.

He snagged her arm, swinging her around. Wondering why he'd pulled her back, her default was to prepare for a kiss. Instead, he nodded toward a door. Their destination?

Blaser hadn't opened this club until after prison. It was strange to be an integral part of something you knew nothing about. She had pored over every detail of this place with him while it was still a dream. Being there now that he had done it, made her sorry she hadn't been a part of the journey.

Before they went through the door, Blaser actually knocked on it. He didn't wait for a response, just went in, but he'd alerted the occupants to his pending entry. Coming in after him, she took in the lockers and strewn clothes. The women's changing area. Women, in various stages of undress, hung around the vast space. He didn't blink at the flesh on show and was probably used to seeing every inch of these women.

He passed the lockers perpendicular to the entrance and with a hand on the small of her back he guided her around to sit on a couch.

"Everyone together," he called.

The women were already gravitating toward him. He had that kind of force in every room. Either men wanted to hit him, or women wanted to mount him. Blaser evoked extreme emotion wherever he went.

"Where's Crystal?" a tiny little woman asked, propping herself on the high arm of another red leather couch.

"Keeping things moving out front," Blaser said.

"I thought that Lyssa and Colt were out there," the little woman said.

"They are," Blaser said, eager to move on. "Suzette just came in, the women are chattering about some shit and—" The women laughed. "Yes, Colt is up to his eyeballs and if I leave him out there on his own too long, he'll kill me."

"Bet you miss Ruger," the same little woman said. "He called me."

"Good, I'm glad to hear it," Blaser said. "That's just made my day, Destiny. Now you want to quit your yapping so

I can get done what needs to be done?"

To the outside eye, he was a guy who wanted to keep things moving. But she sensed his irritation at his younger brother being brought up in such a public forum. The Warners believed family business should be kept inside the family. Maybe this girl was part of the family. Blaser wouldn't want his female cousins getting naked in his club, where he could see them. But if Ruger wasn't in a relationship with Suzette, maybe he was with this woman instead.

"This is Jade."

Bri's attention flew up to Blaser, but he didn't look back. Jade was the name they'd come up with as a cover name for when she worked in the place they were going to start together. It had been her idea for them to use cover names. Although they planned to have a respectable joint. From first-hand experience, it was easier to have a character to disappear into. And no girl would want a customer to track her down either.

Trying to shrug off her surprise, she turned away from him, but still couldn't quite bring herself to look at the other girls. Being there among so many beautiful, confident women was intimidating. Everyone knew each other and had a history together.

The only person present she shared history with had seen her very naked, very often; he'd been inside her body. That in itself might not be so bad, except he'd also seen every other woman in the room naked too, on stage at the very least. How close was he to these women? Other than Crystal, did he have any favorites?

She hadn't been paying attention, so quickly listened in. Other than her introduction, nothing specific about her came up. He talked about a pricing change and said something about an issue with the air conditioning in room C. The meeting seemed routine until he opened it up for questions.

"Crystal should really be here," Destiny said, squirming while the others seemed to be urging her on.

"What's the problem?" Blaser asked.

"Did Lyssa talk to Colt?" Destiny asked.

Bri smiled. This roundabout questioning was leading

to something. It would be driving Blaser crazy that Destiny wasn't getting to the point.

"She's fucking him, so yeah, I imagine they talk. What is this about?"

"I wish Ruger was here," Destiny mumbled.

Suddenly Blaser being riled wasn't funny. These women were genuinely nervous to bring the issue, whatever it was, to him. Either it was a very serious issue, or Blaser was a hardass boss.

"You should be more afraid of Colt than of him," Bri said before actually thinking about speaking up. "Blaser's bark is much worse than his bite. The hard man thing is all an act."

"Who asked you?" he snapped at her and that was enough to bring her to her feet.

"You did not just shout at me in front of these women Blaser Warner," she said, raising her eyebrows, waiting for an apology.

"They're not afraid of me. They just—"

"What?" she asked Blaser. "They would rather talk to Crystal, Lyssa, or Colt about their problem? Who the hell would rather talk to Colt than talk to you? Colt is a prick about everything, he's a superior sonofabitch."

"Colt is a prick to you," Blaser said.

"Because I ruined your life."

"Oh ho," Blaser laughed and shook his head. "It never takes you long to get to that fight does it, Dollface."

"Who is fighting?" she asked, glancing at the spectators. "No one should worry about saying anything to Blaser in front of this many witnesses… he has too many priors."

Sinking back onto the couch, her focus slid downward. A whole lot of eyes were burning into her. Anyone who wasn't already intrigued by the arrival of this stranger would be now.

"It's the alley," Destiny said.

Blaser puffed up when he inhaled. "The camera stays," he said. "I know none of you want it there. I'm not crazy about it myself, but it's for your protection."

"That's what Crystal said," Destiny said. "It just feels

weird to know we're always being watched."

"When you go out someone should be watching you," Blaser said. "You agree with me, Destiny. Don't start rabble-rousing just 'cause you have an audience."

A few of the women started arguing.

"They know that I agree it should stay," Destiny shouted above the others, and they began to quiet.

"Her opinion doesn't count," another girl said.

Bri wanted to jump to Destiny's defense, though didn't know why Destiny's opinion differed from the others.

"Okay, we'll finish this conversation later," Blaser said and got up. "Everyone back to work."

The women started chatting and he took hold of her shoulder to pull her out of the room.

"What was that about?" Bri asked of the abrupt end, which she had a sneaking feeling was for her benefit. "If there's something I should know about…"

"The offices are upstairs," he said, pointing at the stairs but taking her further along the corridor.

Questions queued to be asked, but the music got louder, he opened a door then boom, they were on the main floor. The lit stage to their right was occupied by a woman was dancing topless. More than a few patrons panted, waiting to put dollar bills in her G-string.

Blaser didn't even glance at the dancer, he kept her shoulder, angling her left and right to direct her through tables to a bar. In the same moment they got behind the bar, he let go of her shoulder.

In the rush across the room, her hair had gotten in her face. She flipped it out of the way only to see Colt Warner at the back corner of the bar locked in a clinch with what had to be the good doctor, Lyssa Cutler.

"They're always like that."

Brianna turned toward the voice. A woman on the other side of the bar was gazing at the lip-locked couple too. She took a swig of her drink then looked at Bri.

"Excuse me?" Bri asked.

Blaser had disappeared to the other end of the bar and was serving a customer. Crystal hovered on his periphery, waiting to pounce.

"Really, I mean you'll just be having a normal everyday conversation like it's no big deal and then pow, suddenly they're kissing again. It's getting worse. I don't know what it is. I think it's because he's so desperate to have kids. But Lyssa isn't going to be fooled into pregnancy, you know? I mean she's a sex doctor for crying out loud! If anyone knows the ins and outs of fertility, it's her." The stranger sighed and propped her head on her hand to gaze at the canoodling couple again. "I mean it's kind of sweet really. Don't ever tell him I said that out loud."

"You're not… Suzette by any chance," Bri asked, "are you?"

"Yes," Suzette said, slinking creeped out eyes around to her. "How did you know that?"

"You're Lyssa's best friend, she told me she was at your place this morning. I've heard a lot about you."

"If it's from Colt, it's probably all bullshit, he's never liked me… Though I suppose he did save Lyssa's life, and his brother is giving me a place to stay. Yeah, I shouldn't be so bitchy, should I?"

"It's quite an adjustment, your best friend getting married, that's a big deal."

"It was supposed to be me, you know," Suzette said.

Bri's jaw dropped. "You were going to marry Colt?"

The idea Colt had them queuing around the block wasn't a new one, she'd been around to see how well he did in high school. But Colt had always had a respectability about him—though she called it superiority—it was that righteousness that made him an excellent husband. Whatever their differences, Bri knew Colt Warner treated his first wife fairly, so there couldn't be any doubt that Lyssa would get the same dedication.

"Ew!" Suzette exclaimed. "No!"

"What's going on?"

This time the voice came from the other corner of the bar, where Colt and Lyssa had been. Lyssa was coming over.

As soon as Colt spotted her behind the bar, he

stopped moving. "What the fuck are you doing here?" he demanded.

"Don't swear at a lady," Lyssa chastised him and hooked his arm around her shoulder.

Colt remained intent.

"I need money," she said. "And Blase said—"

"I fucking bet he did, what did you do this time? Shake your tits in his face, let him take you up the ass, what?"

Suzette spat out her wine, but laughter quickly followed.

Lyssa, on the other hand, was outraged. "Who the hell do you think you're talking to?" the doctor asked, moving away from him, folding her arms. "How dare you speak to her like that!"

"You don't know what's happening, Cherrypop. Stay out of it."

"I will not," Lyssa said, undeterred by the fact Colt still hadn't taken his eyes off Bri as though his vision alone could vaporize her. "I won't marry a man who believes it's okay to speak to a woman like that. What if we have a daughter?"

"She won't be anywhere near a place like this or a woman like her, so there's nothing to worry about."

"I sense trouble," Suzette sing-songed.

That wasn't exactly a mystery. Trouble burned neon in the darkened space.

"It's okay, Doctor Cutler," Bri said. "Please don't argue because of me. He's entitled to say whatever he likes."

"Damn right I am."

"He is not," the doctor said. "And please call me Lyssa, Bri."

"She…" Colt said, finally taking his eyes from her to look at his fiancée, though he thrust a finger in her direction. "Is the one who got Blaser locked up, who got Blaser messed up, who got this place raided and you arrested too. Don't fucking expect me to—"

"Oh, so now you're swearing at me? It's not attractive, Colt. Why do you feel the need to do that? Does swearing make you feel more powerful? When you raise your voice—"

"That deconstructing shit is patronizing when we're fighting, how many times I gotta tell you that?"

"And how many times have I got to tell you that shouting and swearing is not the way to get your point across?"

"I'm not shouting," he said, having already lowered his volume considerably. "You don't know who she is and what she's done to my family."

"I know exactly who she is," Lyssa said, slipping onto a stool, topping off a half-drunk glass of wine from the bottle beside Suzette. "Bri and I have met. She's living in your old apartment."

Colt's frown took a while to react, perhaps because he wasn't expecting the statement. "Why would she be staying there?"

"I assume because she made an arrangement with Blaser or Gus. Possibly Ruger, though I doubt that, having Suzie in his place is probably as much responsibility for a female as he can take."

"No one can take responsibility for that," Colt mumbled.

Suzette shot upwards. From her height, Bri guessed she was standing on the crossbar of her stool. "Blaser! Where's my wine? This bottle is empty!"

"Jesus," Colt breathed.

"She's having a hard time," Lyssa said to Bri. "I've tried to tell her that alcohol isn't the solution but…"

"You were the stalked one, not her," Colt said. "You're too understanding, you take on all these ridiculous pet projects and—"

"My best friend is not a pet project," Lyssa said, touching his face. "How would I feel if I lost you? I don't know what I'd do."

"You wouldn't become a drunk," he said, threading his fingers through hers to guide her palm to his lips. "And you're never losing me, I'm not an insane sociopath like her fiancé."

A hand on her hip alerted Bri to Blaser's proximity,

he nudged her aside and bent to retrieve a bottle of wine from the bottom of the fridge.

"If she passes out…" Blaser said to Colt while filling Suzette's glass. "I am not carrying her home again. It's your turn."

Suzette settled down when her wine glass was full; everyone seemed to breathe a sigh of relief. Bri could only feel sorry for the woman if she had lost the love of her life… she knew what that was like.

"Is he giving you a hard time?" Blaser asked her in a low volume, though it was obvious Colt and Lyssa were still listening.

"Actually, he is," Lyssa said to Blaser. "I find it fascinating. Why should you be at all interested in causing trouble with your brother's ex-girlfriend? You do realize it's that sort of behavior which caused all this trouble in the first place. Maybe if any of you sat down with Gary—"

"Sat down with him?" Colt asked. "I'm sorry, are you aware this is the same guy who had his friends molest you and Destiny in that locker room back there? I didn't see you sitting down to talk then."

"I was talking to him actually," Lyssa said. Bri got her answer on why Destiny would have a different opinion about the camera in the alley. "Maybe if you hadn't come in and—"

"Gary…" Bri said. "My brother attacked you?"

"No," Lyssa said. "No, it wasn't your brother."

"It was Zeke and that bastard Marshall," Colt said, garnering more anger. "They rushed Destiny outside, crowded her into that locker room and tried it on with her and Lys. If Ruge and I hadn't walked in—"

"Oh, Ruger was the big hero," Bri said, unable to stop her lip from curling. "Spare me his sob story. I'm not interested."

"That's your nerve," Lyssa sighed out the clarity, her intense intrigue made Bri squirm. "Why is the mention of Ruger so upsetting? Did you have an affair with him?"

"What?" Blaser barked so loud she jumped. "When the fuck did that happen?"

"We… we didn't," Bri said, surprised by how Blaser

loomed so close and grew larger without ever moving from his spot beside her.

"If he tried it on with you or—"

"I wouldn't let Ruger touch me. He wouldn't want to. He hates me now, just like he always did."

"Ruge doesn't trust you," Colt said. "And neither do I."

Maybe if she'd known how much animosity still existed in this family towards her, she would've stayed away. Blaser had always protected her and now she began to see what he'd been dealing with.

Before he went to jail, they hadn't spent much time with Colt and Ruger. They associated with different, shadier, members of the Warner family. Dealing with Blaser's brothers directly was limited to family occasions. They'd mostly ignored her. If they wanted to talk to Blaser, they would pull him aside.

"Cryst!" Blaser called and Crystal was quickly at his side. "Show Bri around, will you?" His hand curled around the back of Crystal's neck as he leaned down to whisper something into the blonde's ear.

Bri tried not to bristle. Her shoulder popped back and her head twisted away. Through the course of their relationship, it had never occurred to her to be jealous. Seeing how close he was to Crystal, and how easily they spoke to each other in a private way, she could only assume they'd had their own intimate relationship. Why did that make her skin sting?

The heat of the air plummeted. Suddenly, she was cold. Blaser with Crystal would just be the icing on her cake. Her life was supposed to get better after they split up; that was the whole reason behind their breakup. It didn't matter which angle her life was examined from, there was nothing better about it, not a single thing. Whereas Blaser, on the other hand, had flourished. She didn't begrudge him his success, but it did leave her wondering why she hadn't accomplished her supposed fate while he was immersed in his.

"Crystal will show you around," Blaser said.

Bri glanced at his hand on the small of Crystal's back and her own spine straightened. He did care for Crystal. There was every possibility she had lost the love of her life to a woman who hated her and everyone else she cared for.

When Crystal moved away from the bar, Bri could only follow on behind her. She was in no position to question Blaser's life choices. He had broken up with her so she could move on. Now she saw their breakup improved his life while hers remained shattered.

SEVEN

AFTER BRI DISAPPEARED through the staff door with Crystal, Blaser propped his hands on the bar to support his weight.

"What the fuck is your problem?" he asked Colt. "She's been through enough, leave her the fuck alone."

"We've had this conversation before," Colt said with sarcasm he didn't understand or appreciate. "A couple of thousand times. She's bad news Blase, do you want me to remind you of all the crap you went through for her?"

"I didn't go through any crap for her. I make my own decisions, then and now. She didn't force me into doing the things I did."

"Bravo," Lyssa said, looping an arm through Colt's. "Blaser is taking responsibility for his own actions. That's what a person has to do in order to move on. He's taking responsibility and look how far he has come since those days."

He didn't know what Colt had told Lyssa about his past. The rate Lyssa liked to ask questions coupled with Colt's strength of desire to please her, he'd bet she knew a lot about every member of the family.

"Yeah, and I've been here to see him do it," Colt said

to Lyssa. "You haven't seen how hard he's had to work. I don't want to see all his sweat go to waste just because he goes cross-eyed over the girl who always led him around by his balls."

"Maybe he likes that."

"Maybe he does," Colt said. "But it's not worth it. She's not worth it. She never gave him any damn thing; all she did was take. I won't watch him dismantle everything just because she makes him feel like less of a man for not giving in to her every whim."

"Is that what it is, Blase?" Lyssa asked him. "You have an inferiority complex?"

"No," Blaser said.

"Oh, come on," Colt said. "You did what you did because you wanted to make her proud. You were showing off for a girl who got off on the bad boy act."

"It wasn't an act. I got stoned, I stole. I chopped cars and beat on people. I was a bastard, Colt," Blaser said, owning what a prick he'd been back then.

"Because you thought it was cool," Colt said. "Because her, Gary, and that damn gang of his thought Mattie was all that, and you were his cousin. You couldn't let the family down, could you?"

"You thought I was showing off for Mattie? What? Do you think that I wanted to be a part of his crew?" Widening his hands, he lowered toward the couple. "Let me tell you something you never knew back then: Mattie asked me to join his crew. He wanted me there through it all, he practically begged me to be his right-hand man. It was a lucrative offer. If I wanted infamy, Matt would've delivered it."

"Why didn't you join him?" Lyssa asked.

His tongue darted across his lips as memories of a very specific night went through his mind. "She told me she'd leave me," he said, confessing something he'd never spoken to anyone. "Bri hated it. She hated every time I went out with her brother. I used to come home to her crying, she wouldn't let me touch her for days if I came home with so much as a scratch on me. She hated that world. The only reason she took any part in it was because of Gary and me."

"Easy to say that now," Colt said. "So it was Gary you were trying to impress?"

"You're very judgmental today," Lyssa said. "Why does he have to be trying to impress anyone? Maybe it's just his personality to be a bastard."

"Because if he was a bastard who wanted to cause trouble, he wouldn't have gotten himself straightened out. I'm damn proud of everything he's done to get here, our parents are too, and if that all goes to shit…"

Some of Blaser's gusto seeped out, he'd never heard Colt admit to having pride in him. They spent so much time butting heads that he forgot his twin actually did like him sometimes. Talking smack about your own brother was different to letting someone else do it, he released some of the pressure on his hands. Colt always gave him grief, but he'd never hesitated to use his influence with the cops when he was in a jam, something he never did for Mattie.

"It's not going to go to shit," Blaser said, cutting his brother some slack. "You have to trust me, and you have to give her a chance."

"A chance? Why?" Colt asked. Blaser braced for what was to come next. "Are you fucking her?"

"Why would he have put her in your apartment if he was sleeping with her?" Lyssa asked.

"This isn't about sex," Blaser said, appreciating Lyssa was sticking up for him. "She was my girl for years. I'm not going to see her in trouble. Gary is in jail, she has no one to look out for her."

"You ran to her after Gary was arrested and she slammed the door in your face."

She had, but he'd stayed right there knocking until she opened it back up for him.

"Because she thought I was responsible for it, she was upset, but she's calmed down."

"Ruger told me you two were sleeping together," Lyssa said.

He mentally retracted his previous gratitude.

"When did he say that?" Colt asked in that cop voice

as though trying to catch him in a lie.

Once again, his irritation bubbled up.

"The night after the rock came through my window," she said. "The same night Gary showed up here and... all that happened."

Colt's eyes came to him.

The accusation in that gaze clenched his fists. "I am not having sex with her. I haven't had sex with her since..."

Recalling the last night they'd been intimate probably wasn't wise, because it reminded him of exactly how it ended... with his arrest. Drifting into the memory, he didn't come out of it until Lyssa's hand took his.

"Since when?" she asked.

"Sometimes it's just nosy to ask personal questions," he said to his future sister-in-law, knowing exactly how inappropriate her questioning could get.

His rebuke did nothing to loosen her grip on his hand or discourage her probing. "It's very clear you still have feelings for her," Lyssa said. "But she's struggling with her own demons at the moment, Blaser. I very strongly urge you to reconsider going ahead with what you're thinking."

"I'm not thinking anything," he said, unsure how the doctor could so easily read his mind.

"Sexual attraction is important in a relationship. You can work to build that element of your bond with her. But it's crucial that you not force her into—"

"I would never force her into anything."

"I know, but something you may think is an innocent advance could remind her of previous experiences. That could be dangerous; it could set back her recovery. Have you sensed any kind of fear from her when you've been in proximity?"

"She doesn't fear me," he said, thinking about the anxiety she'd displayed last night when he put his jacket around her, and how short her temper had been. "She seems more comfortable instigating physical contact than letting me do it."

Lyssa nodded. "That is normal behavior."

"We shouldn't talk about this here," he said.

"No, we shouldn't... But I'd like it if you came into

the office."

Blaser blinked. "Your office? Why would I do that?"

"You care about her, and these situations often affect loved ones."

"I'm not having this conversation with you again," he said.

"What are you two talking about?" Colt asked. "You don't have to sexually deconstruct everyone in the family, Cherrypop."

"Your father and I had an interesting conversation after dinner last weekend," she said.

Colt shuddered. "Was that before or after my mom asked about your cycle?"

Lyssa laughed, resting her head on his shoulder. "Now that was an interesting conversation. If for no other reason than to see all you men blanch."

"Future reference," Colt said. "That's not acceptable dinner conversation."

"I thought you wanted kids," Blaser said, happy to see his brother finally with a woman able to handle him.

Lyssa wouldn't turn on him, she just wasn't the type.

"We do," Colt said. "But my mother doesn't need to know every detail about my fiancée's internal temperature for that to happen. In fact, if I hear them discussing the volume of my yield one more time, there's a chance it will never happen."

Suzette laughed in time with Lyssa. Blaser stepped back to serve another customer. Colt hadn't been happy until he'd met Lyssa. He'd never considered just how pent up and frustrated his twin was until he saw the new more relaxed side of him.

Bri and Crystal came back on to the floor wearing standard Risqué garb, a Lycra skirt and halter top, which drew his attention to her cleavage. Damn, he never noticed his employees' bodies. But, shit, he loved her chest. She was insecure about it because she wasn't as ample as some of the other girls they'd known growing up. He'd never had any complaints. She wasn't flat-chested, she just didn't flaunt herself the way other women did.

The blonde in her hair reflected the white lights flashing on the stage. He stopped to watch her, shaking the coins of the customer's change in his hand. Crystal was explaining something about the stage and Bri just listened. Her perfect skin was so soft, he still remembered the way it felt last night when he'd touched her.

He'd touched her when she was sixteen, made love to her when she was seventeen, and been in love with her from the moment he'd laid eyes on her. The years hadn't dulled her beauty, they enhanced it.

Breaking up with her had been agony, but he really believed he was doing what was best for her. He'd left her alone for years afterwards. From everything he'd heard, she started to get her life together. On the couple of occasions he'd enquired about her when he came across mutual acquaintances, he'd heard good things. She'd worked at an architecture firm doing some sort of admin work and was even dating some guy, which he didn't like to hear, but had to accept was inevitable.

Man, she was beautiful. Being there, around women who were usually semi-naked, had never distracted him. It made no sense that from across the breadth of the room, he couldn't take his eyes from the little scamp whose specialty was tying him up in knots. Other women didn't affect him like she did. Their bodies weren't quite as alluring, their eyes didn't shine quite as brightly, and he'd never got a hard-on at the sight of their smile.

Bri was smiling at a patron. Blaser's fingers closed tightly around the warm coins in his palm. Blood began to move south, and his eyes closed to block out the sight of her glittering, happy eyes. He couldn't want her, he'd been there and done that, and she'd been through too much. Being with her again would only make it more difficult when he had to let her go.

"Hey! Buddy!"

When he opened his eyes, the patron at the bar was holding out his hand. With a mumbled apology, he handed over the coins with a shaking hand. The customer stuffed them into his pocket and stalked off wearing a frown.

Having Bri around wasn't going to be good for business, he could tell that already.

EIGHT

REACHING SUNDAY without further altercation was a relief for Bri. The pressure of living with Erika had been so constant for weeks that she'd almost forgotten what it was like to live without the threat of trouble.

Blaser had been nice to her. He'd gone above and beyond what she would have expected from a regular friend. Maybe because Blaser wasn't a regular friend. If he hadn't given her a place to stay and a job, she'd have been stuck. God knew where she would be without his generosity.

Settling into her new apartment was easy. Almost all the other tenants had been by to introduce themselves. All were variations of scary. All built, mostly tattooed, but so far very friendly. Every tenant worked for or with Blaser in some way, except Suzette. It was awe-inspiring to see how far the one-time ruffian had come.

Closing up at Risqué was almost done, but she'd hung around to catch a ride, as she had the past two nights. Nobody else caught a ride with Blaser, so she assumed they all had their own forms of transportation, or other places to be.

In the locker room, getting ready to leave, she put on her jacket, snatched her purse and slammed her locker door.

When she turned to exit, the door opened. Mattie Warner strolled in.

At about six feet, with slicked back dark hair, he carried an air of affluence, confident in his expensive suit and shiny shoes. "Hello," he said, slipping his hands into his pockets, checking out her figure. "I heard you were back in town."

"Hi Mattie," she said, holding the edges of her jacket together.

Pre-jail, of all the Warners, Blaser had been closest to Mattie. She might not have always appreciated what Mattie was into, but he'd never given her any direct trouble. Seeing such a familiar face, one that she hadn't seen for so long, gave her a spike of nostalgia that took her across the room to him.

With open arms, he welcomed her embrace. The oddest thing happened, tears pricked her eyes and she found herself not wanting to let go.

"It's been so long," she whispered.

"I haven't seen you since before Blaser went inside," he said into her hair.

Maybe that was why it was such an emotional experience. She'd cut herself off from everyone when she moved away. Mattie was a dream. A distant part of her past that was often painful to remember but was also filled with happy memories. Mattie had been a crazy kid, just like Blaser and Gary, he believed himself destined for better things. He'd followed through on those dreams as the suit and shoes attested to.

From the glimmer of surprise on his face when she finally backed away, she could tell he hadn't been expecting such a reaction.

"I'm sorry," she said, poking her fingers into her tear ducts to try jamming the tears. "I don't know where that came from."

"Come here," he said, taking her hand to lead her to the couch. "Gary's in prison?" She nodded. "Does he have a lawyer?"

"Court appointed," she said. "I couldn't even afford to bail him out." That shame enhanced the tears. "I really can't do anything for him.”

"Don't worry about that," he said, moving her hand to his lap as he slid an arm around her. "You've been dealing with a lot on your own."

"Blaser's been great," she said. "And Marshall, but I can't tell him I'm here, you know? If Gary found out I'd come to Blaser for help—"

"Every guy in your life is trying to pull you in a different direction. Maybe you should spend more time worrying about yourself."

Familiar advice. That was something she'd been told after Blaser broke up with her. Eventually, she'd chosen to do just that. Had the guilt of that decision ever left her?

"God, I'm sorry," she said and tried to laugh. "I just went all female on you. Ignore me... Did you need something? If you're looking for Blaser, he'll be out front."

"I'm looking for you."

"For me?"

"When I heard you were back in town, I had to come over and see you. The family is worried about you." Withdrawing her hand, she was annoyed she'd shown him vulnerability if he was about to warn her off at the request of the Warners as a whole. "And I've been hearing whispers about you from the girls. My cousin has always been strict about screwing around with employees. I was surprised he'd employ a woman he's spent most of his life screwing."

"We're not screwing," she said. "He's been a good friend to me, that's all."

"He's been more than that," Mattie said. "But it's not romantic for you anymore?"

"I don't see what that has to do with you," she said. "Are you worried about Blaser's virtue?"

"Blaser can take care of himself especially when it comes to women."

Maybe Mattie's warning wasn't against her, maybe it was for her. She had no idea what Blaser had been like with women since his release from prison.

"You're worried about me?" she asked. "I can take care of myself, Mattie. You don't have to look out for me."

"I'm here to ask you to have dinner with me."

"Dinner?" she said, suppressing the urge to slide to the other end of the couch.

"Yes," he said, lifting her hand to his lap again. "You're an attractive woman and I'm curious… Tell me the time and the place."

Something about the invitation made her uneasy; the word "*curious*" did too. Going out with a curious man usually only led to one thing.

"I'm flattered," she said, wondering why Mattie was suddenly showing interest. "But I'm not looking for romantic… anything right now."

"Nothing romantic," he said. "You're family and it's been a long time. I want to catch up."

"I'm family because I work here at Risqué?"

He couldn't possibly mean her association with Blaser unless he was trying to trick her into confessing lingering emotions.

"And Blaser is looking out for you. If he cares, we all care. You work Thursday to Sunday, so you're free tomorrow. We'll go to Marco's, eight o'clock. I'll meet you there."

"I don't know where—"

"I'll text you the details," Mattie said, kissing her knuckles then rising from the couch. How did he know her schedule and phone number? Blaser better not be giving out those details to just whoever asked. Mattie went to the door and opened it. "I'm looking forward to it."

After he left the room, she gave him a few seconds head start before grabbing her purse from the couch and hurrying out of the locker room to the back alley where Blaser parked the truck.

The girls had informed her he didn't usually drive to work. She had a feeling the truck was for her safety, or at least to give her the illusion of it. The truck was already idling, so she jumped into the passenger seat.

"Do you know where Marco's is?" she asked.

Blaser was messing with the stereo. "Yeah, it's a few miles from here, toward the city."

"Do you want to eat dinner there tomorrow night?"

she asked. "Eight o'clock?"

Losing interest in the stereo, he sat back in his seat, resting a forearm on the top of the steering wheel. "You're asking me out to dinner? You're asking me out on a date? We're dating?"

"Not… no."

Blaser frowned. "I don't understand what—"

"Mattie just came to me. He said I was family."

"And asked you to dinner?" he said and sighed. "That sonofabitch."

"Not asked as much as told," she said. "I'd appreciate it if you didn't give out my schedule so freely."

"I didn't tell the bastard anything," Blaser said. "He knows more than a few of the Risqué girls."

"Oh," she said, wondering again if Blaser "*knew*" them too. To distract herself, she changed the subject. "I told him I had no interest in romance, but he said we were family. I don't want to disrespect him, but I'd feel better if you were there with us. If it's a family meal, that shouldn't be a problem, right?"

"No, I guess not." The edge of his lips curled. "I like the way you think."

"I don't like to be alone with men I don't trust," she admitted.

"You don't trust Mattie?"

"I've never trusted Mattie, he's too smooth, and I know what he's into. I want no part of it."

"You're in your own trouble," Blaser said. "And I got you into plenty back in the day, but you came to me. You still trust me."

"You're different now," she said. "You're not like you were back then and you never pretended to be something you're not. And you saved me from assault in the alley." Displaying her own smile, she hoped to put him at ease. "You proved yourself. If you're uncomfortable and don't want to—"

"I'll be there," he said. "I know my cousin. I know what he's like."

"What does that mean?" Leaning in, he brushed his

lips over hers then retreated, leaving her stunned. "Why did you do that?"

"Staking a claim," he said. "I want you to know I do have… intentions toward you. Everyone will go nuts, but there's no point in me denying it to myself. If I do, I might lose my chance… Mattie's moved up my timetable."

"Blaser," she said on a sigh.

"No pressure and no hurry. You're free to do what you want. If you're not interested, tell me to go to hell… But I don't want to lose out on a chance with you through a dumb miscommunication. So there it is."

He put the vehicle in gear and drove out the end of the alley toward the apartments. Blaser was an attractive guy, six three with defined features and thick dirt brown hair. There probably wasn't a female employee in Risqué who didn't have designs on him at some point. Yet he walked through life with blinders on, oblivious to his own appeal.

Knowing what she did of him now, and his hectic schedule, she could believe what he'd said about not having a girlfriend for a long time. The man seemed to do nothing but work… and worry about her.

"When did you decide this?" she asked, clasping her purse in her lap. "I thought you were just being a friend."

"I was, I didn't help with ideas of talking you out of your panties. But you've been driving me wild for three days, Dollface. I can't keep walking around the club with a boner, someone's gonna get the wrong idea."

"Blaser," she said, enjoying how his name felt on her lips, but wound tight by what he was suggesting. Closing her eyes, she relaxed her head on the backrest and tried to breathe through the tears that hadn't fully subsided since she embraced Mattie. "We can't… I mean… I can't…"

"I'm not asking for sex. I'm telling you, I want to make this work."

"This?" she said, allowing her eyes to open. The motion of the car rocked her head toward him. "You want to go back to the way things were? How do I explain that to my incarcerated brother?"

"While he's incarcerated it doesn't really matter what

he thinks," Blaser said. She sat up, but he pre-empted her complaints. "Don't fly off the handle at me, I'm saying it doesn't matter what he thinks. When a guy tells you that he wants to be with you, your first thought shouldn't be, 'What would my brother think?' should it?"

"What should it be?"

"You know what it should be," he said.

When his hand touched hers, she pulled it back. Odd that she should allow Mattie to touch her but recoil from Blaser.

"You want to know if I'm still in love with you? Is that it?" she said, realizing why Blaser was more of a threat to her than Mattie. In all likelihood, Blaser would get her naked again if he put his mind to it, and she wasn't ready for that yet. "I do love you, Blase. A part of me will always love you. You were my first love, Love."

"Doesn't mean I can't be your last love too."

"You're not ready to settle down," she said. It could be that was more of her hope than her true belief. "Have you told Crystal how you feel about me?"

"Crystal?" he said, frowning. "What does she have to do with it?"

"She's always wanted to be with you Blaser, since way back in high school, you know that."

"This isn't a competition," he said. "You think I'm some dumb prize?"

"If you were then, I'd have won, and I wouldn't be trying to tell you that it's impossible."

"What's impossible?"

"I can't be with you, Blaser. I can't be with any man. I tried it and it didn't work."

"You're talking about the guy you were with in Jersey?"

"Scott? No. I'm not talking about him, that didn't work out, he was still in love with his ex. We called it quits long before I got back in touch with you."

"So what are you—"

"I'm talking about this year. I went on a few dates with a guy after… anyway, it didn't work. I can't do it."

When she'd been freed from her abductors, after speaking to the police, she'd walled herself off from everyone for weeks, even telling Blaser she'd never want anything to do with him again. Once she fathomed that isolating herself wasn't helping, and she'd figured out her own self-help, she had forced herself to date. It hadn't worked out, in fact, it had been a disaster. It was then that she knew being intimate with anyone wasn't going to be an easy step for her.

"It didn't work with him," Blaser said. "But we were great together."

"A long time ago," she said. "And I'm not talking a relationship. I'm talking about sex. I can't have sex."

His laugh startled her. When she caught sight of his broad smile, she folded her arms, wishing to get away from him.

"I'm sorry," he said. "But if you think sex is what's driving me… Lyssa's told me to be patient with you and not to pressure you. I'm not interested in jumping your bones, at least not until you're ready for it."

"Jumping my bones," she repeated. "What is it with Lyssa anyway? You all talk about her like she's some sort of messiah, the girls in the club love her too."

"She's a sex therapist and takes her work everywhere with her. If you give her a chance, you'd like her."

Suzette and Lyssa hadn't been back into the club, but Colt had. Although he couldn't be classed as friendly, he also hadn't given her a hard time. Either Blaser had told his brother to back off or Lyssa used some of her influence.

"I didn't decide not to give her a chance," she said. "She just… she's so direct and… I don't know, maybe it's just because I don't have any experience with therapy."

"You get used to her. I know you and Colt have never been the best of friends, but he's giving you a chance. It would be great if you could do the same."

"Give Colt a chance?" she said. "He could come to dinner with us tomorrow, him and Lyssa."

"Colt at a table with Mattie?" Blaser said. "I'll ask him, but I doubt he'll be open to it."

"Would you at least invite Gus?" she said as he pulled

into the apartment parking lot. "He's family too, right?"

"And you're trying to diffuse any tension between Mattie and me before it boils over. 'Cause he's making a move on my girl, and I might take exception to that. You're smart."

Climbing out of the vehicle, she fished her keys from her purse wondering if she'd inadvertently discouraged him. But when she started up the stairs without saying goodnight he followed on her heels.

"Bri, babe, I'm sorry if—"

When she got to her door, she spun around and grabbed a handful of his tee-shirt to yank him down. Shoving onto her tiptoes, she forced her mouth to his, cutting off his words, making her own intentions clear. Pushing closer, she relaxed her hands on his pecs and he walked her back until he squeezed her against her front door.

This was the same mouth she'd learned how to kiss with when she was a kid. Every part of her remembered the first kiss they'd shared as teenagers. Blaser's mouth was more practiced than hers then, but he was three years older. Some kind of anxious energy had transferred to her that night, and right there, against that door, pressed to the same hot, hard man, she experienced the same sensation.

As a teenager, she hadn't recognized it for what it was: unsated sexual tension ready to explode. Much as they both wanted to heighten the intensity of this kiss, they had to smother that instinct. There was no chance of anything more than a kiss happening tonight.

With a gasp, she lifted her head and smiled at the flames flickering in his eyes. Movement to her left caught her eye.

"Dax," Blaser said in acknowledgment of their amused neighbor.

Dax just shuffled past them, holding up his hands. "I saw nothing," he said, smirking.

Listening to Dax descend the stairs, she took a stifled breath, still squished between Blaser's solid form and her door.

When Dax was gone and they were alone again, he asked her, "Why did you do that?"

"Staking a claim," she said, matching his smile. "I want to, Blase. I mean I wish that I could… I have no intention of involving myself with any other man. My reluctance… it's not about you… you know? I don't want to play games; I want to be straight with you. Intimacy isn't as easy for me as it used to be… There's so much that we should talk about, that… I don't know if it's a good idea for us to… do this again."

"You said you wanted to."

"Yeah," she said. "Because it's you and… it's us."

"Ignoring what happened to you won't make it go away," he said. "You have to work through it, forget about our relationship. You need to process it for your own sanity, don't let those bastards control you anymore."

Being in that secure place, the world couldn't get to her. Blase made her feel so safe. While he was near, nothing bad would happen to her. She'd always known that. He'd been the one to make everything right in her life for as long as she could remember.

"After my failed attempt with that guy a few months back, I made a promise to myself that I would get to know a guy properly before I was intimate with him. If the guy wasn't interested in taking the time to get to know me and be patient with me, then he wouldn't be worth my time."

"Again, proving how smart you are."

Steeling herself for the answer, she almost didn't want to ask but she had to. "Are you interested?" she asked. "I know we already know each other pretty well, but… will you be patient before demanding we get naked and sweaty? I can't tell you how long it will take. It could be a day; it could be a year. I want to be with a man I can trust and rely on, Blaser. I'm so tired of bullshit."

Stroking her arms, shimmers of heat followed the path of his caress which stopped only when his hands were on her face, holding her eyes on his.

"I'm interested, very interested," he said. "Naked and sweaty can wait. I'll keep myself for you… not that I'm inundated with offers."

"You're not oblivious to how hot you are, Blaser.

Women fall over themselves around you."

"Like I said, I haven't had time for women."

"I'm flattered that you would take the time for me."

"You're special."

"You have always told me that I'm different," she said. "What makes you so sure this is right?"

"I've known it since before you looked me in the eye," he said.

Such a statement was profound given how old he must have been when that clarity struck him. Older and wiser, he still trusted that instinct. She understood that innate connection too, sexual attraction wasn't the only spark between them.

"You'll come to dinner tomorrow and promise not to leave me alone with Mattie?"

"You're scared of him?" he asked with growing suspicion. "What happened in the locker room tonight?"

"Nothing like that, I just… I know what his business is, or rather what it's not."

"Legit," he said. "He's not going to get you involved in any trouble. I promise you. No one will get away with hurting you, not ever, you hear me?" She nodded. "Okay, I'm going to kiss you goodnight, then I'm going to watch you go inside. Tomorrow night I'm going to pick you up at seven thirty and we'll ride to the restaurant together with Gus."

"One big happy family," she said.

He exhaled a laugh. "Yeah," he said. "Enough about them and back to my plan."

Lowering his mouth to hers, she parted her lips and held herself close to him savoring the sweep of his tongue and his embracing arms around her. Being encompassed in his strength let her relax in a way she'd been unable to for a year. Her attraction to him was as tangible as it ever had been. That had been obvious since Erika moved aside and Bri caught sight of him in the apartment doorway. After so many years apart, she'd been unprepared for their physical connection to remain so visceral.

"If I don't stop now," he said, trailing his lips to her jaw. "We'll still be here when Dax gets back."

"Where would he be going at this time of night?" she asked.

"I don't ask questions."

"I've heard him going out at this hour before. He's usually gone quite a while; we've got some time."

"And when you're ready, I plan to take advantage of that," he said and took a step away. "Goodnight, babe. Go inside."

"I'll see you in daylight," she said and unlocked her door while he watched her go inside.

On closing the door, she went to the kitchen window to peek out the drapes at him descending the stairs. In his profile, the breadth of his smile was humbling. Special was definitely a word she'd use to describe him too.

NINE

"WHAT'S MATTIE'S GAME?" Gus asked the next night while standing in Blaser's living room buttoning his shirt. "Asking out your girl… Wait, is she up for grabs? You might have given me the heads up first."

"Don't even think about it," Blaser said, lounging on his couch. "Mattie played the family card, so we're playing it right back."

"You know he'll have a reservation for two," Gus said, reeking of mischief. "Champagne in a high hat, the works."

"You like seeing your brother get what he's due, don't even kid yourself."

"Won't hear me objecting. A front row seat to seeing the arrogant jerk put in his place? Yes, please."

Blaser stayed on the couch when there was a knock at his door because Gus went over to answer it. On the threshold, Bri thrust an envelope inside, but when Gus took it, she paled. Clearly, she'd expected him to answer his own door.

Gus looked in the envelope. "I don't know what Blaser told you, but I'm an even five hundred for the night.

It's more if you want to cuddle after."

"It's rent," she said on a laugh, examining his shirt. "Why are you half-dressed?"

"I've not been messing around on you, sweetheart," Gus said. "I missed a button."

"Can I come in?" she asked him.

Gus stayed in her way and looked over his shoulder for the permission she sought.

"Yes, she can come in," Blaser said. "Move, idiot. I'll kick you out if you piss her off."

Gus laughed and moved aside, Bri came in wearing a brown dress that clung to her hips and flared to halfway down her thighs. Zeroing in on her long, tanned legs, his mouth began to water. She came straight to him, dropped onto the couch at his side and rested the length of her body on his with her arm relaxed on his thigh.

When he lowered his arm from the back of the couch and slid it around her shoulders, she wriggled closer. He hadn't been sure how open Bri wanted to be about what they'd discussed the previous night, but she was making it damn clear who she belonged to and that was okay by him.

"Let me put this in my place," Gus said, holding up the envelope. "I'll write you a receipt."

Gus dashed out and pulled the door over but didn't close it.

"I was supposed to come and pick you up, Doll."

"I thought you might want to keep business and pleasure separate," she said, turning her body toward his, her breasts pressed into his ribs.

"You show up looking like you do, all a guy thinks about is pleasure."

"Is Gus okay with this?" she asked.

"Gus likes to watch when his brother is humiliated, so yeah, he's fine with it."

"Humiliated?" she said. He regretted his choice of words. "I don't want to upset Mattie. I've already got people after me, I don't need to add to that."

"Have you had more trouble I should know about?" he asked, touching a shining strand of hair that coiled over her shoulder.

"That you should know about? No."

"I don't like that distinction," he said, noting how she was facing him but managed to avoid eye contact. "Tell me."

"Marshall called," she exhaled. "Gary heard that… I've been made at the club."

If that was the trouble she was worried about, he could breathe a sigh of relief. "You're safe at the club," he said. "I pay security well to make sure my girls are safe. I'll put word out they should keep a special eye on you."

"To make me different from the others? They already think you favoritize me."

"After three days they've picked up on that?" he teased. "They're smart girls."

"Don't tease me, Blase," she said, turning away.

From the way she moved, it appeared she was going to get up and leave. Instinct drove him to reach for her, to hold her near, but he was in two minds about whether grabbing her would upset her. Except, instead of going away, she rested her back on his torso and closed her eyes.

"I've missed lying in your arms," she confessed, bringing his arms tighter around her. His cock reacted to the words before his ears heard them. Knowing they were about to have company, now wasn't the time to push her. He changed the subject. "Gus is as suspicious as I was."

"Suspicious of what?" she asked, twisting around enough to look up at him.

"Mattie asked you out because he wants to seduce you."

"No, I told him I wasn't interested in romance with him."

"Did you tell him you had romantic interest in me?"

"I sort of skirted the issue," she said, laying her temple on his arm.

The peek of those eyes beneath those long lashes sent more of his blood south until he was solid in his jeans.

"No skirting next time," he said, pleased her chest was against him again. "Your actions tonight told Gus that you're my girl. Did you mean to do that?"

"He's family," she said. "Maybe we shouldn't flaunt it at the club."

"I have a rule against dating employees."

"What about tenants?"

"Our tenants have always been male," he said, taking the liberty of touching her knee when she crossed her legs toward him. "It's never been an issue until now."

"Will it cause you problems?"

"We'll work through it. But once Mattie knows, all the club employees will know. Word gets around."

"I'm not ashamed to be with you," she said. "I'm happy for them to know. But I don't think we should change our behavior and parade our relationship in front of the Risqué girls."

"Okay."

"Though once we start sleeping together, I might not be able to keep my hands off," she said, toying with a button on his shirt.

"I'll schedule extra break time for both of us."

"Dating my boss might come with perks," she said.

"You ever done it before?" She shook her head. "Then this is new territory for both of us. I've never dated an employee."

"Is Mattie going to cause trouble for you about this?"

"Let him try."

"He's the money in the family, isn't he? How much sway does he have?"

"Mattie needs me running this place or it would go to shit. Gus is great at doing what he's told, but not so great at taking initiative."

"But you have the garage and the club. So even if he takes this place away from you…"

"We'll be fine," Blaser said. "I can take care of you now, legitimately."

"That's not what I'm worried about," she said. "I can pay my own way and shoulder some of the responsibility, but… I don't want to cause more rifts in the family. We're going to have to deal with a lot of grief from Gary. I would hate to upset your family too. If Mattie kicks you out of here, the family will know why."

"Don't worry about my family," he said. "The only person we need on our side is Ruge. Everyone listens to him, don't ask me why but they do, and Ruge is going to be fine with this."

Now she did sit up and edge away from him. "There's something… something you should probably know before you talk to Ruger about us."

"What?" Blaser asked, shifting to the front of the couch, resting a hand on her knee. "Doll?"

"He might not… I know something about…"

"About what?" Stroking her pinkie finger didn't prompt her to lift her head, apprehension tickled his instincts. "The Warners will accept our relationship, no one is going to cast me out. You don't have to worry about me, babe. Is that it? Is that what you're worried about?"

"Blaser's the business brains in our family," Gus said, pushing open the door and nodding out. "Come on, let's get moving."

Gus' interruption cut their conversation short. When she shot to her feet with determination in her spine, he knew that the mood of the moment needed for that particular confession was gone. As he stood up, he linked his fingers through hers to lead her out to the truck. Gus got into the back, Bri got shotgun.

The restaurant was in a nicer part of town, in the direction of Lyssa's townhouse. Colt had refused his invitation, just like Blaser had said he would. As long as Mattie's associations were illegal, Colt wouldn't give him the time of day and he wouldn't want Lyssa associating with their cousin either.

Mattie would be in the restaurant, no doubt ready for seduction. Thank God Bri had been confident enough to ask for his and Gus' company. Whatever Mattie's intention, humor or sinister, Blaser wouldn't have Bri deal with it alone.

TEN

INVITING BLASER TO DINNER with Mattie may be a mistake she would live to regret. From the first glance at Mattie in Marco's, she could tell he was angry. The private table lit by candlelight was a good clue he'd intended for the night to be more romantic than he'd admitted. Though it was because a part of her suspected his motives weren't entirely familial that she'd asked Blaser to come along in the first place.

Asking Gus to join them was a smart move. Having only Blaser there would've put Mattie on the defensive; it would have seemed predatory. With Gus there, the misunderstanding seemed more innocent.

"I should've called ahead and changed the reservation," she mumbled to Blaser who rested a reassuring hand at the small of her back to guide her through the tables.

"Let him fume," Blaser growled from the corner of his mouth. "Look at this setup. I'm going to skin the bastard."

"Don't even think about causing a scene," she said just before they reached the table.

Gus had got there first and was already talking to the maître d' about a second table.

"I didn't realize this was a communal affair," Mattie

said when they reached him.

"When you said family, I just assumed…" The innocent tone was an act, but she hoped he bought it. "Is it a problem?"

"No problem," Blaser said before Mattie could reply.

He swept her around and into a seat that was already at the table while the staff got the second table set up beside it.

"Easy," Gus said when the staff went away and Blaser took a seat next to her.

"I'm surprised you're here, Blase," Mattie said. "Your precious club will survive without you for a whole night?"

"Every man deserves a night off once in a while."

"Once in a while is right. When was the last time you took a vacation? Prison, was it? You weren't sentenced to hard labor in there, were you?"

Mattie was trying to paint Blaser as a workaholic who wouldn't have time for her.

"I love a man with a sense of responsibility," she said and leaned over to kiss Blaser's cheek, much to his surprise, and probably the surprise of everyone else around the table.

But she didn't see them, she only saw Blaser and the grateful, wondrous glow in his eyes.

"I thought you two weren't together," Mattie said. "You look enraptured."

"We weren't flaunting it," Blaser said, bowing to kiss her hairline, then picking up his water glass to drink.

"You're sleeping together?"

Maybe it was the disgusted incredulity he failed to disguise, or maybe it was the possibility of Mattie trying it on with her later, but the response she gave was a total lie.

"Yes," she declared.

Water might have come out of Blaser's nose, but she was too busy watching Gus laugh.

"Classy restaurant and gutter talk," Gus said. "This is a great night already, Matt. How about you tell us about the last woman you fucked?"

Oh, Bri regretted getting riled. Tension brought her shoulders high as she hid behind her menu. A hand on her knee brought her attention to meet Blaser's gaze. With that look, he reassured her, telling her he accepted the lie and understood it. While his understanding was appreciated, her embarrassment remained. It might be a different story if she could go home and ride him senseless, then it wouldn't be a lie anymore. But she couldn't, she just wasn't there yet.

And it was as the men discussed the menu that she made her decision. She needed to embrace help, and there was only one qualified person in her circle who could offer it.

ELEVEN

"JUST RELAX," Lyssa said, but it didn't make Bri feel much better.

Since making the decision to work hard to get herself to a place where she could be intimate with Blaser, it had been all she could think about. Her appointment with Lyssa had been scheduled for that afternoon anyway, so it made sense to follow through.

She'd been ready for the meeting way ahead of time and had fidgeted around the apartment killing time until walking over to Lyssa's. Now that her heart was in it, she felt different about therapy. Blaser was to thank for that. Not only was she grateful for him connecting her with professional help, she was also grateful that their new "relationship" provided the impetus to face the horror from her past.

As it turned out, Colt was on a job, so she didn't have the threat of him looming nearby. Had that been set up by the doctor for her comfort? Maybe.

Lyssa greeted her and ushered her into the neat, professional office to seat her on the leather couch opposite the angled armchair.

"I don't really know what to do here," Bri said, hands

folded on her lap. "I mean… I don't know what to say."

"Just think of this as a time for us to get to know each other," Lyssa said. "I understand you grew up around here?"

"Yes," she said. Trying not to squirm, she kept her eyes fixed on a spot on the rug. "Gary and I came from what I guess you'd say was the wrong side of the tracks."

"Is that your description of your childhood home? Or someone else's?"

"It was no secret we weren't from a great family. My dad used to drink, somewhere in the middle my mom started taking drugs. I don't remember when exactly."

"That must have been very difficult for you and Gary."

And it was when Lyssa said her brother's name that she looked up. There was no judgement in the doctor's eyes, but Bri shook her head. "This is stupid."

"Why do you say that?"

"You're going to marry Colt, who is, in all likelihood, going to stand up against my brother in court. I can't reveal my life to you."

"You don't have to say a single thing you're uncomfortable with," Lyssa said. "But what you say in here will always be confidential."

"How can I believe that? I've seen you and Colt together."

"I love him, nothing you can say in our sessions will change that. But he respects what I do. The day he asks me to divulge personal patient information is the day I tell him to stop meeting beautiful women in dark alleyways."

Huh, interesting point, intrigue made her frown. "What is it Colt does now? He stopped being a cop around the same time he got divorced, right?"

Lyssa nodded. "Now he does what he did then, but without the rules."

"So he meets clients and investigates their problems?"

"He's a little more niche than that," Lyssa said, picking up her clipboard. "You decided to keep your appointment with me today. I'll be honest, I wasn't sure you would."

"It's Blaser, I… he really trusts you," she said though the answer was only half true.

"Blaser is a great guy," Lyssa said. "I think he struggles to believe that himself."

"That's true. He always thinks the worst of himself, he's always been the same. I think that's part of the reason he got sucked into crime, he didn't believe he was worth fighting for anything better."

"But he had you."

"Yeah," Bri said, reaching for a cushion on the couch beside her to pick at the corner. "He tried to protect me from it. But he… I think I was part of the problem, he wanted money to take care of me. Blaser hated to see Gary and I struggle, so he sort of moved in with us for a while. I know he begged his parents to let me move in there, but they wouldn't have it."

"His parents were concerned about youth pregnancy I imagine."

"That was no less likely to happen," she said. "We had sex anyway, lots of it."

"Ruger was in the house too, and he is the youngest. Maybe they didn't want to set precedent."

"God forbid Ruger be inconvenienced," she said, trying not to grind her teeth. Just the mention of his name stirred an urge to scream. That was something she'd need to get over if she wanted to be any part of the Warner family.

"Ruger upset you? Did you two have an argument? He hasn't mentioned—"

"No, he wouldn't mention it. You don't know what he does, none of you do. I know that you're clueless because I was too, completely clueless until they took me."

"They?"

"The Sniveller and some guy called John…"

"They're the ones who assaulted you?"

"The Sniveller did," she said, closing her fingers around the edge of the cushion. "I should never have been there."

"With them?"

"I blamed Blase at first, you know?" she said, closing her eyes on the memory. "I sat chained up in that cell cursing his name because if he'd just gotten to the restaurant sooner, if I hadn't gone outside… But it wasn't his fault that I was there. I know that now."

"It wasn't your fault either."

"No, it was Ruger's fault that I was taken," she snapped. "I was there because he walked away. They wanted him to work for them and he refused, he walked away, and that's when they took me. I was an example of what they could do, what they were capable of. He didn't have a girl of his own, so they took his brother's. Neat for me, huh?"

Lyssa put the clipboard aside and slid to the edge of her seat. "Are you saying you were kidnapped and held prisoner in order to encourage Ruger to do something they wanted him to do?"

"Yes," Bri said, angry with herself when moisture slid from her eyes.

"I can't believe he would know something like that and do nothing about it. Did you see him in—"

"No," she said, sniffing and brushing a nostril with her fingertip. "I didn't see him. As far as I know, Ruger never knew I was there, he'd already left their crew by then. They were human traffickers. They were going to sell me to the highest bidder to scare him into coming back. They wanted to show Ruger what they'd done, prove they were serious, so he'd have no choice except to work for them."

"How on earth did you free yourself from that if Ruger didn't—"

"A cop saved us," Bri said. "A group of us, of women, were being transported. The cop ran us off the road, he was looking for his own girlfriend. Apparently, this group made a habit of abducting the women of those they wanted working for them. It greased the skids and ensured their compliance."

"Brianna," Lyssa exhaled. "I am so sorry you went through that experience. It must have been horrendous. Did you go to the police or—"

"There were investigations and I talked to cops; I told

them my story. But by then all the men involved were dead."

"So no one was prosecuted?"

"No one that I had contact with. I know the feds went after those higher up in the chain, but that was nothing to do with me."

"You told the police about Ruger's involvement in—"

"No," she said, releasing a laugh. "Is that your main concern, doctor? No, I didn't get Ruger into any trouble. I played dumb about why they took me. I only know because John told me, him and his buddies really had fun letting me know I'd been kidnapped because of my boyfriend's brother."

"Blaser. They believed you were in a relationship with Blaser?"

"That night was our first official date, supposed to be," Bri said. "I was so excited about the idea of dating Blaser in a grown-up way. As opposed to how it was when we were kids, just showing up to fall into bed with each other, you know?" Lyssa nodded. "I sat in the restaurant waiting and he didn't show, so I went outside to call him and that's when they took me."

"So you blamed him for being late and allowing you to be taken?" Lyssa said.

"Except now I know he didn't know anything about it."

"How long did they have you?"

"Just over a week," Brianna said. "The first couple of days were terrifying, there was no food, and it was so dark. There were others… no one knew what was happening."

"I can't imagine how scared you must have been."

"I kept thinking about Blaser, about how he'd think I stood him up. I just… I couldn't decide if I should hate him or feel sorry for him… and then… one night I… they took me out and fed me, and I was so grateful, but this…" Her lip curled in disgust. "I told him to stop, I begged, and I…"

"It's okay," Lyssa said. "Just take your time."

"It was just that once, but it was… I switched off, I tried to kick and fight, but it was useless. My hands were tied, and he hit me so hard I passed out. When I came to, he was…

I just had to block it out."

"You did what you had to in order to survive," Lyssa said.

"I felt like it was my fault," she said, biting her lip. It was hopeless, the tears came anyway. "And Blaser... I knew he'd... I couldn't let him near me when I was so filthy... I couldn't bear to have him turn away from me. He had never turned away from me and if he rejected me because... because of what The Sniveller did to me." Covering her face with her hands, she tried to count her breaths in and out to stop herself from losing the battle with distress. Her body shook and her quaking fingers only reminded her of what it was like to be on that stinking floor with that slimy bastard on top of her.

"Take your time," Lyssa said.

From the proximity of the voice, Bri could tell that the doctor had moved. When she took her head out of her hands, Lyssa was beside her holding a box of tissues.

"I'm sorry."

"Don't apologize," Lyssa said, tugging out a couple of tissues. Bri took them to wipe her face. "You're doing really well, and everything you felt, those are perfectly normal reactions to such a horrible violation."

Lyssa kept hold of her hand.

After taking some time to measure her breaths, Bri managed to compose herself. "I told Mattie Warner I was sleeping with Blaser," she said, choosing to switch to a different topic.

"This was last night during the family meal? Why did you do that?"

"I think Mattie wanted to... I don't think he intended for it to be a family meal. I asked Blaser to come because I worried... being alone with men who have ideas of intimacy is difficult for me."

"Mattie is apparently an intense character," Lyssa said. "Colt didn't want us to come because he doesn't get along with his cousin."

"They're opposite ends of the same spectrum," Bri said. "Colt has always been the moral sort with a strong set of ethics. Mattie isn't interested in a rule unless he's finding a way to bend it or making it up himself. If I had your job, I'd say Mattie seeking me out at Risqué, asking me to dinner, was his way of bending the family rules."

"Family rules?"

"As far as the Warners are concerned, I've always been Blaser's property. Mattie heard I was back in town and not on Blaser's arm…"

"So he thought he would take what was Blaser's?"

"Mattie doesn't really want me, we never got along. I mean, we did, on the surface, but not really."

"Why not?"

"I didn't want Blaser to have anything to do with him," Bri said. "I knew what Mattie was into was illegal, but Blaser is so big on family… and Gary was getting him into all sorts of trouble. I guess Mattie thought it was hypocritical of me to object to him… which I guess it was."

"You were trying to protect Blaser," Lyssa said. "You shouldn't allow yourself to get drawn into their alpha male pissing contest. If either of them wants you, they'll have to prove it in their own way and win you over. If you're not ready or interested—"

"I want to have sex with Blaser," she said. Lyssa clamped her lips shut. The glitter in the therapist's eyes implied maybe she wanted to smile or laugh. Would that be in joy or surprise? "I'm sorry to be so abrupt, I shouldn't have… I shouldn't have said that."

"You can be completely honest here," Lyssa said, squeezing her hand. "Can I ask if you've been with a man since the attack happened?"

Bri shook her head and dropped focus to her knees. "After it I just wanted to curl up, you know? I didn't want to see Blaser or anyone. He called me for months and… I just shut everyone out."

"But you came back here?"

"I'd come to the conclusion that I wasn't going to settle in Jersey, not after what had happened to me. But I was trying to get better, to get over the issues caused by what I'd gone through. I bought books and worked through the steps, trying self-talk to make sure my anxiety didn't get the better of me and that I didn't automatically go to a negative place. I was really determined not to let him win."

"That's very good. It sounds like you've been using cognitive processing approaches."

"Gary had been asking me to come home forever," Bri said, "so I did."

"You've been through a lot," Lyssa said. "I'm sure Blaser understands he has to be patient."

"He does, but I don't want him to have to be."

"If you force yourself to go further than you want, it will set back your recovery. Have you two been close to intimate since you've been back in his life?"

"We kissed," Brianna said. "And we admitted we have feelings for each other and that we want to try to be together."

"That's great," Lyssa beamed. "I tell my clients that communication with your partner is the most important thing. Sexual intimacy is always better with emotional intimacy. You and Blaser have proved you have trust in each other by admitting your feelings openly. You already share a history, emotional intimacy could really help you to move past this… We're going to get you through this, Brianna."

Something about the way Lyssa said her name attracted her attention, the sincerity in Lyssa's eyes brought tears to her own. "I want him to be happy."

"Which is what he wants for you too," Lyssa said. "I'm going to talk you through the various techniques we can use to help you. We're going to decide together how to move forward, okay?" Bri nodded. "And if you want Blaser here, for any of this, we can include him whenever you're ready."

Lyssa left the couch to return to her seat and Bri relaxed. The woman was very comforting and accepting, which reduced her nerves. As much as she didn't relish discussing such a difficult episode, the space felt so safe that she didn't worry about being judged.

She had no idea how long it would take, but at least it was movement in the right direction. Blaser would be patient. He'd waited this long to have her again; he wouldn't mind waiting a while longer.

TWELVE

HER NEWFOUND RELIEF drained out of her not long after she left Lyssa's office. They made plans to meet again, and she'd been looking forward to seeking Blaser out and singing the praises of his future sister-in-law.

Positive thoughts withered and died when she saw Rafe on the corner of the block, near her apartment building. By the time she noticed him, he'd already seen her eliminating her ability to run and hide.

The last thing she wanted to do was to talk to the guy. But he'd shown up himself as opposed to sending a henchman, that had to be good, didn't it? If he'd wanted her beaten or worse, he would've sent someone. He wouldn't be there in broad daylight, so close to her apartment where there were people who'd react if they heard her scream.

"You're a clever girl," Rafe said when she stepped onto the sidewalk, and he came to meet her.

"I am?"

"Yes, the Warners put word out this week you're under their protection. You moved into Mattie Warner's building, smart move."

It hadn't occurred to her that affiliating herself with

Blaser could start a gang war. But now she got why she'd blipped on Mattie's radar. If Blaser declared she was under his protection, it would be like sending a memo direct to the most allied criminal member of the Warner family, Mattie.

"I'm only here because a friend was kind to me," she said to Rafe. "Your idiot goons got me kicked out of my last apartment."

"This friend of yours is a pretty old friend. From what I hear, you're paying him in kind." Rafe's hand rose, she tensed when it came toward her and stayed completely still when it moved through her hair. "I thought maybe coming down here in person, we could come up with our own arrangement."

"That money is nothing to do with me," she said, batting his arm away. "Erika and her boyfriend borrowed it, not me. I'm not paying back their debt and damn sure not in that way."

"I'll give you a week," he said. "Ten grand."

"You can't be serious," she said, trying not to gape. "They can't have borrowed anywhere near that amount."

"Consider that an opening payment," he said, examining her figure. "With interest, the debt gets higher every day."

"It's not my debt."

"Maybe get in touch with Erika and figure something out with her, 'cause if you don't   "

"If I don't, what?" she asked, glaring up into his beady eyes.

"Gary could find himself in more trouble."

"More?" she said.

Gary was already in jail facing charges. How could Rafe make it any worse?

"I know more about Gary's business than you," Rafe said. "I know a whole bunch of people who could go to the police with new stories, proof what your brother is really capable of."

The charges on Gary's sheet were theft offences and providing the police with false information. Yes, he was facing time, but she didn't believe it would be lengthy time.

"What do you plan to do?" she asked.

"You never heard about the shooting, did you?"

"The shooting?"

"Gary shot your boyfriend and boasted about it to the police. Your boyfriend refused to give a statement and denied the whole thing. The charges didn't stick. Maybe if my boys told the cops what they saw… attempted murder is a serious offense. Gary already has a couple of assault charges behind him, he could be looking at a lotta time…"

"Why would you do that?" she asked, sorry her desperation was so obvious.

"Now we're looking at repayment of a debt and hush money…" He hissed in a breath between his front teeth. "We could be looking at a long-term payment plan here…" Rafe's finger met the outer edge of her arm and began to slide up, she yanked it away from his reach. The move angered him. He snatched hold of her to haul her close, bending down to growl into her face. "You're going to give me what I want. I'm going to see I get every cent back and if you've got no dough, you better practice that technique with your boyfriend 'cause I'll be taking advantage of it for a helluva long time."

"Hey!" An intimidating male voice closed in beside them.

Her attention flashed around at the same time Rafe was hauled away.

"Dax," she said.

Not having been introduced, she wouldn't expect him to come to her aid. But there he was throwing Rafe against the long since forgotten billboard on the corner.

"You stay the fuck out of this," Rafe snapped at him.

"You go for a girl from my building, you're asking for trouble," Dax said, planting an arm across Rafe's chest. Despite his struggling, Rafe didn't budge. "Do you want to come see the boss?"

"That don't intimidate me," Rafe said. After another shove, he gave up his fight. "You talking about Blaser? He's a nobody."

"A nobody who cares about this chick. You better be sure you can take him and his crew before you approach this girl again, hear me?" Rafe didn't respond, just tried to spit fury through his expression. Dax increased the pressure on his arm and got closer. "Are we clear?"

Much as it visibly pained him to do so, Rafe nodded. Dax released his prisoner and shoved Rafe down the sidewalk, putting his own body in front of hers. He stayed right there watching Rafe traverse the street then cross and disappear into an alley. Still Dax didn't move. What was he waiting for? Should she speak first? A car sped out of the alley and flew down the block, around the corner. Only then did Dax turn to look at her.

"Thanks," she said, hating the fact he'd had to help her.

"There's more to you than meets the eye, isn't there?" he said. "Come on."

She wasn't quite sure where they were going, but when he started to stalk down the street toward the apartments, she trotted along behind him. They were both going in the same direction anyway. She stayed near but wasn't sure if they were actually going somewhere together or not.

His white tee-shirt strained around his biceps both covered with black tattoos. Wondering if they meant anything, she carried on across the apartment parking lot with him, worrying the whole way. She was with a man she didn't know. What were his intentions? Were they any better than Rafe's?

"You're married, aren't you?" she called out, having fallen a couple of steps behind him.

He glanced back at her. "Yeah."

"I haven't met your wife," she said, hoping the wife wasn't a figment of everyone's imagination.

"You're about to."

"I am?"

He ran up the apartment stairs, taking them two at a time. His stealth and speed were impressive. As fast as his honed physique moved, he barely made a sound.

"Babygirl!"

They were already on the upper floor of the apartments. Forlorn want welled up in her at the sight of her own front door. All she wanted to do was disappear behind it and wait for Blaser to find her.

The door next to hers was Ruger's, or more accurately, Suzette's. The next door along opened. A beautiful, busty brunette poked her upper body out. "Don't holler at me like I'm an animal," she said. "You couldn't have walked the extra three steps and opened the door to come in and talk to me like a civilized human being?"

"Stop the shit and come out here," he said. "The girl here's got herself into some crap and I'm not in the habit of asking strange women into dark apartments with me."

"Actually, you are, tough guy," the brunette said, stepping out onto the balcony, "but it's a habit we're trying to break."

"This is Ivy," Dax said, folding his arms and leaning back on the railing. "Tell her what's going on."

"Don't bark at her like that," Ivy said and shook her head at him. "Geez, you have no idea how to behave around normal people at all."

Dax muttered something Bri couldn't make out. Ivy completely ignored him.

Bri took it upon herself to fill the silence. "Your husband was very kind just now," she said, hating to owe anyone a favor. Maybe talking him up to his wife and winning him some brownie points would even the score. "He's a very nice man, he was… gallant, you should be proud."

Ivy's smile quirked. "I'm proud, but nice and gallant aren't words anyone should use to describe Dax. Though if you're in trouble, he can fix it."

"Fix it?" Bri asked.

"Can I?" he asked. "I charge a fee to fight. I don't beat up lowlifes on the street… anymore."

"You will if they're intimidating a woman who can't defend herself," Ivy said then looked at her. "You're Blaser's friend, aren't you?"

"Yes," Bri said. "I should probably go and… I can go find him."

"He's at the garage," Dax said and pushed away from the railing. "I'll get him."

She wanted to object because it would mean owing

him yet another favor, but he strode away with such purpose, it felt rude to stop him.

"Your brother's in jail?" Ivy asked.

This building and its tenants were a concentrated model of small-town life. Everyone there was related to each other or worked together. It was no surprise everyone knew everyone else's business.

"He's in jail, what do you care?" Bri asked, knowing it was unfair to be so defensive, but she was sick of being scrutinized.

"I don't," Ivy said. "Just trying to make conversation. Why don't you come in and tell me about the trouble Dax just got himself tangled up in?"

"You don't have to worry about Rafe coming after Dax. He likes to think of himself as a big deal, but I don't think Dax would have any difficulty taking down the idiots who work for him."

"I don't think he would either," Ivy said. "That's not why I asked."

"Why are you asking?"

"You showed up here in the middle of the night and Blaser put you into his brother's apartment which wasn't even cold," Ivy said, coming closer. "Word is you and Blaser used to be tight... like down and dirty tight."

"Yeah," Bri said, shrinking in the shadow of the woman's confidence.

Ivy wasn't much taller than her, maybe only an inch. Although her breasts were generous, the rest of her was slight. She probably carried less weight on her hips than her. Yet, she stood so tall and met Bri's eyes in a way that awed her. Nothing scared Ivy, maybe that was what it took to be on the arm of a man like Dax.

"I saw a guy pick you up the other day, outside the parking lot, who was that?"

"Marshall," she said, believing Blaser wouldn't employ anyone she couldn't trust. "He's a friend of my brother."

"The brother who is in jail?" Bri nodded. "Getting yourself involved with more than one guy is a bad idea, especially the sort of guys around here. If Marshall is your brother's friend and you're messing around with Blaser too, that's gonna lead to trouble."

What was the point in arguing? "Thanks for the advice."

Lyssa hadn't been at all judgmental, a sign of her training. Ivy seemed to be all about judgement and had no reservations about voicing it. Everyone wanted to give her free advice, even without invitation.

"Look…" Ivy said when Bri began to move toward her apartment. "I didn't mean to sound… I shouldn't stick my nose in. But Blaser's pretty clear about everyone around here looking out for each other. It seems to me that you're surrounded by a bunch of guys, all of them want something from you. So if you want a friend, like a girlfriend, who has no interest in seeing you naked, I'm here if you want to talk… And, by the way, I'd think twice about talking to Suzette… she's a nut. Certifiable."

Talking to Lyssa had helped, and she was a professional, but Lyssa didn't know anything about the reality of her life. Crime and scum were what she'd grown up with. Unless you'd lived that life, you couldn't explain it to anyone.

"Did you grow up around here?" Bri asked.

Lyssa was a doctor, so didn't give out much personal information. Maybe, if it could work both ways with Ivy, they could forge a real friendship that wasn't in any way tied to her past.

"Not around here," Ivy said. "But ex-cons, doing anything to get by… yeah, I grew up around that."

"Do you want to come over for coffee?" Bri asked and the women shared a smile. Having a friend on her doorstep, a female one who wanted nothing from her, could make a difference. Until she tried it, she couldn't be sure. The women headed for her apartment, but Bri whirled around to face Ivy. "Sorry to ask such a personal question but, before we go on I should…"

"No, I won't share Dax," Ivy said with an icy glare that quickly gave way to a smile, Bri's tension burst out in a laugh. "I'm messing with you, what is it?"

"You don't use drugs or owe anybody money… do you?"

Ivy shook her head. "No, I don't. But I think you've just explained to me what your trouble is, ex-boyfriend?"

"Ex-friend," Bri said. "I'll tell you all about it, but I'd love to know how you snagged a guy like Dax first."

"You got it," Ivy said. "It wasn't easy. Let me tell you, the story will blow you away."

THIRTEEN

BLASER HAD BEEN OUT on a tow. As soon as he pulled the truck into the garage lot, Dax came out and headed straight for him. Immediately, it was obvious something was up. The second Dax mentioned Bri, he was enroute to the apartment block, getting the rest of the story on the way.

He didn't knock, it didn't occur to him, he went straight into Bri's apartment to find her seated on the couch with Ivy, Dax's wife, drinking coffee. Their abrupt entry interrupted the women's laughter.

When they silenced, Dax blew out a short whistle. "Come on, Minx, out of here," he said. "Man's got to sort out his female."

"Yes, Master," Ivy droned.

The women shared a look, then laughed again. Ivy put her cup down and exited with Dax, just like she'd been told to.

"Do you know the story of how they got together?" Bri asked, taking her cup and Ivy's into the kitchen to wash them. "It's amazing."

"Fuck their story, what happened to you?"

"Nothing happened to me," Bri said. "I went over to

Lyssa's—"

"Lyssa," Blaser said, shaking his head and marching over to her. "You're telling me that Rafe approached you and Lyssa? Colt is gonna go nuts."

"Like you are?" Bri said, turning to lean on the counter as she dried her hands. "I'm okay, Love. Dax came along and scared him off."

"What did he want?"

"Dax?" she asked being deliberately obtuse.

"Not Dax, Rafe. What did Rafe want?"

"His money," Bri said. "He wants ten grand in a week and if I don't deliver, he'll send his men in to testify against Gary and invent some story about him shooting you."

Some of Blaser's anger gave way to an awkward reality. "Gary did shoot me," he said.

Given how honest she'd been with him, it was only right he be honest in return.

Her ease vanished in a flash, to be replaced with a panicked concern. "What? When?"

"It doesn't matter," he said, reducing the space between them. "I told the cops it never happened. They can't charge him if they have no evidence."

"But they will have evidence if Rafe's men rat him out. Oh God, Blaser, this is terrible."

That he'd been shot, or terrible that Gary might pay for it?

"Was Lyssa hurt?" Blaser said, taking the focus away from his altercation with Gary might alleviate some of her worry and guilt.

"Lyssa wasn't there. I was on my way back here, Rafe was waiting on the corner," she said. "Can I see it?"

"See what?" he asked, considering how to respond to the threat encroaching on his territory.

"Where he shot you."

"You don't believe me?" he snapped then instantly regretted his strong reaction. It took her aback, he didn't bark at her. Not at Bri. "Babe, I don't want to see you hurt."

"I can't believe he… Why would he…?"

"He heard we were seeing each other."

"I heard what happened at the club. Was the shooting before or after, God…" she stumbled over the last word. "He shot you, Gary, actually… he actually…"

She sank to the floor, her hands rising to her throat. Impulse took him down with her. Dirty and greasy from the tow job, he couldn't reach out to her like he wanted. Being restricted formed an ache in his chest, squeezing air from his lungs.

"He wasn't trying to kill me," he said, remaining on his knees, speaking in a soft tone meant to soothe because he couldn't do it through touch. "We were fighting, arguing. He was waving the gun around… It was an accident."

"An accident?" she shrieked. Her wide, wet eyes leaped to his. "That's worse, he could've killed you! Oh, Blase!"

She crawled to him, throwing her slender arms around his neck, dropping her weight to them. When she buried her face against his flesh, goosebumps skittered over him.

"Lys fixed me, Doll. I'm safe. I'm fine."

"But you could've been killed," she said, the cloud of her warm breath wormed its way into his coveralls.

Squeezing his eyes closed, he was losing control of his blood flow. Despite his best attempts, it was routing south.

"Lys is a good doctor," Blaser said, fighting to keep the subject on something un-arousing. "She patched me up and kept on at me 'til I was all fixed up."

Her small fingers skimmed from his neck to the pops on his coveralls. One popped open. He clenched his jaw. The next popped and he closed his fists. The third went and he swayed away, but she still hung off him with one arm. He was stuck there, being undressed by the woman he'd been naked with more than any other.

"Doll," he murmured, allowing his mouth to settle in her hair. "I could tell you he shot me in the groin. Would you still want to see it then?"

"I've seen your dick before and you're not modest," she said, but he could feel her heart hammering against his body.

"Look at me."

Any time she was nervous, she wouldn't meet his eye. But he wanted to be sure she heard and understood him. The rush of her breath came out twice, then she lifted her head to look at him, her dainty digits maintaining their position on his chest.

"It will make me feel better to see it, Love, to see that you're okay."

"It was my shoulder and it's fine. There's no hurry for us to get naked with each other. We'll get there when you're ready. I'm your guy, okay?"

"I went to Lyssa again because... I want to get past this. I told her I wanted to be with you... I want to be with you, Blase."

"You are with me," he said.

Maybe he shouldn't have asked her to look at him. With their eyes locked, he worried his vulnerable adoration for her was exposed.

Shifting to her knees, she rose higher until her plump lips cushioned themselves on his. He'd never experienced sensory overload with anyone other than her. Every part of him, every inch, became alive and aware. He wanted to touch her, wanted to get hold of those slim hips and lower her onto the vinyl floor. He wanted to kiss the creamy, sweet skin on the side of her neck and find out if that sensitive spot behind her ear still made her mew out a blissful breath of gratitude. That sound always made him want to work harder for her.

For however long it took her to work through her trauma, he would support her and be patient. The last thing he wanted her to think was he was a horndog only out for one thing.

When her lips widened and her tongue touched his lip, he let her in. Like a teenager learning how to do this for the first time, he didn't want to push her. He held back, ready to let her take the lead. Her fingers slid inside his coveralls and spread over his collarbone.

Her lips departed his and her forehead landed on his shoulder. "I'm sorry about this," she said.

"About what?"

"I know how you kiss, Love, and that wasn't it."

A wave of desperation tried to force him to grab onto her and possess her forever. "You think I don't want this?"

Leaning back, she dropped to her haunches then sat on the floor, staring straight at his groin and the conspicuous lump straining his coveralls. "I think I've brought a criminal onto your property and started a war between your crew and his."

"I don't have a crew anymore."

"Dax says different," she said but carried on. "On top of that, my brother put a bullet in you and tried to ruin your business. Why, oh, why would you want anything to do with me? Your family is right, Blase. I'm bad news."

"None of this is your fault," he said, touching her face. "None of it. What matters is we're together. We found each other again."

They'd found each other again a year and a half ago. The wait to have her back in his arms had been torturous. At times, he'd almost given up hope. But now that he had her, he wasn't ever going to let her go again.

Breaking up with her had been madness. Despite his best intentions. He shouldn't have left it so long to speak to her again. Every move made to bring them back together had been hers. Now it was his turn to hold them together.

He'd gotten grease on her face but seeing the physical markings of his possession only fired him further into a frenzy of want. The build-up of panic and passion collided until he forced himself to stop touching her.

"I have to get to the club soon to open up. Will you let me buy a takeout lunch and we can eat in my office? It's not romantic, but—"

"Sounds great," she said. "I'm flattered you would ask."

"Better get used to dinner on the fly, we've got a lot of businesses to run."

"It will get easier now that there are two of us to share the responsibility. We were always a good team."

"Yeah," he said. "We were… I better get back to it."

Leaving her there, alone on the floor, was difficult,

but he had no choice. If he kept touching her and losing himself in her beautiful face, he might be tempted to push boundaries.

He kissed her quickly and got to his feet, taking her up with him. With a brief goodbye, he left the apartment and closed the door. The garage wasn't his first port of call, that honor was awarded to the apartment two doors down.

Knocking, he waited for an answer. "I owe you one," Blaser said when Dax opened the door.

"Good," Dax said. "I like it when guys owe me."

"That why you did it?"

"Ivy says I'm desensitized to that kinda shit, and I love to prove my female wrong."

Blaser couldn't work out how to take this guy. If he meant what he said, then he had to assume Dax had seen some scary shit. Reading between the lines, he took it to mean the comment was more about his wife and her perceptions.

"If I wanted to scare this piece of shit off our turf…, would you be interested?"

"There's a lot of muscle around here, Blase, you don't need me."

"You got a problem? Squeamish or just scared?"

"You won't bait me into a fight," Dax said, one corner of his mouth slinking up. "And if you ask me, it's not a fight you want either."

"Why do you say that?"

"Last time you got in a fight, you got shot," Dax said. "Either you pay this guy what he wants, or you end him. No fight, the end, you get me?"

Pay him off or kill him.

Blaser didn't like those options. "I'm no murderer."

"You're no fighter either. I know you're pissed he came after your woman, but if his associates saw her brother shoot you, somehow, they're all connected. You think her brother would be happy to hear what this guy is doing to his sister?"

"Gary's got no influence," Blaser said. "Even if I had a way to get word to him, Gary couldn't do anything about it."

"Then you're back to my original suggestion, pay him

or end him."

"I can't pull that kind of cash together that fast," Blaser said. Selling one of the businesses would be an option, if he could close the transaction fast. Probably not. His savings were on the sparse side. Everything he earned was poured back into the businesses.

"If it's money you want," Dax said, lowering his volume and pulling the door closer to his back. "I know how you can raise it fast."

"How?" Blaser asked, ready to try anything.

"The basement of the club," Dax mumbled, keeping his eyes trained to Blaser. "How many can you get in there?"

"The capacity?"

"Yeah," Dax said.

"Why do you need to know that?"

"Because I've got a lucrative hobby. You provide me with a venue, and I can fill it to the rafters. Invitation only. If you want to make yourself a quick buck, I'm the only guy you want in the ring."

"In the ring?" Blaser said. Dax wanted a venue. From his fitness level, it was obvious he could handle himself. But Dax wasn't talking about obtaining licenses and inviting the masses, which meant he was talking illegal. "Does Ivy know about this?"

"Yeah," Dax said. "I'll handle the wife if I have to. Are you interested?"

"I don't know," Blaser said. "How risky are we talking?"

"If your guys know how to keep a secret, it's not risky at all. It's just one night, a one-time event. You'll have enough to save your girl and pay off a few debts too."

The notion was tempting. It would give him a chance to show Bri he could take care of business for her. That was the same thought he'd had throughout his youth, right before he screwed up.

FOURTEEN

UNDERGROUND FIGHTING. Blaser had seen a few rounds in his younger days and always thought it was brutal. Two guys in the ring, no weapons, and don't hit a guy while he's down, those were the only rules. He had no idea there was so much money in it. Dax laid it out for him, there on his doorstep and Blaser turned him down flat. He'd promised Colt and Ruger there would be no illegal activities at the club… but he'd made that promise before Bri needed him.

"It's the only way I can make enough money to pay Rafe," Bri said. "You must be able to see that."

Except he couldn't see that because he wasn't following what she was saying, he was too busy thinking about Dax and his offer. They were in his office at the club, eating the picnic Bri had put together for them at short notice.

"Sorry, Doll, I was somewhere else," he said, not ready to admit he'd been considering a brief return to his old ways.

"Dancing," she said. "If you let me dance in here, I can make more money. I mean, I won't make ten grand in a week, but it's worth a shot… There's no other way I can get close to giving him what he wants. I have nothing worth selling."

"I could sell the truck," he said.

There were plenty in the junkyard he could fix up to get running, if he could ever find the time to do it… and afford all the required parts upfront.

"Is it worth ten thousand?" she asked with a tinge of hope, but his wince made her sigh. "Then there's no point getting rid of your only mode of transportation."

She could be so vibrant when she laughed, he thought, watching her scrape her plastic fork through her wilted salad. Right then, she had nothing to laugh about. The whole situation made him feel pathetic, weak, useless, he wanted to take care of her, but he'd never earned big bucks.

Even with his businesses and their success, he wasn't rich. His income was higher than it probably ever had been, and it still wasn't enough to provide what she needed. Back when they were teenagers, he had promised she would never need to go back to that, that he'd always take care of her. How could he break that promise? He couldn't.

"I'll be safe dancing in Risqué," she said. "You have great security, and you can keep an eye on me. No one will step out of line. I haven't heard of any problems with patrons around here, everyone seems decent."

Every man was decent until the surge of arousal met that of anger. He could never tell which customer might let those urges take hold of him.

She carried on. "You've been taking me home every night, so no one will approach me after my shift either. I'll be completely safe… I know you think I'm not capable, what with what happened to me, but dancing is different to sex. I'll go out there on stage, do my thing, and go home. Just another day at the office, that's all it will be."

The fact she was mentioning the negatives betrayed she'd over-analyzed the idea of getting naked for an audience. A horny, slobbering, eager audience of strange men. Her trauma made her edgy; taking off her clothes would only lead to feeling more vulnerable. It didn't matter how much she tried to convince him otherwise, he knew her better than that.

Besides his own personal aversion to other men

enjoying the body he craved, the minute she got onto that stage with the music pumping and the lights flashing, she would freeze. Dazed, her inability to see what was beyond the dazzle would paralyze her. As the owner of the club, as her boss, he didn't care if she didn't complete her act. But Bri would take that embarrassment and magnify it in her own mind until she couldn't show her face at the club again. That didn't work for him.

Now he had her back and had admitted his desire for them to be together, he was determined to keep her. Dealing with Gary, and his objections, would wait. Dealing with Rafe was the number one priority. He could try to track Erika and the boyfriend down. Then what? He wasn't the type to kidnap them and drag them back to Rafe to let the sadist do his worst.

Rafe had made this Bri's problem. That made it his problem. Bri wouldn't have to dance to raise the money. Mattie would have the capital. If he went to his cousin for a handout, he'd have to be prepared to owe him for life. Mattie would own him, and he wasn't the type to let go easily.

"What do you think?" she asked.

Once again, he'd been drifting in his own thoughts so didn't know what she'd last said. "I think I can take care of this," he said. "I can get the money we need to get this guy off our backs for good."

"How do you plan to do that?" she asked, a suspicious edge to her tone. Though her eyes remained on him, her face turned away, examining his expression for some sort of tell. "You better not be planning to fight, Blaser Warner. I don't care how much trouble we get into. I don't want you getting hurt."

Taking her hand, he tossed her fork aside and got closer, until they were almost nose to nose. "Trust me to take care of this, Bri. Once I do, we'll put all this behind us and promise to hide from trouble if it ever tries to seek us out again. We're going to live normal, boring, toiling away at the hard graft lives until we're old, grey, and done with life. How does that sound?"

"Like quite a feat," she said, but he was pleased to see her smile again. "Can you pull it off?"

"You trust me, don't you, Doll?"

Her pleased expression bolstered him, she did trust him and was relieved he could fix the mess. One tiny indiscretion on an otherwise spotless record couldn't be held against him. Since he left prison, he'd been whiter than white. No one ever needed to know about this once it was over.

FIFTEEN

HE HADN'T WRESTLED with the decision for long. The way he saw it, there were two choices, have the fight and pay off Rafe or… Dax's other suggestion. He'd go to prison for a helluva lot longer for one than the other.

Dax didn't need to fight at Risqué. If he did, it would be as a favor because he could pull in a crowd no matter who was getting paid to host the event.

Of all the things he could get himself mixed up in, providing a venue for a clandestine fight was one of the safest. Other than unlocking the doors, he didn't technically need to take any more to do with it.

Certain, he took off from the club as soon as the shift change was done. Leaving Crystal in charge, he'd promised to be back soon, then rushed back to the apartments.

"I'm in," he said to Dax when he opened his front door wearing only a pair of jeans.

"Cool," Dax said. "I'll call my guy and set it up. We'll talk tomorrow."

Dax tried to close the door, so he slapped a hand onto it, preventing it from shutting in his face. "I need to do something first, and I need back up."

"Knock on the next door," Dax said. "I don't enforce anymore."

"Anymore?" Blaser asked. "I'm not asking you to enforce, I'm asking you to watch my back."

"Already did that for your girl today," Dax said. "Don't you have brothers?"

"Colt is the moral type and Ruger isn't around. I just need back up."

Dax's form loosened and his brow came down. "What you planning, Warner?"

"Dax!" Ivy called from within the apartment.

"In a minute, Minx," he called back and came out onto the balcony, pulling the door closed behind him. "If you're going to crack this guy's skull, why set up the fight?"

"I want a figure," Blaser said. "I'll let him know we plan to pay him because it's fair, money is owed and he's going to get it."

"Brianna didn't borrow the money," Dax said.

"How do you know so much about it?" Blaser asked with creeping suspicion.

"Ivy told me, they talked about it this afternoon. I know what's going on."

"I could go over there and tell the guy to back off, but this is Bri's safety we're talking about. I don't want that bastard thinking he can harass her any time I'm not around. He'll get his money. We're not going to be hot heads; I'm going to be the bigger man."

"Why? I'd go in there and kick the—"

"Because that's what I did when we were kids," Blaser interrupted. His hand went through his hair, and he turned his back on Dax to exhale. "I was an idiot growing up, anytime anyone disrespected me or my girl, I went for them. I started a war, and that meant neither of our asses were safe. I was immature, a punk kid, and didn't want anyone calling me a coward, so I fought. They slashed my tires, so I broke their windows. Their tags appeared on my walls, so I returned the favor. It's bullshit, childish games. I want to move on with my life."

"You did time inside," Dax said, materializing beside

him, leaning back on the railing, folding his arms. "For what?"

"Criminal damage and auto theft," Blaser said. "I had a couple of priors."

"Felony?" Blaser nodded. "You did two years?"

"Almost. I didn't do myself any favors inside. I got into it with a guard after Bri and I split."

"Not smart."

"No," he said, curling his fingers around the railing, flicking some flecks of cracked paint out the way with his thumbs. "You didn't get that from Bri talking to Ivy this afternoon."

"No, I didn't. I like to know who my wife is spending time with. None of your guys have priors against women."

"No," Blaser said. "I'm not interested in helping out scumbags, but I know it's tough to get a fair shake after you've been inside. I give guys a chance, but I wouldn't risk it on a guy who didn't respect women and kids. I took Ivy's word that you've never been violent."

Catching a sideways glance, Blaser watched a small smile form on Dax's face, but he lowered his attention to the concrete floor as though to hide it. "Not against women or kids."

"I'm beginning to figure that out," Blaser said. "Tell me how you know so much about the underground fighting circuit."

"I've been a part of it since I was a kid," Dax said. "It's a good way to earn decent money."

"Yet you live here and both of you work for me?"

"Yeah, well Ivy doesn't like me getting in too deep. We're in a transitional phase."

"Transitioning to what?"

"More like from what," Dax said. "I'm not quite sure where we're gonna end up, but I know for sure we're not going back."

That would be a story for another day. He needed to get back to the club, and still had his errand to run. "Are you with me?"

"We go over there, scare the guy, and come away with a figure. After you pay up, he's meant to leave you alone?"

"I don't care about me, but Bri, yeah."

"And if he doesn't?"

"Then we'll look into your option number two."

Their eyes met. From the serious energy Dax emanated, he knew exactly what that meant. "You'd kill for her? Die for her?"

"Dying for her would be easy," he said. "Killing for her is harder, but yeah, I'd do it. If it was the only option."

"Okay," Dax said, pushing away from his leaning perch to head from the door. "Let me go untie my wife and put on a tee-shirt."

"Untie her?"

He paused in the doorway and glanced back over his shoulder. "She's still in training; it takes time to get them into shape."

"I heard that!" Ivy called.

Dax snickered as he went a step inside. "It's naughty to listen to conversations that don't involve you," he called into the apartment. "You know what that means."

Blaser didn't want to ask what that meant. "I didn't realize I was interrupting," he said.

"It's okay, she'll keep," Dax said. "Give me a minute."

He went inside and closed the door, leaving Blaser on the front balcony waiting for his backup to arrive. It had taken some time to cobble together where Rafe was. After a couple of phone calls, his old buddies had eventually come up with the goods. He hadn't told Bri or Colt where he was going because they would try to talk him out of it. Either that or want to come with him. He didn't need the distraction of looking after someone who couldn't handle themselves. Dax exuded capable efficiency and wouldn't need anyone to watch his back.

Not involving Colt was deliberate. He didn't want his brother connected to anything illegal. The guy was getting his life together with a fiancée who adored him. They had a nice house and were trying for a kid. No, he wasn't going to drag Colt into the mess or endanger all his brother was working for and all that he had achieved.

If, or rather when, Colt found out what had happened, Blaser knew his twin would ream him out for it. He'd take the riot act over watching his brother lose even the tiniest piece of his happiness. Colt believed he was irresponsible and always one step away from screwing up monumentally. Maybe that was true. One thing that wasn't true was Colt's belief of his motivation.

Colt thought that he screwed up on purpose, because he liked to play gangster, or wanted to piss people off. Neither was true. Blaser didn't want to screw up. In fact, he often envied how together Colt was, how moral his life had been. Colt was a good guy, such a good guy that he could be relied on and really deserved to find happiness.

Was the same true for him? Who knew? He wanted Bri and wanted them to be happy. But would he ever deliver the white picket fence for her? There he was at thirty-five still creeping around in circles with criminals, threatening those who threatened his kin, doing illegal shit.

Dax came out of the apartment and closed the door, fully dressed and wearing a scowl, his demeanor totally different. The jet-black hair and piercing blue eyes coupled with the solid form made Dax formidable. Thank God the guy was on his side.

"Was she pissed?" he asked as they made their way downstairs.

"She's always pissed," Dax said, waiting for Blaser to unlock the truck and grant them both entry.

"She is?"

Throughout the short time he'd known her, Ivy had always been the picture of polite and hard-working. He couldn't remember her complaining or hearing anyone complain about her.

"Nah, that's not fair," Dax said. Blaser started the truck and got them on the road. "She likes to push my buttons and I let her."

Arguing really was foreplay for the couple. They were both dynamic characters, it would be quite a show to see them interact with each other. While both Dax and Ivy had jobs with him, he'd rarely seen them together. They didn't advertise their relationship but didn't know if it was their intention to conceal it.

"Bri says your story is pretty amazing."

"My story?" Dax asked. "What does she know about it?"

"Ivy told her, how you guys met."

"We met in Vegas," Dax said as if that was explanation enough.

"Married the same night?" Blaser asked, wondering if the story was a drunken mistake turned good.

"Not even close," Dax said.

He didn't expand, so he let it dissolve into the air. It might be a good story, but that wasn't the time to hear it. They were going to tell Rafe he'd get his money. After that, they'd expect him to back off.

Blaser doubted Rafe wanted to start a war. Getting involved with a family like the Warners would be too complicated for a punk kid like him. If nothing else, Mattie's name held notoriety. If it came to it, if they were at make or break, he wouldn't hesitate to get his cousin involved. Mattie would argue he'd outgrown this kind of disagreement and liked to be the savior. It would make him feel big and clever to show how quickly he could dispense with Rafe.

Bri would hate him getting himself involved and Dax too. Once she found out, she would scream to high heavens and point out how she didn't like to owe anyone anything. He wouldn't mind highlighting that so long as they were together, they shared the burden of everything. Fixing the problem with Rafe was just his way of ensuring they got to be together without anyone coming between them.

SIXTEEN

BRI WASN'T SUPPOSED to be working that night, but she couldn't stand being alone in the apartment any longer. Going to see Blaser seemed a little too needy, she didn't want to hang at the bar waiting for him to look her way. The other girls would probably judge her and assume she was only there to supervise her boyfriend, ensuring that his eye didn't wander.

Instead of sitting around overthinking it, she went to Ivy's door and asked if she wanted to join her for a drink. As it turned out, Dax wasn't working or home, so she agreed. They shared a glass of wine while Ivy changed and did her makeup, then they made their way to the club together.

Neither of them paid to get in, maybe because half of them worked there, or because both of their men worked there, but she wasn't complaining. Except when they got inside, Blaser wasn't behind the bar. As much as she wasn't here for him, to see him, she was surprised by his absence.

Another of the security men was working the bar and Crystal seemed to be running things. Colt and Lyssa weren't there, which was something of a reprieve at least. It might have been too intense to see her doctor socially after the session they'd had. And she really wasn't in the mood to have another fight with Colt.

"I should've told you he wasn't here," Ivy said, leaning in close to shout because Destiny had just taken to the stage and the music was loud.

"Who?" Bri said, playing it cool.

"Blaser. He came over to our place a half hour before you showed up."

"I didn't realize he and Dax were close buddies."

"They weren't," Ivy said, sipping her cocktail. "At least not until today."

Blaser's friendships were usually superficial, at least they had been back in the day. He always told her you could never really trust anyone unless they were family, or they'd proved themselves. Dax must have proved himself.

"Did he say where they were going?"

"No," Ivy said. "But Dax said they wouldn't be long and Blaser won't stay away from the club for longer than he has to. I wouldn't worry."

Anything that took Blaser away from Risqué had to be serious, especially since their dinner with Mattie last night diverted his attention from the club for a couple of hours. After dinner, Blase had taken her home and then returned to the club. He really wanted to make the place work and he was terrible at relinquishing control.

He said he didn't like to burden others with his responsibilities, but what he really meant was he didn't trust people not to let him down. That in itself was very sad. He could rely on her. She would prove that by not being just another of his obligations.

Destiny finished her act and Ivy talked about her own time on the stripper pole. Something they had in common. It was a surprise to hear how much experience Ivy had in everything. Especially given Ivy was three years her junior.

As Ivy and Bri tried to convince the bartender to let them perform on stage, Dax and Blaser came in.

"Nobody has to know," Ivy said with a persuasive lilt, leaning over the bar toward the bartender. "I want to see if I've still got it."

"I don't think so," the bartender said, laughing.

"Your husband would skin me alive."

"Skin you for what?" Dax asked, approaching Ivy's side as Blaser went around behind the bar.

"Don't worry about him," Ivy said. "I can handle Dax."

Dax moved in behind his wife and closed his arms around her, placing his own hands on the bar, pinning her chest to it. Ivy kept on grinning. Dax buried his face in her hair and began to whisper. The smile on Ivy's face completely disappeared. The intense expression that took its place was worrying.

"What are you doing here?"

Blaser's question stole Bri's attention from the couple. "I didn't want to sit in my apartment alone all night, so I asked Ivy if she wanted to have a drink with me. Where were you?"

"We went to see Rafe."

"You what?" Her enjoyment fled as she stood up. "Why did you do that? What do you mean 'see Rafe'? Did you hurt him?"

"Never laid a finger on him."

Bri was smart enough to pick up on the distinction. "Did Dax hurt him?

"Are you kidding? His enforcing rates are ridiculous."

Glancing to the side, she intended to ask Dax what went on and if he was still involved in criminality. But Ivy's eyes were closed, her head resting back on her husband's shoulder. The look of bliss on her friend's face could be tracked to Dax's hand... up his wife's skirt.

Not the tattletale, Bri tried to seek out Blaser to see if he'd noticed what the couple were doing, but he was busy getting a debrief from his security man, preparing to take over bar duties again.

At least two minutes went by before Blaser came back to her.

"We're going to take off," Dax said, lifting Ivy off her stool. "Bri, you wanna come with us or are you gonna wait for Blaser?"

On arriving it hadn't been her intention to be there

until closing time, but she also wasn't going to crash what the couple had started, so she smiled and shook her head. "I'll wait."

Dax and Ivy said their goodbyes and disappeared out of the club. As soon as they were gone, Blaser bent to rest his forearms on the bar, bringing his face to within an inch of hers. "Colt has a widescreen TV in his office. If you want to hang out up there, you can."

With Dax and Ivy gone, Colt, Lyssa, and Suzette not around, he'd be staffing the bar without distraction.

"You don't want company?" she asked.

"I've worked plenty nights in here without friends at the bar, besides Crystal's around somewhere. If I need entertainment, she'll do."

"Crystal," Bri said. Finding her courage, she asked the question she'd been pondering. "Have you had sex with her?"

"Crystal's my best friend," he said, glancing back when a patron shouted for service. "You don't have to worry about her, Doll. Go upstairs and find yourself something to watch on the TV, I'll bring you a drink in a minute."

Reaching under the bar, he produced a key which he slid toward her then disappeared to serve the customer. Bri wasn't satisfied with his answer, but she'd just been dismissed so couldn't push the issue. Not in that minute anyway.

SEVENTEEN

LESS THAN A WEEK LATER, Dax gave him the nod. This was it. They were going to raise the money Rafe wanted. In one night. Blaser provided the venue, meaning he got the largest cut of the door money. The fighters got their money from the bookies who made a fortune from the audience coming to watch the show.

The type of men who frequented Risqué on a daily basis were very different to the men there that night. The place was filled with money and muscle, each of which was easily differentiated from the other.

Blaser had nothing against his usual patrons, they were mostly mid-level types ranging from working to middle-class. Men who liked to blow off some steam with a drink and a good view.

The spectators of a fight liked to bet big. Those guys dressed well, drank expensive alcohol, and had no problem flashing the cash. Others were tattooed, some were bulky biker types and others were lean and athletic, but they all mingled, happy to stand around shouting at the sparring men in the ring.

Dax had delivered on his plan, much to his

amazement. He'd planned to serve drinks upstairs, play music, offer a quiet lounge for those who wanted it, but no one did. No one had been in the main club at all.

Patrons came in the security covered rear entrance and went downstairs straight away, fighters went into the locker room upstairs, except Dax who had been dealing with bookies and then retreated upstairs to Blaser's office to make a phone call.

The timing of the night couldn't have been better. Colt and Lyssa were having dinner with his parents. When Lyssa and his mother got together, talk of babies and procreation took over. They would stay late, and Lyssa would expect Colt to perform when they got home because her impetus to have a baby would be at its height.

Bri didn't work Monday nights, and he told the rest of the girls to take the night off too, feeding them a line about fixing the problem with the air conditioning. They were happy to accept as they'd been whining about it. To ensure no questions were asked, an engineer would come fix the unit in the morning.

Blaser ran upstairs to let Dax know there was another fight in progress. Dax's contacts had pulled the event together in record time and had done it with amazing ease. Blaser was beginning to understand from whispers around the joint that Dax was something of a legend, a bigshot in this arena. Dax kept his secrets well hidden leaving Blaser to speculate about what other talents his latest employee might be concealing.

Entering his office, he was surprised to see Dax at the desk, on the phone, his head bowed, resting on his palm.

"Babygirl, you don't want to be here," Dax said into the phone. "I'll be home in a couple of hours… no, you don't… you don't… you're jerking my chain, Minx, what have I told you about riling me…?"

Blaser cleared his throat because he didn't want to overhear anything too personal. Dax straightened and held up a hand.

"Babe, I've gotta go… yeah, yeah, don't forget your place." Dax hung up without waiting for a response then pulled himself in at the desk.

"Ivy, I guess?"

"Yeah," Dax said. "She's pissed I wouldn't let her come."

"Why wouldn't you let her come?" Blaser asked, closing the door and leaning against it.

"She talks too much," Dax said. That wasn't true. "I also told her to make sure Bri stayed home tonight. You haven't told her about this, have you?" Blaser shook his head. "None of my business, but if you ask me…"

"Ask you what?"

"Ivy's a pain in the ass. She bitches at me and never lets me get away with anything. She calls me on my bullshit."

"Romantic," Blaser mumbled. "What's your point?"

"There's something sorta cool about her accepting all the crap, you know? I've done some low shit in my time. Some real bottom of the barrel scum-sucking shit, you know? She accepts it and loves me anyway. For as much as she gives me crap, she gives me as much love, I can't get her to stop fucking telling me it."

Blaser smirked just to give him some shit of his own. "I had no idea you were such a sap."

"Bri finds out about this after it happens, she'll freak and probably dump you," Dax said, dropping his hands to the table to push up onto his feet. "If Ivy taught me anything, it's that a real man owns up and takes responsibility. Lying to her isn't protecting her, man, it is teaching her she can't trust you. After everything she's been through with this Rafe guy, and her friends screwing her over… she needs to trust her man."

"You need to start working more day shifts, dude. You're watching too much of that daytime shit."

"Whatever," Dax said, crossing toward him. "But I got my female down the aisle, you can't even get yours in your apartment."

That was a point he couldn't argue with. The wisdom would've come from Ivy. Seemed the couple really did share everything.

"Would you tell her?" Blaser said. "I promised her I'd stay on the up-and-up, promised my brothers too."

"Lying and going back on a promise? This is gonna

come back and bite you in the ass."

Blaser didn't need Dax to tell him what he already knew, but he hadn't seen any other option. "Even if I lose her, at least I know she'll be safe."

Dax's mouth remained flat, but his cheek twitched. "Yeah, that's what I tried to tell the Minx, but she knows best."

Dax slapped his shoulder and reached for the door.

"Wait," Blaser said. "Is Ivy going to tell Bri about this?"

"Nah," Dax said. "She'll say anything in the world to me, but Mrs. Harrow knows how to keep a secret, believe me on that."

Removing himself from Dax's path, Blaser let his new friend depart then exhaled as he looked into his office. Dax seemed like a decent guy and that was worrying, there was no way he was the lawful type. Making the decision to throw his lot in with a criminal on a level far above anything in his past was dangerous. But he would risk it all for Bri.

For this one decision, this one night, he could be locked up, lose the businesses and any remaining support he had in the family. And if Bri decided to turn her back on him too, he would be left with nothing. But she would be safe, and that was all that mattered.

TONIGHT HAD BEEN A MASSIVE learning curve. Superfluous to the action, fight after fight had taken place in his basement while he looked on. The fights grew in length as more experienced fighters took to the ring, set up by Dax's associates it was little more than some gym mats cordoned off by rope wound around the building's existing support pillars.

Down there wasn't used for anything except storage. The clutter had been removed by the guys Dax brought in earlier in the afternoon before the event got started.

Choosing to keep an eye on things was more about protecting his own interests than curiosity. The third fight had just wrapped. Money was being exchanged and counted out under the watchful eye of monitors. Everything worked on a hierarchy scheme based on experience from what he could tell. Participants wouldn't get far in this sphere if they weren't fair and honest… at least as honest as crooks could be.

The audience he strolled through most probably guessed he was just security. No one paid him much attention and he was happy with that. The fewer people who remembered his face, the better. Blending in was the key to success in most criminal ventures at his level.

He hated that he had a level and Dax's words from the office were playing on a loop in his head. Bri wouldn't be happy that he'd lied by omission. His belief that he could talk her round was based on who she was when they were together, not on who she was now.

Considering how her reaction might be different, given all that she'd been through, he passed a group huddled around a bookie. Lifting his head to check his path, he saw two people in the corner who wouldn't have been granted entry by his men: Gary's friend, Marshall, and the blond with the eyebrow scar, Bri's attacker from outside Risqué on the night he put her in Colt's apartment.

Struck by the fact they were hidden in a shadowy corner, he wondered if they were there to spy on him. But that left the question of who they'd be spying for, would it be Gary or Rafe? Something smelled off. To ensure Bri would be safe from even her own family, he would have to get to the bottom of it.

Dax had mentioned an alliance before. If Rafe's men witnessed the shooting or heard about it after, they had to be somehow aligned with Gary and his crew. Figuring he couldn't just stalk over there and start a fight, because that would probably end with him being ejected from his own club, he spun around with ideas of seeking out Dax.

He'd been away from crime for too long and wasn't used to acting alone. There was a time he'd have recognized every face in the room. Now they were nothing but strangers.

Everyone there lived their lives surrounded by debauchery and greed. He was detached from that, floating above it… at least he had been. Now he was right back where he started, and it made him sick.

Before he got to the stairs, the entrance became the focus of everyone in the room. Pausing to seek what had the audience's attention, he found they were watching Dax descend the stairs behind a skinny blonde woman with red streaks in her hair. From the holler that went around the basement, it was obviously Dax's turn to fight. Acting on his discovery would have to wait.

EIGHTEEN

IT WAS SURPRISING HOW QUICKLY Risqué could be put back together. After Dax's fight, people quickly gathered their money and dispersed. By their practiced actions, he could tell they were an elite, almost close-knit group of people. Each one got admitted by invitation because they'd proved themselves or been vouched for by someone. This wasn't your standard fight club; this was premium pay-per-view.

They didn't leave in droves. Another clue they knew what they were doing. They staggered their exits, not making it obvious to any onlookers that something was breaking up. Since vehicles weren't allowed to park outside, there was little indication from an external point of view that the hundred or so people had been in Risqué.

The fighters left after their fights, so by the time Dax was done, the men brought in to work security had put the locker room back together. The ring was dismantled, and everything returned to its previous position. Just like that, it was as if nothing happened.

Locking up was the last thing to be taken care of, and he did it with a pounding heart. They'd got away with it. With the money bound in brown envelopes in the safe in his office, he had more than covered Bri's debt. He wasn't hanging around. He wanted to get home and pretend the whole mess hadn't happened. His sweaty palms and pounding adrenaline betrayed he wasn't cut out for a life of crime anymore.

The buzz had been part of the thrill when he was younger, he'd loved it. Now it just made him anxious. He'd broken his promise to people he loved. He couldn't get on his righteous high horse when Colt judged him, not anymore, because it turned out his twin had been right all along.

Racing back to the apartments, he jumped out of his truck and got inside fast, praying no one was interested in what was going on at that time of night. As soon as he got inside his apartment, the quivering anxiety took on new meaning. Bri was standing there at the end of the hallway, wearing his tee-shirt.

"Babe, I—"

"Don't," she said. With one step forward, she came into the light, streaks of wetness stained her cheeks. "Where were you, Blase?"

It was like going back in time. Exactly like it. This had been his life for years, coming home to find the woman he loved crying because she didn't know where he was or if he'd been safe.

"I… I, uh…"

"I want you to think before you answer me," she said. "I want you to think about it because if you lie to me—"

"I was at the club," he said. "I was at Risqué." That wasn't a lie, but it wasn't the whole truth either. It should have occurred to him that Marshall would've ratted him out. Getting her away from him would have been Gary's first command to his subordinate. "I didn't know that… how did you get in here?"

"I told Gus I was planning a romantic surprise," she said, wiping her nose on the back of her index finger as she sniffed. "Maybe the next time you consider lying to me, you should let your cousin in on it first."

He had chosen to tell as few people as possible for two reasons, he didn't want to drag anyone else into the trouble, and because it was harder for a large group of people to keep a secret. Gus was a great guy, but no criminal mastermind.

"How long have you been here?" he asked.

"All night."

"What did you have planned?"

"There was no plan," she snapped. "I knew you were up to something. You don't think I know you, Blase? Ever since that night you said you went to Rafe's you've been quiet, whispering with Dax, you've been distracted. I know the signs, Blase. I notice when you get tunnel-visioned and everything else falls away from your focus. Every time I tried to ask you what happened at Rafe's, you gave me an excuse or dismissed me. I knew it. I knew you were up to something."

"So you came in here to spy on me?" he said, shrugging off his jacket to toss it toward the couch.

"There was nothing to spy on. I already knew something was going on. I came here to give you a chance. I came here because I wanted you to tell me, I wanted to see if you would be honest. And I wanted to make sure that you were safe."

Taking his eyes away from her, he strode into the kitchen and opened a cabinet to pull out a half-drunk bottle of bourbon and a glass. Pouring a measure into the tumbler, he threw it back into his throat, then shoved the glass away and swiped his hand across his mouth to remove the remnants of liquid.

He spun around and held open his arms. "You're right," he declared. "You were all right about me all along, there, are you happy?"

"Am I happy?" she retorted. "God damn you, Blaser, this isn't what I wanted!"

"I'm sorry, Doll, but right now I don't give a fuck what you want. My objective was to keep you safe and that's not an objective I'll ever apologize for."

"I don't need you to take care of me!" she said, moving into the kitchen, stopping on the other side of the table. "I don't want you to risk everything you've built for yourself just because I came back into your life. I didn't come to you because I wanted to be saved!"

"So why the fuck did you come back?"

"Because I love you, Blase! You know that! I came back because I finally had the chance to get close to you again without Gary and without trouble. I wanted us to work! I wanted to make this work because you're the only man I've ever loved!"

"Great," he said. "There's no problem then, we can make this work."

"No," she said shaking her head. "We can't. Because I wasn't the one who was right, they were. All of them, out there." Extending her arm, she pointed out of the front of the apartment. "Colt and Ruger. All of your family and mine. We make each other worse! I am trouble! I make you a worse man just by being around! All you did tonight was prove them right!"

Fear seized his throat when she turned for the door. Leaping around the table, he caught up with her and snatched her arm to pull her back. "Don't walk out."

"I have to leave," she said, fresh tears skimming her cheeks, she wouldn't look at him.

"No, I'm sorry, okay, you're right. I shouldn't have…"

"It doesn't matter," she said, lifting her arm out of his hand. Slowly, her chin rose until her glistening eyes landed on him. "I'm bad for you."

"No, you're not. You make me better. You give me something to love so much that I would give it all up. I would risk everything in my life for you, Bri. Not because you ask me to but because you're the only one I would sacrifice myself for. You're my girl," he said, brushing the tears from her cheeks then taking hold of her head. "You've always been my girl, Doll. I should never have ended our relationship. I should've made you wait for me."

"I wanted to wait," she said. "But you were right to do what you did. Tonight has proved that you are a better man without me."

"I am no man without you," he said. "I think all along I wanted to prove to you that I could do it, that I could provide for you in the way you deserved. Every night I came home to you like this, crying and wondering where I'd been. I thought I needed to do what I did to keep you, to provide for you, to stay on Gary's good side. I don't need to do any of that anymore, Bri. I love you."

"How can you love someone who brings out the worst in you?" she whispered.

"You bring out the best in me," he said. "You make me live. Before you came back to me, I was only going through the motions. Each day blended into the next, life had no purpose, but you… you give me purpose: to make you as happy as I can. I failed in that tonight, but I won't do it again."

"Is that a promise?"

"Yes," he said, hoping if he smiled, she would too.

"Just like the promise you made to Colt that you wouldn't do anything illegal ever again?" His smile dropped. The nausea returned to his throat, bringing with it a tingling that stretched from his jaw to the back of his neck. "We can't do this again, Blase. When will the cops next come for you? Tonight? Tomorrow? Maybe in five years when we've got two kids, then what do I do?"

"That's it," he said, experiencing unfamiliar desperation. "No more, Doll. I promise. Can't you see tonight was for you? I raised enough cash to silence Rafe. We can put all of this behind us, for good."

"Until when?" she asked. "What if I see a pair of shoes I like that you can't afford? Where is the line, Love? You make decisions to go out there and do these things, then claim that it's in the name of love. Why can't you see that I love you for who you are not for what you can give me?"

"I see that," he said, dipping to kiss her. "I see it, babe, I'm sorry."

Covering her mouth with his, he wanted to show her the love she had declared. The stark focus with which he saw things was jarring. Bri was the most important priority. She wasn't interested in him fixing the messes, she wanted him to be by her side, that was all she needed from him.

A gulping cry made her retreat, but he kept her face and kissed her again. Moving her back they came up against the front door. He pressed deeper, opening his mouth to devour the woman he'd craved every day of his life. Holding her face, he tipped her head higher and came lower to tilt the other way. The mass of their muddled tongues forced her to suck in a long breath through her nose then she seemed to still. Had he taken too much?

He relaxed, reducing the pressure and giving her some more room. "Bri," he said on her mouth.

Her hands came to his shoulders. When she pushed, he gave her space and met her eye. "I…" she said, fluttering those lashes, liberating the last of the tears that remained in her drying eyes. "I think I can do this."

Hope and primal want delivered him a piercing spear to the gut. But he wasn't going to push her. "Can I make love to you?"

Although he could tell by her stiff form and wide eyes that she was nervous, she nodded. "Take me to your bed, Love."

The emotion of the night was high. There was enough adrenaline rushing through them to distract from her reservations about sex. But he had no intention of pushing her further than she wanted to go.

Taking her hand, he led her through to the bedroom and saw from his rumpled covers that she'd already been sleeping there. She really had been here all night.

Seating her on the bed, he crouched in front of her. "If you want to stop, if you don't like something I'm doing—"

"I know," she said, covering his forehead with her hand and arcing it down around to his cheek. "I know, Love."

So much remained unresolved, but if she was ready for this, if she needed him, then he had to give her what she wanted.

NINETEEN

BLASER LOOKED SO INNOCENT crouching before her. He was anything but. Her fear for his safety was real. Bone deep. The pacing, the jumping at every sound, the ache to know he was safe, it was all familiar. Just like the old days.

Living through it again may be impossible. Whatever was next for them, if anything, Blaser was the only man she could imagine getting physical with. Trusting him in bed was natural. Her love for him raged with unparalleled intensity. No other man would match or surpass that strength of feeling. If she couldn't be intimate with him, she couldn't be intimate with anyone.

Reaching for his nightstand, the first thing he did was open the drawer to fish out a condom. He tossed it on top before closing the drawer. An interesting start. She'd always been on the pill when they were together. A condom would be a novelty. Was he proving his maturity? His willingness to be responsible? Giving her a physical cue of what was about to happen?

From the way his measured gaze came back to her, that last one was his point. By showing her something only needed for sex, he was communicating his intention and giving her a chance to back out.

The tentative approach demonstrated how he respected her and what she'd been through. They hadn't been together for years. Breaking their drought was for both of them. She needed patience and he needed to see confidence in what lay ahead.

Giving him that signal, she didn't hesitate to take off her tee-shirt, baring all to the man she wanted to be intimate with, even if it was for the last time.

The wariness in his eyes vanished. Desire began to pound, charging the air until it emitted an electric buzz. This was it; they were going to do it. She wanted it. So much.

Without losing her fix on his gaze, she dropped the tee-shirt, put her hands on the mattress and slid backwards to lie down on his bed. The bed may be different, the bedroom too, but this was them, in their space, nothing felt more right.

Rising to his full height, he examined her figure for a second before crouching to unlace his boots, ridding himself of them and his socks. While submerged in comfort and heat, she began to move, anticipating what it would be like to revisit their past. In their relationship, he hadn't been slow or shy about taking what he wanted, his current restraint only heightened her craving. Who knew respect could be such a turn on?

Passion overwhelmed her fears about what sex could mean. She wouldn't give her attacker power over her anymore. Lyssa had explained that the steps she'd been taking in the last year to minimize the lingering effects of the trauma were a form of self-help stress inoculation. Now it was time to reward herself and there was no better prize than being with Blaser.

The doctor's pride in her progress drove her to repeat the full story again and again. The prolonged exposure was meant to desensitize her. Although still in the early stages, she could already tell it was going to help.

Blaser stripped off his tee-shirt and her mind blanked. Wow, she sunk her teeth into her lip, exploring the defined chest of the man she'd first shared her body with. Now he was going to be her first all over again.

A fresh scar on his shoulder interrupted her feast of admiration. Her lip slipped from between her teeth as reality bled back in. That was the mark he'd refused to show her before. The proof that her own brother had put a bullet in the man she loved. Blaser could've died for her, and she never would've known it.

Leaping to her hands and knees, she crawled across the bed and grabbed hold of him to bring him down next to her. Tracing the jagged edges of the flush pink mark, she kissed the indentation and then his collarbone and his jaw.

"I'm so sorry, Love. You bled for me… for us."

"You're the only one I'd bleed for," he said, tipping up her chin to kiss her again.

This kiss started slower than the one in the living room. His rough lips traced over hers then closed to form a gentle suction which he released and adjusted to a different angle.

The approach was different than before. His kiss fired the same drive, the same want to be joined, the need to unite her body with his. But his slow, careful kisses betrayed a reverence, a patience he would never have displayed as a younger man.

He had changed and so had she. With maturity came a greater understanding of what they had with each other. The depth of their love and respect wasn't normal. As their younger selves, they could never have appreciated what it was to find someone to bond with so easily. That night was bittersweet. In returning to the Blaser of old, he had proven her negative effect. Everyone was right about them, she caused him to take risks and be bad.

His warm hands glided onto her waist. The slight moisture they brought with them made her wonder if he was nervous, or if he was still worried about her and how being intimate with him might affect her.

To be so esteemed was humbling, but she didn't want to be treated like glass, she didn't want him holding back for fear he would break her. She took her chance to spur him on and reassure him by unbuckling his belt and pushing his jeans and underwear from his hips.

The sound of denim hitting his floor, accompanied by the thud of his belt buckle, made him withdraw from the kiss. Instead of questioning her, he removed her hand from its resting place over his gunshot wound and lowered it to the girth of his erection. After pumping her hand a few times, he let her go and swept her hair away from her breasts to cover them both with his hands.

Being seduced by him inundated her senses. The gratification of his mouth was just the same. Having been without it for so long, the significance heightened. These lips had been hers for so many years, they'd kissed her more than any other female, he had always belonged to her.

Without realizing it, she had continued to work her hand around him, squeezing her fist and pulling him toward her, mimicking the action she wanted him to feel in her body. Their position gave her space to flee at any time. Neither of them had more power than the other, they were simply free to explore each other.

His mouth glided from her shoulder to her neck. When she gave him more room, he went straight for a certain spot behind her ear. She smiled at the evidence he remembered her as well as she did him, and that brought back every joyous memory of their unity.

When she breathed out a mew of pleasure, his lips curled into a smile against her.

"Still there," he exhaled into her ear.

She laughed. "Only for you," she said and grabbed his face to kiss him.

Nostalgia poured through her senses, drowning her in the love they'd nurtured from the moment they met.

He swayed forward, easing her back, she broke their kiss before he could lie her down. Kissing her way down his body, she kept her hands on him, preventing him from coming forward. She kissed his chest, closing her eyes, reveling in the sensations of longing. At one time, she'd had unrestricted access to this body any time she wanted it. She hadn't appreciated it; she hadn't appreciated him.

She'd let him get into trouble because it was easier, it kept the peace with Gary. It was on her that she didn't put up a fight for her love. She should have. Blaser solved the problem with Gary by giving him his own way, and she hadn't blamed her brother or rebelled against him. If she had put her foot down and told Gary to get lost maybe Blaser wouldn't have ended up in prison at all. Maybe they would have had a future.

Slinking down to kneel on the floor, she directed his pulsing want toward her mouth and blinked her eyes up to his. Fluttering her lashes, his throat bob was an encouraging sign. How could she still have such impact on a man after he'd had her so completely? With a smile, she parted her lips and breathed him in as far as she could take him.

This technique allowed her to acquaint herself with him again. She liked the control, liked that she could pleasure him at her own pace and in her own way. Drawing back and forth she sucked on him, using her circled fingers to squeeze his base, and come up to meet her lips when they reached their limit.

"Oh, God, Bri," he said.

Their gaze was broken when his head went back.

Recognizing the signal he was close to his own release, she stopped and sat back on the bed.

"Come here," she said.

The greenlight fired him to action, but before he got her onto her back, she put her hands on his shoulders, using her own force to stop his advance. "Babe?"

"I want to be on top," she said, more confident that her memories wouldn't resurface if she didn't put herself in the same position.

Except, in truth, she wasn't sure of anything more than desire. Anxiety seeped from her pores. This was it, she was going to do it, let a man into her body.

He accepted her request without question and sat up against the pillows at the head of the bed to roll on the condom he'd put on the nightstand in preparation for this moment. He was ready, and despite the narrowing of her throat and the prickle in her sinuses, she moved forward and climbed on top of him.

"I want to touch you," he said, asking for direction.

There was no question he knew what he was doing with a woman, but he didn't want to step over her boundaries. The show of further respect boosted her courage.

The whisper of his fingertips floated above her outer thigh. The slight movement of air raised her awareness, but there was nothing negative in it. Contact with another human being, a man who loved her and had no interest in overpowering her, brought new wetness to her eyes.

"I love you, Brianna," he said.

Opening her eyes, which she hadn't meant to close, the sincerity he exuded drew her mouth to his again. He touched her inner thigh, tracing circles that got ever wider until they met her outer labia.

"I'll go slow," he said.

Speed wasn't the first thing on her mind, she wanted him to touch her. The wait to experience his caress increased the pounding urgency. He kissed her, taking the time to warm his tongue to hers and loosen her body. His fingers slid into the softer, thinner flesh, furrowed in perfect fashion to lead his fingers to her clit. When they made contact, she yelped and he froze, but she exhaled a laugh against him and dug her fingers into his pecs.

"That was good," she said. "You feel good."

Taking control of the kiss, her focus stayed on his mouth, but his hand kept going. Increasing the pressure on her clit, he rubbed in faster, longer strokes until his fingertip dipped into the well of moisture slickening the passage that she wanted him to occupy. He brought the moisture to her clit, then down he went for more until he'd coated all of her with her own juices.

His finger went deeper each time. Although the digit wasn't as thick and stiff as what she needed for ultimate pleasure, she was moving, riding his hand. Momentum gained until his finger wasn't retreating anymore, she was moving up and down on his hand and his finger was actually in her.

Pure joy at getting this far increased her pace. She was doing it, she was with him, with Blase and it was working. Pulling up, she was surprised when on her next descent there was a second finger. Accepting it propelled a cascade of heat to shoot up inside her. When unfamiliar orgasm stole her oxygen, she gasped for more then stilled, sinking down onto his hand, grinning at him.

His hand wasn't enough. Impatient for more, she shoved it aside, grabbed his dick and rose, resting her other hand on his shoulder. He nodded either in permission or pride, but it gave her the last push to take her chance.

Calculating her angle and releasing pressure from her knees, she squeezed her eyes closed and guided his head to her center. Her muscles tensed of their own volition. Frustration clenched her further. The problem wasn't as easily forgotten as she'd hoped. For all the work she'd done, and with how sure she'd been about Blaser, she really believed this was possible.

Unshed tears from her months of celibacy tried to escape. Before they could, his lips touched hers and her eyes opened.

"Don't close your eyes," he said, curling his fingers around her hips. "You forget who you're with when you're not looking at me. Don't think about the memories of what was, think about here and now, and how much we want this. I love you and I want to be with you. It doesn't matter if it's now or in five years, I'll wait. We'll get there eventually. You've come so far tonight. I'm honored that you would trust me like this, open yourself to be vulnerable with a guy when I know it isn't easy.

"You are so strong, Brianna Wilcox. Keep your head up because with those beautiful eyes fixed on me baby, that's all the pleasure I need. You're as perfect as a doll with the face of an angel and the heart of a saint. I love you and I will always belong to you. My heart is yours and no one will ever take it away from you."

Having held her attention so thoroughly, she hadn't managed to blink yet. When she did, wet tears tumbled free, tears of joy, because she believed every single word he said. What had she done to deserve such dedication?

Squirming on the pressure between her thighs, she felt the thickness of him in her. Inside her. In speaking to her so sincerely, he'd relaxed her body until she slid down onto his in a final perfect motion of oneness.

Another yelp, more tears, and she threw her arms around to kiss him with all that she had. Gratitude and love came together, and her anxieties fled.

"I love you too, Blase," she whispered, bringing herself up and lowering onto him again.

Being with him, moving on him, using her body to prove to him the strength of their bond, it was all that she needed. This moment was meant to be. Every second of the last six and a half years they'd spent apart had been leading to that second. They were destined to collide like this. Every step of their lives paths was designed to make them appreciate what it was to be so completely loved by another. It was such a tragedy their love could have no future.

Slanting her mouth over his, she kept moving, kissing every joy and agony of their time apart, building to their release. The sweep of his enlivening hands spurred her into moving faster. His hands played with her breasts, fondling and massaging, then slid to her waist and hips, directing their movement.

Letting him take over some of the strain, he worked her body, giving her a rest until he dipped forward and kissed her nipple. Flicking his tongue over her sensitized peak, she fell against him, plummeting into the pulse of orgasm. The hard impact winded her tired lungs and exhausted thighs.

Blaser again took her hips and spread his to part hers further, giving himself more room. He drove up into her and back out. Putting her on her back would've been easier for him, but he didn't, he maintained the position she'd requested.

When orgasm began to build again, she bounced back onto her knees to move in time with his thrusts until the volume of his grunts increased and the rhythm revealed he was close to his own climax. Trying to withhold her own was useless. The gates were open; her body welcomed the release.

With her mouth wide and her head flung back, she shouted his name propelling him into his own orgasm, he pushed all of himself into her and panted until the last of his seed was released.

His body flopped down with hers on top of it. As he

wriggled down to take them into a lying position, they remained locked together, their sticky bodies still joined. The strength of his embrace protected her.

She closed her eyes and tried to relax. Letting go of the obvious was too difficult. While he arranged them into a position for sleep, she went along with it, but spending the night wasn't an option. If she stayed in his bed, she would never want to leave it. She couldn't be weak, not anymore. Putting up a fight, taking a stand, was right. Keeping the peace wasn't enough, not anymore.

TWENTY

BLASER'S DREAM of the future featured one star: Brianna Wilcox. Already his subconscious was making plans and his physical self was ready to put them into action when he opened his eyes.

Turning over in the bed, he reached for her, hoping for some morning fun before they discussed what they wanted their life together to look like. The bed beside him was empty.

Sitting up, he looked around the room, expecting to see her nearby, except he was disappointed. "Bri!" he called out, assuming she was in the bathroom.

When there was no response, he got up and searched the whole apartment. The only thing he found was a note on the kitchen table, *"Give me time."* Reassured he didn't have to panic she'd fled town, he assumed she was upstairs in her apartment.

His initial impulse was to get dressed and go straight up there. Doing that might be too much. He couldn't pressure her. Though, at the same time, he didn't want her to think he wouldn't be supportive.

Dropping the note, he ran his hands through his hair and fixated on the door. She had left him in the early hours.

Had she slept at all? What was she struggling with? Their physical intimacy or the argument that came before it?

She needed space. As much as he wanted to go to her, to crowd her, he had to show her respect and that meant being understanding of her wishes. There was no way he'd sleep again, so he put on coffee and jumped into the shower. He would get ready for the day. After he was sure she would be awake, he'd check in on her, if for no other reason than to make clear that running away wasn't an option.

Giving up on their relationship had cost him. Walking away from each other wasn't best for either of their lives. What he'd done at the club the previous night could fuck everything up.

He would go to her and explain what had happened. Let her know he was wrong. If she forgave him, he'd never get involved in anything illegal again. She wasn't the cause of his mistake, but she could be the remedy. Without her, there would be no point in making a success of his life. His success was all for her and now he wanted to share it.

TWENTY-ONE

BRI HADN'T MANAGED to get much sleep at all. Her thoughts warred with her emotions and, after last night, she had her hormones to contend with as well. Sleeping with him had seemed like a great idea at the time. In the new day, it only complicated things.

As soon as she heard the first glimmer of movement elsewhere in the building, she decided the time was respectable enough to visit a neighbor.

Locking her own door, she went two down and knocked. The rapping sounded much more urgent than she'd intended it to. Her nervous energy was desperate to escape in any way that it could.

Dax opened the door. Disappointment made her body sag, except her interest in the bruise on his jaw and the cut on his cheek made her forget her own troubles.

"What happened to you?" Bri asked Dax.

Yawning and scratching his corrugated abs at the same time, Dax propped himself on the doorframe. "She's a bitch when she only gets one orgasm a night," he said. "What do you want?"

"Ivy did that? Ivy… she hits you?"

Bri had been around domestic abuse and would never have figured a guy like Dax would take a beating from a woman. From anyone. From the look of his injuries, she would assume that Ivy put up quite the offense.

Snatching his hand, looking for defensive wounds, she instead saw fresh white bandages, wrapped around his knuckles. Dropping his hand, she took a step back, blinking at the predator she hadn't known lived on her doorstep.

"Did you hurt her?" Bri whispered, terrified by the ordeal her friend must have endured while she was downstairs making love with Blaser.

Dax boosted himself off the doorframe unaffected by her accusation. He just yawned again. A hand appeared over his tattoo, Ivy drew him back to come into view, giving Dax silent permission to slink off back inside.

"I put up with a certain level of his jerkiness," Ivy said, "but he'd lose me if he hit me in anger."

Bri didn't know why anyone would hit another person except in anger. A few of the jumbled pieces fell into place.

She pounced forward, into the doorway. "He was with Blaser last night, wasn't he?"

The jovial expression on Ivy's face greyed, her new friend just went on guard. "Don't ever ask me about what Dax does or where he is. Even if I gave you answers to your questions, you would never understand them."

Ivy began to close the door, but Bri moved against it, putting herself over the threshold. "I had sex with him."

The door stopped and Ivy's curiosity brought her forward. "What?"

"Not Dax," Bri stuttered. "With Blaser. I'm sorry, I… my question wasn't really about Dax, it was about Blaser. I know he was doing something illegal last night. I know he broke the law and… he promised so many people he would never do that again. But he risked it all, Ivy. How can I turn my back on him when there's a chance he could lose everything because of me?"

"Then don't turn your back on him," Ivy said, then sighed. "You should come in for coffee."

"Won't Dax—"

"He'll be sleeping already," Ivy said, moving out of the doorway to welcome Bri in. "He's not a morning person and he was out late."

"But you were both awake when—"

"I like morning sex," Ivy declared, going to the coffee maker to load it up. "We have a sort of deal where I get mine then he gets to sleep for as long as he likes. With Dax, that can be a long time. He's more of a night person."

"What does he get in exchange," Bri asked, seating herself at the kitchen table when Ivy put mugs on it. "Other than sex, I mean."

"He likes to get his at night when he comes home from work. So I stay awake, or get up, to welcome him home."

"You two seem so…"

"What?" Ivy asked, making toast and pulling out eggs, which she proceeded to split. "What do we seem?"

"In perfect sort of sync, I'd guess you'd known each other forever if I didn't know how you actually met."

Ivy whipped up the egg whites and began to make an omelet. While it was cooking, she poured coffee into Bri's mug. She tidied up and washed the dirty dishes before sitting down opposite her at the table.

"We have known each other forever," Ivy said, slurping her own coffee. "We might not have physically met, but we came from the same place, surviving on the streets and doing what we had to in order to get by. Dax fell on his feet for a while, if you could call it that, and I didn't. Though I managed to stay on the right side of the law, for the most part."

"But Dax didn't?" Bri asked, watching Ivy rise to split the toast and omelet onto plates.

"Don't ask me about Dax," Ivy said, licking a spilled drop from her finger then presenting Bri with the food.

"I just… Blaser got himself into such a good place after he came out of prison," she explained while Ivy tucked into her own food. "He promised his brothers he wouldn't break the law and then as soon as I come back into his life, it's one of the first things he does."

"How do you know that he did?" Ivy asked, washing down her food with some coffee.

"I waited in his place last night and confronted him."

"And he told you what happened?"

"Not exactly, I didn't ask for specifics. But I know he did something he thought would help with the Rafe situation… Everyone told Blaser I was bad news, and he stands up for me every time. But from the outside looking in, everyone will assume I put him in this position on purpose."

"The trouble wasn't yours to start with," Ivy said, pointing to Bri's plate, urging her to eat. "This Rafe guy shouldn't be coming after you, but he is. The only way to get rid of him is to run away or stand and fight. You chose the latter, you have to own that."

"I do. If I had run away…, where would I have gone? My brother is here, or he will be, and Blase… we never got the chance to try again. We were supposed to… we agreed to… he came to Jersey, where I was living and…"

She wasn't eating anymore. Staring at the food on the plate, she began to feel numbness overcome her again. This wasn't like it used to be, she wasn't numb because of the terror or disgust of the attack, now she felt detached from it, like her life had moved onto a different chapter. Except that new chapter may be about to end as quickly as it had begun.

"What?" Ivy asked. "What is it, Bri?"

"I was raped," Bri said. Ivy stopped eating. On that confession, she pushed her plate aside and waited for her to continue. "I was supposed to go on a date with Blaser, but he was late. I went outside and… I was grabbed off the street. They kept me for more than a week. It only happened once, but the disgusting, sniveling bastard took over my life. I let him take over for more than a year."

"But last night, with Blaser," Ivy said. "Was that the first time…?" Bri nodded. "Wow."

Ivy was one of the few people who could understand her ordeal to any degree. She too had been kidnapped and held against her will, though she hadn't endured a full-on intimate assault.

"I had to do it. I mean, I was mad at him for lying

and getting involved with crime again, but… I love him and something about being there with him, in the night, in that apartment, with his hands on me… It just felt right. It might sound crazy…"

"No," Ivy said. "I understand. Hell, I fell in love with the man who was supposed to break me. Our hearts and bodies sometimes overrule our heads."

"But it's so complicated," Bri said, shoving away her own food and sinking her head into her hands. "There are so many people involved and so many things going on. I have a brother in jail and a gangster after me for money. Blaser is trying to run legit businesses that he may well lose now that he's broken the law. He could go back to prison… his family could… they're going to hate him and it's my fault."

"They're not going to hate him."

Sitting back, she kept a hand on her cheek. "He promised Colt and Ruger he would never be involved in anything shady again."

"Who says they have to know?"

"Asking him to be dishonest—"

"You don't have to ask him to do anything," Ivy said. "He's a grown man, Bri. His family have to realize he's made his own decisions. You know what it's like to be forced to do something against your will, and I do too. Implying you've done the same thing to Blaser insults both you and me."

That made sense. Although she still felt that her influence caused Blaser to do what he did, that wasn't at all the same thing as being forced to act at gunpoint.

"I suppose so…"

"I went through this with Dax. He made his own decisions, and until he took ownership of those decisions, he was going to let other people direct his life and his actions. I left him to prove to him he would lose me if he let others keep control of his life. You know what it did? It scared the shit out of him. Almost as soon as I was gone, he came after me. He made the decision to take control and make his own decisions."

"Blaser has control of his life," Bri said. "It's not him I'm worried about. It's his brothers and his liberty I'm worried about."

"You didn't make the decision for him. He chose to break the law and you chose to let him know you aren't happy about it. Other people can go to hell. If they choose to shun Blaser, that's their decision. You can't make it for them. The only thing you have control of is your own decisions, your own actions… Have you spoken to anyone about the rape?"

"Lyssa."

"Colt's girlfriend, uh, fiancée," Ivy said. "I remember her."

"She's a therapist who specializes in sexual dysfunction. Part of that involves dealing with abuse victims. Blaser told her about what happened; he recommended I go to her. I've only been a few times, but she's really great."

"Good." Ivy smiled. "That's great. She must know what she's doing if you screwed Blaser's brains out last night, right?"

Appreciating the smile, Bri returned it. "I can't keep going to her if I stop seeing Blaser."

"Sure you can," Ivy said. "She's a doctor."

"I'm not sure I'll be welcome. Colt already doesn't like me and… once he finds out what Blaser did, he'll be mad."

"Lyssa isn't the type of person to let Colt dictate to her, she's a strong woman."

"Yeah, well…" Bri squirmed in the face of her next confession. "I told Lyssa something quite personal about who was involved in what happened to me… I think if Colt finds out I made that accusation—"

"What accusation?"

"The youngest of the three Warners, Ruger…"

"Never met him," Ivy said. "He's been gone since I got the garage job."

"He gets along with everyone. Everyone in the family loves him because he's such an easy-going, happy-go-lucky guy, except…"

"What?"

"He disappears for long periods of time for his job, and no one really asks questions. I don't know what Colt thinks he does. I didn't think much of it myself… but Ruger, he was the reason I was taken. I never told anyone until I told Lyssa, but if she tells Colt… Colt is so close to Ruge. It could tear their relationship apart if they blame me—"

"Who the fuck cares about their relationship? It's not your fault that Ruger lied to his family. If you ask me, all that proves is Blaser isn't as different from the rest of them as they make out."

That good point silenced her for a minute. If Ruger was taking part in criminal activities, and had during Blaser's law-abiding years, that sort of meant that Ruger was actually the worst of the bunch.

"Babygirl!" Dax hollered from another room.

Ivy tsked. "I'm entertaining, tough guy! Jerk off if you're horny, I'm busy!"

"Don't sass me!"

"Spank me later," Ivy called back then leaned across the table. "You know Blaser better than all of them. Do you think he loves you?"

"I know he loves me," Bri said.

Noise from the end of the hall startled her. A door slammed and the shower went on.

"It's just Dax getting ready," Ivy said.

"Blaser told me he loved me last night."

"Do you want to be with him?" Ivy asked. Bri nodded. "Then go get him, girl. Stop letting sense overrule what could be your future. Blaser's not a bad guy, he's hot and he's a sweetheart. You just have to put your foot down and tell him you don't want to be with a guy who could be dragged off to jail any minute. You're already dealing with your brother being in prison."

"And my father too."

"You want a guy you can rely on. Maybe Blaser hasn't always made the best choices, but he's always come through for you."

"I have to tell him about Ruger. I can't lie to him. I haven't sat down with him and given him details of what happened. Talking to Lyssa… she says talking about it helps, and she's right. A few weeks ago, I would never have told you what happened. I thought I had to keep it to myself. But if I'm going to be with Blaser, I have to tell him everything."

"I would agree with that," Ivy said. "If the Ruger thing comes out later, he'll know you lied."

"Maybe I should do it with Lyssa," Bri said. "She said we could have a joint session, if I do it with her, she'll know how to control it, won't she?"

"Maybe," Ivy shrugged. "Talk to her and find out what she thinks. If she already knows the details and the players involved, she can probably give you advice."

"Someone will tell Colt," Bri said.

"Maybe someone should. I don't know him well, but he can't go shouting his mouth off about folks being pure white when his own family is dirty. He's making a fool of himself for one thing. You guys will all know this big secret and he'll be the only one in the dark…"

When she said it like that, it made sense to give permission to Lyssa to talk to Colt, as family instead of as a doctor. A knock on the front door drew their attention. Ivy was up and on her way to the door in an instant.

The shower went off as Ivy peeked through the peephole, then she pushed away from the door. "Dax!" she hollered, then opened the front door to Blaser. "Who are you looking for?"

"Who am I…?" Blaser trailed off when Ivy opened the door further.

Bri got up from her seat to offer a feeble wave.

"I didn't realize you were here," Blaser said to her. "How are you doing?"

"I'm… I think I'm okay."

"Good. Great. Glad to hear it…"

If the awkwardness wasn't already apparent, Ivy's laugh put it there. "Dax is just getting out of the shower," she said when a door in the hall opened and another closed. "Maybe he's getting dressed now… We were just having some breakfast, you know, girl talk."

Blaser's focus flashed to Bri, and she had to drop hers. Now he knew she'd confessed to Ivy what they'd done last night. A few seconds later, the bedroom door opened, and

Dax came striding toward their tense group.

"I got your message," Dax said to Blaser.

Dax smacked Ivy's ass with so much force, Bri jumped. He squeezed her butt, stooping to jolt his wife's head aside with his own, giving himself access. After licking up the side of her neck, he bit into her earlobe and whispered something.

"Go to hell," Ivy said with a smile that didn't match her words, shoving Dax on his path toward the exit.

"Let's go," he said to Blaser.

The men departed together.

"What was that about?" Bri asked when Ivy closed the door.

"I can honestly say that I have no idea," Ivy said. "But they'll come back to us eventually."

Bri had meant Dax and Ivy's display. Maybe that was their normal behavior since Ivy was over the exchange already.

"I guess," Bri murmured, going back to the table with Ivy.

"Finish your breakfast," Ivy said. "After that, call your doctor. I say you should get going on that plan of yours. When Blaser gets back, tell him to meet you when it's time."

"I'm supposed to be seeing Lyssa this afternoon," Bri said.

She'd attended therapy every other day over the last week, far more than she'd expected to. Lyssa obviously subscribed to the Warner philosophy of putting family first. It was humbling that Colt's fiancée thought of her as family.

Ivy topped off their coffee. "Tell her you'll be bringing company, and, in the meantime, you can tell me all about your night with Blaser."

Ivy's playful smile made Bri laugh. She was pleased to have a friend who was nothing like Lyssa. The doctor had to be impartial and objective during their sessions. Ivy didn't have that constraint. Lyssa wasn't from the same background as her either. Ivy was. Spending time getting to know more about this woman would be fun, she'd never had a truly reliable girlfriend before.

Any time she got close to colleagues, shame about her

past and upbringing kept her vague, meaning there was always some level of distance. Ivy had seen it all, and she'd married Dax despite his jaded past. Bri could say anything she wanted in Ivy's presence and would never succeed in shocking the woman. It was liberating.

She hoped Ivy and Dax planned to stick around for a while but wouldn't question their plans yet. For now, her concentration had to be on the afternoon. On telling Lyssa about last night. On persuading Blaser to join her at the session.

That afternoon the truth would come out. Either it would bring them all closer together, or it would tear them all apart.

TWENTY-TWO

"I REALLY THOUGHT these days were behind me," Dax said, getting out of the truck to stride onto the sidewalk.

Blaser fell into step beside him. "Tell me about it."

They'd already visited the corner apartment building. Twice in one week was more than he liked. After this exchange was over, he never wanted to lay eyes on Rafe again.

Dax went into the extended entry corridor first. Without internal lighting, they relied on the daylight that drifted through the shadows from outside. Pond dwellers like Rafe should be stuck in dank places like that. The sad fact was that even the money Blaser was about to hand over wouldn't change much for the crook.

They went up the stairs and along another corridor to Rafe's door. Shoulder to shoulder, Blaser made brief eye contact with Dax to get a nod of agreement before knocking on the door. He could be dramatic and burst in but taking men like Rafe by surprise was likely to get someone shot.

"Amateurs," Dax muttered when a chain slid aside.

The door opened.

"We're here to see Rafe," Blaser said.

Without giving the short man on the threshold a

chance to say anything, he barged the guy out of the way, going inside with Dax at his back.

They knew the layout from their previous visit. He went straight into the living room. Rafe was on the same couch as before; the greasy dealer didn't flinch when he tossed the paper-wrapped money into his lap.

"It's all there," Blaser said. "This is done."

Rafe picked up the packet and ripped open the top to finger the bills. "Came up with that quick."

"Disappointed?" Blaser asked.

Rafe's usual guy wasn't around. The two loitering thugs were new, but he didn't doubt the blond with the eyebrow scar reported back about fight night.

"That I don't get to take your little chick for a test drive? Sure, but I guess that's still up for debate."

"No debate," Blaser said. "Leave her alone. You stay away from everything and everyone that's mine, get it?"

"Or what you gonna do about it? You're a washed-up has-been, no one is afraid of you anymore."

"This isn't about fear, it's about smarts," Blaser said. "You want to piss me off? My brother still has a bunch of contacts in the law who could make things difficult for a wannabe like you. You ran away like a pussy when my buddy here stepped in. You're nothing without your men around."

"You think?" Rafe snarled.

Examining the men in the room, Blaser scoffed. "You wanna shed blood over this? We'll do it right here. Just make your move…" No one twitched. "You don't touch Bri again. You've got your money. And if you think about escalating this, about trying to get to her behind my back… maybe a few of my prison buds and I will come back to teach you what it is to start a real war. You go after a woman on her own, why? Because you're too fucking scared to stand up to a guy who could kick your ass."

Rafe thrust his hands to the arms of the chair to propel himself up. "She owed me—"

"What? She owes you squat," Blaser said, sneering at the shameful picture of the prick.

In this shitty apartment with a couple of guys hanging

onto him because he had the means to supply drugs for them, there was no real loyalty and definitely nothing to fear. Leaning in close, he almost wanted Rafe to hit him, to start a brawl just so he had an excuse to punch the slimy little fucker.

"You have your money. If that's not good enough, come knock on my door. We'll see how many guys come out of retirement to teach you a lesson about respecting women."

Rafe's teeth clacked as he worked his jaw, he glanced to Dax, somewhere in the background, then his attention came back. "Fine, we'll call this even for now. But you step out of line again and—"

"And nothing," Blaser said, with a light shove he made Rafe stumble back into his chair. "Go back to your cartoons."

Ignoring the onlookers, he turned and gave Dax the nod to leave the apartment. They got all the way outside again and into the truck before either spoke.

"You think he'll leave Bri alone?" Dax asked.

"If he knows what's good for him," Blaser said. "We'll keep an eye on her, between the apartments and the club, there's always someone around who will look out for her. At the first sign of trouble, I swear to God, I'll knock his fucking teeth out."

"Would have been interesting to know you back in the day," Dax said.

"Why's that?"

"You showed a lot of restraint in there. If some guy had approached Ivy like that…"

"I wanted to beat the shit out of him, but I've done time already. If I go inside again, I lose everything. I just got Bri back, I can't ask her to go through that again."

"Time to settle down?"

"You're married," Blaser said, figuring that Dax must have made a similar decision about his future and going straight.

"Married? Yes," Dax said. "Settled…"

His phone rang and he pressed the receive button to play the call through the built-in Bluetooth of the car. "Yeah?"

"Are you busy later?" Bri's voice seeped from the car

speakers, and he had to suppress a shiver.

"Booty call?" Dax asked. Blaser frowned at his new friend, but the clear expression on Dax's face knew what he was doing. "Just letting her know I'm here, in case things get kinky."

Bri's awkward laugh concerned him. After declaring he had just got her back, he didn't want to find out he hadn't had her at all. "Will you come to Lyssa's with me?"

Therapy. She wanted him to join her at her therapy session. Pouring out his heart to his girl in front of his future sister-in-law wasn't on his bucket list. But it would be hypocritical of him to encourage her to go then refuse to take his own advice.

"Sure. Text me the time and I'll get cover at the club."

"Thanks," she said and ended the call.

"Family get together?" Dax asked.

"Something like that."

Blaser wouldn't divulge Bri's secrets though he was sure her "girl talk" with Ivy would contain some details. He didn't know how many of them Ivy would pass on to Dax. Being included in her therapy had to be a positive sign. As he drove back to the apartments that's what he kept telling himself. Except… if Bri had something to say to him, shouldn't she be able to say it in private?

He'd have to steel himself because he'd never heard the specifics of her ordeal. Somehow, he had a feeling that the afternoon was going to be filled with details, most of which he'd probably end up wishing he'd never heard.

TWENTY-THREE

BRI HAD JUST FINISHED recounting the particulars of her experience last year up until her liberation. Blaser hadn't even questioned her when she asked him to join her therapy session. Granted, he'd been fidgety on the drive over, but nerves showed he cared about their relationship and about her.

Lyssa was professional in accepting them both into the office and facilitated the discussion. Bri glanced over at the doctor, then they both went back to watching Blaser's back, as he stood facing the blind-covered front window.

Squeezing the tip of her pinkie, she released and squeezed, each time with increasing pressure. "Say something, Love," Bri said.

Blaser didn't respond, so Lyssa spoke up. "What do you feel, Blase? It's natural to be angry or—"

"Angry?" he said, spinning around to face the women. "Anger is bullshit, that doesn't even begin to… I…" His attention settled on her. After a breath the tightness of his expression loosened. "You went through all of that, alone, and… I'm sorry, Doll."

He could have trashed the place. He could have gone

storming out of Lyssa's office with murder on his mind. But he didn't.

His restraint helped alleviate some of her tension. "It wasn't your fault," she said.

"I am angry," he said. "I'm pissed as fucking hell and if you want me to go out there and—"

"He's dead," Bri said. "All of them are dead."

"I know and I know anger won't help you. All I want to do is support you. Tell me what you need and it's yours, I'll do it."

Relief suffused her blood. The first part of the tale was over, and he was still there, still with her.

"This is really good," Lyssa said. "You're both doing really well. Blaser, your patience is admirable, you're absolutely right that anger doesn't change the situation. We need to focus on taking positive actions only. Brianna has educated herself and recognizes the root of her anxieties. She has worked to overcome those anxieties and control her fears."

"It started with talking to myself," Bri said. "In my head, I would... I would tell myself when I was being irrational and try to calm myself down by talking myself through possible outcomes. I couldn't be scared all the time; it would've paralyzed me."

"From what we've discussed, it's clear she already uses many techniques we teach in therapy, about stopping damaging thought processes, mental rehearsal and such. She has even forced herself to engage in stressful or worrying behaviors, such as spending time outside, being out in the dark, and even going on dates and getting close to men."

"She's strong," Blaser said.

"There were cops and counsellors at the police precinct," Bri said. "I had to talk to various people about what happened. I wasn't much use, I knew that. By then everyone was dead, so there wasn't much of a case, I guess."

None of the information moved Blaser enough to return to the couch. He stayed where he was, too far away from her, just listening. Bri wished he would come to her; contact would make her feel better. But until she had told the full story, she wouldn't ask anything of him.

"It's all a form of stress inoculation," Lyssa said.

"Lyssa has helped me to see that telling the story makes it easier to endure. It's like it desensitizes me to hear it over and over again, it helps me to detach. I've told Lyssa a few times, and I told Ivy too. I... speaking the words and getting it out there, making myself face it, I don't feel ashamed of it anymore. I see it's not something to be embarrassed about, I was a victim, and I won't let him continue to wield power. I am the only person who can give him that power over me. I won't do it anymore. I won't."

"I'm proud of you, Doll," he said.

"She is doing very well, making great progress," Lyssa said. "But I should highlight these things do take time. There's no reason to assume her comfort level with intimacy will change. She may be ready tomorrow; it could be next month or next year. You will still have to be patient with—"

"You didn't tell her?" Blaser asked.

Bri was already examining the pinkie she'd been playing with and breathed out before looking at Lyssa. "We had sex last night."

Lyssa looked at each of them in turn. "That's terrific," the doctor said. "Really fantastic news."

"I mean I... we had a few issues and I... it was only once and I had to be on top, and... well, we... I thought it wasn't going to happen. I just seemed to clamp down the minute I tried to put his dick—"

"Bri," Blaser said, rolling his eyes away from Lyssa.

"Sorry," Bri said.

This was where your doctor being your future sister-in-law probably wasn't a good thing. Disclosing too many specifics could get creepy for him.

"Don't worry about sharing details," Lyssa said. "And don't cut her off, Blaser. You can share anything here."

"You're marrying my brother."

"Your brother doesn't even know you're here," Lyssa said.

"Yeah, but he will later, right?" Blaser said.

"If you didn't want to come, you should've said so," Bri said. "You encouraged me to come here, you said we could trust Lyssa."

"We can," Blaser exhaled. "I'm sorry, okay. Talk about my dick as much as you like."

He turned his back on them. Lyssa's tight mouth and narrowed eyes remained fixed on Blaser's rigid form. His discomfort was irrelevant, Bri wasn't going to talk about his dick anymore. That could wait until the next session when Blaser wasn't present. She'd come to trust Lyssa and believed she didn't discuss patients with her fiancé. The final reason for bringing Blaser remained. The last of the truths had to come out.

"There's something else I have to tell you," Bri said. "I don't know where we're going, or what's going to happen between us, but… I have to be honest with you. I told Lyssa and Ivy knows too…"

Curiosity brought him around. "What is it?" Unsure exactly how she should say it, she took her time and once again began to stroke her pinkie. The delay must have concerned Blaser because he came back to the couch and sank down at her side, covering her hands with his. "You can tell me anything."

"It wasn't random," she said, and he frowned. "I thought… I mean I know everyone thought it was a random attack, wrong place, wrong time, but it wasn't."

"It wasn't?"

"No," she said. "I know you shoulder a lot of guilt. You feel if you had come to the restaurant earlier, I wouldn't have been outside when I was. But it didn't matter. They already had me in their sights and… They were coming for me, and they would've got me. If not at that time, it would've been later."

"It wasn't random," he said. His head tilted as he thought about it. "You mean someone was out…? Someone was after you? Out to get you?"

"Yes," she said.

"Why?"

That was a good question. She opened her mouth to answer it, but her nose began to tingle.

Her attention swung to Lyssa. "I can't say it."

"Yes, you can," Lyssa said. "You can say it, just take your time."

Lyssa wasn't going to do it for her. The only option was to look at Blaser again. The concern on his face was touching. As soon as she told him the truth, he'd either think she was lying or want to kill his own kin.

"You know Ruger disappears for long periods of time?" she said.

"Ruger?"

"Yeah," she said. "Well, it turns out…" Sucking her lips into her mouth, she prepared to confess the secret she'd held onto for so long. "He gets things for people… people who can't go through legitimate channels."

"What?"

His hand left hers. The chilling air that took its place dug her nails into her palms.

"His clients are criminals. I don't know if what he does, or how he does it, is legal, I doubt it. He's some sort of black-market courier. He sources things people need, difficult things that are not easily found, and then he brings them to the person who needs them."

"Ruger," Blaser said, his body rocked away from hers. "But he's… he's not…"

"He is," she said. "I know you didn't know what he does, and I know that he's close to Colt. I don't know how much Colt knows—"

Blaser shook his head as he shot to his feet. "No, he's a good kid. There's no way he was, that he could…"

"Take your time," Lyssa said.

Blaser's attention whipped around to land on the doctor. "You knew about this? I can't fucking believe that—"

"I wouldn't break a patient's confidence," Lyssa said.

"Did you tell Colt?" Blaser asked her.

"No, but she'll have to," Bri said.

"I do not," Lyssa said, sitting straighter. "I pride myself on—"

"Take off your doctor's hat for a minute," Bri said. "I can't have everyone knowing except Colt. He'll feel like an idiot when he does find out. Look at Blase, he's pissed and confused, how can I ask him not to talk to his brother about it? I don't think I should be the one to tell Colt because he doesn't like or trust me. But someone will have to tell him."

"That could negatively affect his relationship with Ruger," Lyssa said.

"It could," Bri agreed.

Talking to the doctor was giving her a reprieve from looking at Blaser struggling to comprehend this news. It was no surprise it was difficult for him. Everyone thought Ruger was harmless and she had just rebutted that.

"Wait a minute," Blaser said, angling to look at both women. "What has this got to do with what happened to you?"

"He was working for a man named Victor," Bri said. "Ruger got a couple of things for him then found out what he was up to... Ruger walked away, said he wanted nothing to do with it. If Victor wanted someone working for him, he got what he wanted, by finding out who was important to that person and kidnapping them. He did it with several others. That's how he manipulated his people to get his own way. He did it to Jansen, he did it to Rushe, he—"

"Rushe?" Lyssa said.

She hadn't expected to be interrupted. In the doctor's defense, she didn't look like she'd intended to talk aloud.

"Does that name mean something to you?" Bri asked. "Do you know him?"

"He helped Lyssa out once," Blaser said.

"You know him too?" Bri asked.

"I had no idea that Ruge was into... Where the fuck does he get off trying to dictate my life when he's involved in shit of his own? Serious shit. They took you because you meant something to me, and they thought it would make Ruger come back?"

"It turned out not to matter," Bri said. "We were rescued while we were being transported. Not long after, all of them were dead. Victor, the Sniveller, all of them..."

"I can't fucking believe this," Blaser said, sitting down and immediately standing up again. "Where's Colt?"

"He's working.

"Where?"

"He's at the club, Risqué, in his office," Lyssa said. "But I don't think that…"

Blaser rounded the couch, pulling his wallet from his jeans. He snatched out a few bills and tossed them onto the couch beside her. "Get a cab back to the apartment. I'll come find you when I can."

"No," Bri said. Leaping from the couch, she had to run to catch up with Blaser before he got to the exit. Plastering herself against the door, she blocked his route, holding her hands far apart on the wood at her back. "Please don't go to Colt."

"He has to know what a motherfucking, piece of shit—"

"No, Ruger didn't know about it. He didn't know! This wasn't his fault. It wasn't his, it wasn't mine, he was a victim too!"

Trying to calm Blaser brought her clarity of her own. Her animosity toward Ruger still existed, but her upset wasn't about assigning blame to him for her trauma. What upset her was the lies. Others in the family looked up to Ruger. The younger cousins idolized him, had since they were kids. Blaser was seen as the bad seed. Even now, after putting his criminal past behind him, Colt and the family still watched and waited for him to screw up.

"A victim?" Blaser said.

"Yes!"

"He should have—"

"What?" she argued, ensuring Blaser didn't ramp up his anger. "He couldn't work for lowlifes like that. He did the right thing by walking away. Everything had fallen apart before they had a chance to use me against him. Ruger never knew. They took me because… I don't know… because the geography suited them and because I was the only girl associated with your family who fit the bill."

"Fit the bill?"

"Yeah, my age and body type, and… I don't know, they were traffickers. I was supposed to be sold—"

"Sold?" Blaser shouted and grabbed her arm to wrench her aside. "If Ruger had anything to do with this, I'm getting to the bottom of it. I don't give a fuck what those bastards told you. I won't believe any of it until I get it from him."

With another yank, he moved her out of the way and stormed out. A few seconds later the front door of Lyssa's townhouse slammed. The women remained in breathless silence, only to be broken when Lyssa pounced from her chair.

"What are you doing?" Bri asked.

Sprinting around the desk, the doctor snatched up her phone and began to punch numbers. "I'm calling Colt, because if I don't, he and Blaser will beat the crap out of each other… Once I've done that, I'll phone Ruger."

"You can get in touch with him?"

"I have his cellphone number," Lyssa said. "And if he has any sense, he'll get back here as soon as humanly possible."

"Colt won't believe Blaser," Bri said, rushing to the desk, "and he won't believe me."

Lyssa listened to the phone ringing. "He'll believe me," she said. "But until we get Ruger home…"

Colt must have picked up because Lyssa elevated the mouthpiece and turned her back. Left to deflate and examine the bereft space that remained where Blaser had been, she had whiplash. The Warner family could be ripped apart by this revelation. Her mounting guilt was difficult to ignore. Reminding herself the situation was not caused by her, she thought of what Ivy had said.

Victor and his men chose to take her from the street. Ruger chose to earn his living in the way he did. She couldn't lie to Blaser. If she did that, there would be no future for them. She could be a martyr, walk away and keep the secret from the man she loved, but it would come out in the end, it would have to.

Besides that, it wasn't fair Blaser continued to believe he was the only screw up in the family. Apparently being bad was Ruger's norm and it was a secret he'd kept well.

***

LYSSA ASKED BRI to stay at her place, but she couldn't. After the next patient arrived, Bri left Lyssa to her day job and headed to the club. Chances were high she'd walk in on a fight, but riling Blaser and setting him free was irresponsible. She had to explain to Colt what she'd seen and why she knew what she did.

Paying the taxi driver, she climbed out of the cab, intent on getting into Risqué. Music was playing and security let her in, but there was no one at the bar, not a soul. She wasn't there for a drink or a show, so she went backstage and ran up the stairs to enter Colt's office.

The brothers were there, sitting on perpendicular couches in front of a low table. The physical fight she had expected was nowhere in sight. The room wasn't trashed. Neither wore bruises or blood.

"You're not fighting," she said, expecting an explanation from Blaser.

"I told him everything," Blaser said. "What happened to you, Ruger, Rafe… last night…"

She herself didn't even know the specifics of what had happened last night, but now wasn't the time to ask questions.

"I'm sorry to interrupt, I just wanted to… well, I was just checking you both were… you know…"

"Don't leave the club," Blaser said. "Hang around and I'll take you home when we're done."

TWENTY-FOUR

SHE JUST ACCEPTED his request with complete faith and walked out of the office. Lyssa must have completed their session. He'd expected Bri to show up sooner but finishing her time with Lyssa gave Blaser the chance to tell Colt everything. Yes, there had been shouting but it helped he knew his twin so well, he'd balanced each reveal to measure his response. He'd just finished when Bri came in.

Colt's phone made a noise, a text flashed up, and he twisted the phone to read it. "Ruger's on his way."

Lyssa had called before he arrived. No one managed to get hold of Ruger, so Colt left a voicemail telling him to come home.

"He better be ready to give us answers," Blaser said. "I'm so fucking ready to—"

"We've got to wait and hear his side."

"You really think there's an explanation for what Bri went through? I believe every word and I'm telling you now if you think about defending that fucking asshole for all the—"

"You're going to hear him out," Colt said. "Just like I heard you… I can't believe Lys knew all this. I need to have a conversation with the future Mrs. Warner."

"I told Lyssa about the rape, and she offered to help. Bri has been a patient and Lys is a professional. She hasn't been lying to you through choice, its professional ethics. You know, your specialty."

Colt didn't respond, he got up to cross to the fridge in the corner. He pulled out two beers and came back to hand one over. Popping the cap, Colt downed most of his.

When he lowered it, Blaser had to ask, "You're not going to give me shit about what happened in here last night?"

"Yesterday I would have but… I thought we could trust Ruger," Colt said. "If the kid's got himself mixed up in something dirty…"

"If you want me to buy you out, it'll take me some time…"

"Putting conditions on the Risqué investment wasn't about the money," Colt said, returning to his seat. "It was my idea to add the stipulations because I didn't want you throwing your life away. Ruger didn't seem bothered about provisos, I thought he was just being a nice guy, obviously there was more to it… maybe I should have picked up on that… But you've done good… That's why I got pissed when you started hanging out with Bri and moved her into the apartments—"

"None of this is her fault," he said, sick of people implying Bri was to blame for any of what he'd done.

Colt sat back on the couch, lifting his feet onto the table. "Whether it is or not, if we find out Ruge, our brother, is into shady shit, we can't judge her brother, can we? And if it turns out she's right and what those asshole traffickers said was correct, well, then I guess we owe her an apology…"

Out of everything he might have expected Colt to say, suggesting an apology wasn't one of them. "She almost paid the ultimate price, just because she loved me… They could've gone after Eva; I don't understand why—"

"She and Ruger were only involved for a couple of months, and she went back to modelling in Italy. Tough to get your hands on someone there."

That was a fair point. "She doesn't blame me or Ruge," Blaser said. "Now that the secrets are out, I think she's sort of relieved… Lyssa sure is good at what she does."

"She's just a sucky waitress?"

"Fucking hopeless."

The men shared a smile, then Colt tossed his bottle in the trash. "Take Bri home, let her know we're handling this."

"We?"

"She's a Warner now, isn't she?" Colt asked. "You're in love with her."

"Yeah," Blaser said, done denying it.

"I'd heard you were protecting her, didn't know why. I also heard that Mattie got her brother a new lawyer, you set that up?"

"No, Mattie tried it on with Bri, but she played him like he played her. I guess the lawyer came before he knew he wasn't getting into her pants."

"It's weird you saw Marshall and Rafe's man together last night. What did Bri say about it?"

"That's a conversation we haven't had yet."

"Have it now," Colt said. "Take Bri home, when Ruge gets into town, I'll let you know. We'll sit down, just the three of us and figure this out."

Glad that he'd been honest, Blaser started for the door and his woman. "Okay."

"Hey," Colt said just as Blaser opened the door. "I'm sorry about Bri."

"Thanks, we're getting through it," he said. "She's amazing, not the scared kid she used to be."

"And I'm sorry that…"

"What?"

"You should've been able to come to me about the Rafe stuff. I'm sorry I've been such a judgmental prick. You make your own decisions; you don't need me to do it for you."

"You were just watching my back."

"Yeah, most of the time you're an ass, but I can come to you if I have to… I'm sorry you couldn't do the same."

"Screwing a therapist agrees with you," Blaser said, showing a half smile.

"She's the best, man. Lyssa's… she's just the best."

"I'm going to drive Bri home, call me if you hear from

Ruge."

"Same."

Ruger would contact Colt first. Knowing the truth, it was odd they were so close. Colt would be good cover for someone trying to appear clean, but he couldn't believe Ruger would be so conniving.

Content, for now, to get Bri home, he'd suck it up and tell her about fight night. After that, they'd wait for Ruger to arrive and slot in the final pieces of the puzzle.

TWENTY-FIVE

"HOW ARE YOU DOING?" Bri asked when they pulled up to the apartments.

Blaser turned off the engine and curled his fingers around the steering wheel. "I have no idea," he said. "I was happy when you invited me to that session with Lys, 'cause I thought… I thought it was us, moving forward, but…"

"You didn't expect to find out what you did about Ruger," she said. "I was pretty shocked myself."

"You've been sitting on this for a year," he said, his body remained forward-facing, but his eyes sloped around to her. "How the fuck can you stand to look at any of us?"

"I've had a year," she said with a feeble shrug. "At first, I was shocked, and I did want to blame Ruger. Every time I let myself get into that destructive thought pattern I… I realized the only way I could've kept myself out of it was to never have anything to do with you again. Except, I wouldn't change our past, Blase."

Shifting closer, she squeezed her fingers in-between his on the wheel. "I went through what I did because I meant so much to you. Once you strip away everything else, I love that, I want to mean something to you."

"You do," he said, twisting to cup her face. "You do mean something to me. I love you."

"I'm pissed that Ruger hid this from all of you for so long," she said. "We could have been prepared for what could come hunting for us if we'd just known it was a possibility. More than that, I don't like how you've been snubbed, and he's just stood back and let that happen."

"Don't worry, I'll be pointing that out to him," he said, still stroking her face.

"I'm surprised at how well Colt took the news."

"I told him about the…" Blaser started. "I told him what happened to you first."

"That I was raped," she said. "You can say it aloud."

"I don't like to… I don't want to remind you. I don't want to remind myself."

"Lyssa is right, it helps to say it out loud. We're not going to let him, to let them, have any control over us anymore." With that said, she pulled his hand from her face and took it to her lap. "We could go somewhere and park for a while if you want…"

Her coy school-girl act earned her a smile, and he breathed out a laugh. "Most of the places we used to do that are condos and shopping malls now."

"We'll just have to find some new places to make out then."

"I'm not sure I'd trust myself."

"I trust you," she said. She had been so preoccupied with her own issues, she hadn't considered whether or not Blaser enjoyed himself. "And we did okay last night, didn't we?"

"Last night was incredible, right up until I woke up alone."

"I'm sorry," she said.

"Why did you run out on me?"

"You promised never to break the law and you did. What you did last night could have ruined your life and everything you worked for. And you did it because I was in trouble. If I'm bad for you, I'm not staying."

"Colt understands… I think. I told him about the

rape and about Ruger. I think those were enough to shock him into shutting up, so in for a penny, I told him about Rafe and what went down last night. He knows everything. There's nothing that can come back and bite us on the ass now."

"I don't get why he was so understanding. Colt used to be so…"

"Lyssa has chilled him out," Blaser said. "And we've seen some shit together recently that… Shit that proves what you said about Ruger is true and taught him sometimes rules need to be broken to protect the people we love."

"But he hates me."

"It was never about you," Blaser said. "He didn't want me to fuck up and you know what, he was right. A lot of what I did when I was a kid was showing off. I did want to impress you and I did want to keep Gary happy so he wouldn't cause trouble in our relationship."

Ivy and Dax passed the truck to go upstairs, back into their apartment. "Dax was with you last night," Bri said, looking at the couple's front door. "Does Ivy know what happened?"

"Yeah," Blaser said. "But she wasn't there. Dax left her at home… and she was supposed to make sure you didn't come near the club."

"You're really on an honesty kick, aren't you?"

"I don't want you to walk away again, and I don't plan on giving you any excuses."

New, responsible Blaser was refreshing. He'd never shied from telling her he loved her, but he'd always thought that he knew best and had a habit of taking control, just like Gary did. While Blaser's antics the previous night were an up-to-date example of that, he hadn't been so forthcoming in the past with details.

"What did happen last night?"

"Dax is a fighter," Blaser said. "He's been part of the bareknuckle circuit since he was a kid. I provided the location, and he provided the event. We went to Rafe's this morning to give him his money and tell him to back the fuck off."

"And will he?"

"I think so," Blaser said, creeping satisfaction took

over his expression. "Rafe knows what went down in Risqué last night. He knows who Dax is now and his reach. The last thing he wants to do is piss off a professional fighter who has influence with others."

"How do you know Rafe knows what happened?"

"The guy who attacked you was there," Blaser said. "With Marshall. They were skulking around."

"The man who attacked me was with Marshall?" she said, falling back into her seat. "Why would they be together? Marshall is supposed to… he told Gary he'd look after me."

"I thought Marshall ratted me out to you when I came home to find you in my place last night."

She shook her head. "I haven't spoken to Marshall. I just knew that something was up and when you closed the club… That was too suspicious."

"Why didn't you just show up at the club?"

"Because I had no idea what was happening," she said. "You could've had some private poker game going on or something. Walking into the middle of that and throwing a fit wouldn't have benefited either of us."

"Smart thinking."

"If there's one thing I'm used to, it's crooks. I've been around enough of them in my life. My father is one, my brother, and my lover too."

"I'm retired," he said, holding up his hands. "Turns out I'm not as turned on by being bad as I used to be."

"Good," she said. "Because if we're going to make this work, I need to know all that is behind us."

"Promise," he said, leaning over the center console to kiss her.

"Except parking," she said, taking her hands to his chest. "That's one illegal activity I approve of."

"Good."

The next kiss was longer, and his tongue edged into her mouth. When she responded and coiled her arms around him, he took hold of her waist to pull her closer, wrapping her in his arms. The awkward angle made her spine ache, but she didn't care. The kiss was good enough to soothe all her pain.

"I'd suggest taking this into the back seat," she said.

"But it's sort of public around here."

"Can we go inside?" he asked, and she nodded.

He released her and came around the truck to open her door for her. His parents had taught him good manners. As silent as his father usually was, the Warner boys had certainly learned how to be gentlemen. He helped her out of the truck and locked it up. Their twined fingers remained together, nothing awkward or inappropriate about their link anymore.

TWENTY-SIX

WITH LINKED HANDS they went into his apartment. As soon as the door was closed, he tried to go into the kitchen, but she dropped her purse, kept his hand and didn't let him choose their destination. Leading him into the bedroom, she slipped off her shoes and cozied up to him, coaxing him toward the bed. She caught his tee-shirt and let her fingers find their way underneath to his abs.

"Do you have time for this?" she asked.

Usually, he spent all his time working. Afternoon delight, well, evening delight, wasn't often scheduled as far as she was aware.

"I told you I'd shoehorn in an hour if you needed me to," he said with a grin that made her laugh.

Being together was different with everything out in the open. Last night sort of felt like a goodbye, like it was her last chance to be intimate with the man she loved. If she believed her influence would ruin his life, then she would've walked away to give him the best shot at keeping his legitimate future together.

With the indication Colt was going to accept them being together, a weight was lifted.

Sitting on the bed, she wriggled back and reached up to pull him down over her. He kept his arms locked, remaining high above her, but the way they'd fallen meant their legs alternated, giving her a solid thigh to push her pelvis up against; a stimulator to grind her core into.

"Do you want to be on top?" he asked.

The joy of a few moments ago gave way to serious concern that irritated her as much as it impressed her.

"Just kiss me, Love. If I need to switch, then we'll switch," she said. "But I want to feel you, the weight of you on me. I've missed having your body protecting mine."

Glad that he trusted her, Bri sighed when he bent his arms to bring his lips to hers again. The missing urgency of the previous night began to build as soon as their kiss took hold. Thoughts of therapy and family faded away. The need of her body took over. Lifting his tee-shirt, she made him remove it, breaking their kiss for only a moment.

Her hands searched the hot flesh he'd revealed, and she imagined kissing every part of him. Touching his chest, she thought about how the unyielding muscles would taste and how he would react to her tormenting him with her mouth.

His hand skimmed down her hip to her leg, curling his fingers beneath her thigh he elevated the limb to pull it around his hip, and pushed his groin down into the soft heat of her body. She tensed. There was no fear in feeling the erect length of him nudging and massaging itself at the tingling apex of her thighs.

Want consumed her. Parting her legs further, she met each of his caresses with her own. Tempted to progress to the next level, she didn't want to take too much control, fearing Blaser would assume she was uncomfortable. Showing him trust was important.

His mouth advanced south. When he kissed her breasts through the fabric of her dress she whimpered and arched up, trying to urge him to erase the fabric from between them. But he didn't, and her breasts weren't his destination, they were merely on the path he traveled.

Gathering her skirt, he continued to kiss her body

through her dress until he reached her lower abdomen. Pulling her dress up over her hips, he exposed her belly and kissed down her left hip to her pubic bone then back up the diagonal formed by her other hip.

"Blase," she whined.

He caught the elastic of her underwear in his teeth and dragged it down as far as he could. He kissed his way across to the other hip and pulled down the other side, spending time kissing the sensitized skin he exposed.

The tingling groove where her leg met her body was on blazing alert. He knew just how to torture her; the trigger spot was the same one he'd learned when they were young. Letting his lips just meet her body and no more, he blew out a light breath that made her spine bend, trying to urge herself nearer to those tormenting lips.

Provoking another whimper, Blaser buried his head against her, then rose to pull off her panties. She'd thought he would look at her, maybe smile to offer reassurance, but he was too fixated on the glistening pink flesh he'd revealed.

Coming down on her again, he lifted her legs over his shoulders and licked the length of her slit then sucked on her clit and flickered the tip with his tongue. If he kept pampering in that way, with that salacious tongue of his, they wouldn't need an hour, it would be over in just a few seconds.

Curling his arms around her thighs to hold them over his shoulders, he planted his hands on her hips to keep them still enough for him to feast. And feast was exactly what he did, nibbling her creases, he licked her clit, increasing the pace of his tongue until she was panting out. Her dress was loose enough to allow her to move it up out of the way to fondle her own breasts as he sucked her into him again.

Yelping at the strength of his mouth, the spike of pleasure forced her body to try leaping away, but he was too strong. She was held there until he delivered the last of the climax that clenched in her chest and stuck in her throat.

It was so powerful, her eyes began to water. Her hips bucked despite the steadying pressure of his hands. He let her pelvis rise and fall and stimulated her each time she came into contact with his mouth. All she could do was hold her breath and ride the endorphins pumping through her body.

Once the wave crested, she flopped, spent and exhausted though she'd done nothing to cause such lethargy. Blaser's arms fell away, and she reached out for him, forcing herself to sit up and grab his wrist.

"Come here," she said, yanking his body down on hers. "I'm spent."

How would they ever follow that?

Blaser rolled to his side, holding them together and she began to psyche herself up for the next showing.

Pounding on the front door made them both sit up.

"Who is that?" she asked.

Her heart hadn't regained its regular pace yet, but it ratcheted up at the urgency of that knock.

"No idea," Blaser said.

She watched him get up and leave the room, smiling when she realized he was still wearing his boots. Fumbling to pull down her dress, she didn't bother seeking her underwear, just went after Blaser to discover who had interrupted their delight.

Her smile and memory of what they'd just shared fled when she got to the hallway. Blaser lifted his hands like in surrender and backed away from the front door. Her brother, Gary, came in holding a gun out in front of him, aiming it right at Blaser's heart.

"Gary!" she screamed, running toward him, but he didn't take his eyes away from Blaser.

"Get in the car," Gary shouted at her, walking into the apartment, forcing Blaser to walk backwards.

The door stayed open, but she had no intention of using it.

"No!" she replied and tried to run over to get in front of Blaser, but he caught her with a straight arm, holding her back with strength she couldn't beat. "Gary! Stop it! What are you doing?"

"Saving you from this prick. Didn't you hear me the first time, Warner?" Gary demanded of Blaser. "I told you to keep away from my sister, didn't I?"

"I came to him," Bri said, beseeching her brother.

"Put the gun down, Gar! I love him, I want to be with him!"

"Get your ass in the car, Bri!"

"No!"

"You get your ass out there now or I'm going to aim lower this time!"

Gary wouldn't listen to reason; he'd come with one thing on his mind. And just like Blaser used to, Gary thought he knew better than everyone else. Her brother was a control freak, she'd always thought his arrogance came from a place of love. That he wanted to take care of her because their parents hadn't. But now she wasn't so sure it was about her at all.

Anger burned in Gary's eyes and although she couldn't see Blaser's expression, she knew he didn't return that resentment. Any anger Blaser had towards Gary was for what he had done to her and those he cared about.

She didn't know how Gary got there, or why he wasn't in jail anymore, but his actions proved he didn't fear going back.

"I should've got rid of you when I had the chance," Gary said. "Get in the car, Bri! You don't need to see this."

Gary was going to pull the trigger. It didn't matter a damn what she said about it. Talking him down wasn't a possibility, her brother had never listened to her. Bri's gaze darted around the room as she searched for options, except none presented themselves. Blaser and Gary carried on their stare out.

Shoving away Blaser's arm, she backed off and ran for the door. Blaser might think she was following Gary's orders and leaving him to his fate, but she wasn't. Running up the stairs, she battered on Ivy's door, not giving a damn if she brought out all the neighbors in the process.

Ivy opened the door.

Bri grabbed hold of her. "Where's Dax?"

"Inside," Ivy said.

Bri appreciated Ivy gripping her arms because she needed the extra support. "He's got a gun; he's going to kill him!"

"What? Who?" Ivy asked. "Where are you—"

"Downstairs! Please! Where's Dax?"

Ivy was shoved aside in that move that took Bri with her. Dax muscled them both out of the way and was immediately on his way down the stairs.

"It's okay," Ivy said, pulling Bri forward into a hug.

Bri sobbed and clung to her newest friend, overwhelmed by shock and adrenaline. Her love was being held at gunpoint by her only family. The blast of a gunshot startled them both. Together, hand in hand, they ran down the stairs to find out who had been on the receiving end of that bullet.

Praying it wasn't Blaser, she felt the tightening grip of Ivy's hand. Had she just caused the demise of Ivy's love? Bri would never forgive herself if an innocent man was hurt because of her actions.

The door wasn't closed, but it swung on its hinges. The women shoved it aside to take in the scene. There was no blood. Dax was on the floor, holding Gary down by the throat and Blaser was on his feet, a few feet from where she'd left him.

The singular focus on Dax's expression fixated on the man he held down with little effort. Pressure of knuckle and thumb was all he needed to subdue the gunman. Searching the space, the gun was under the kitchen table, obviously having skittered away from her brother. A hole in an upper kitchen cabinet door revealed where the shot had gone.

Blaser was at her side, he stroked her hair and pulled her into his arms. Talking to Gary would fall to her. She peeked out of Blaser's embrace. Dax still had him pinned, and Gary wasn't fighting as hard anymore.

"Let him up," she called, shoving out of Blaser's clinch. "Please, don't hurt him!"

"Don't hurt him?" Ivy said. "Who is he?"

"He's my brother," Bri said.

Dax either wasn't listening or didn't care. He held on until Ivy went over and crouched beside him, grasping his elbow and dipping to break his eye line. She whispered something and Dax released his hold, stood up, and tucked her under his arm.

Gary coughed and rolled onto his side.

"Thanks," Blaser said to Dax, who didn't react to the gratitude.

"Someone might want to grab the gun before he does," Dax said, saying nothing more before taking Ivy out of the apartment.

Blaser did as Dax suggested and retrieved the gun then emptied out the bullets. While he took it out of the room, she crouched beside Gary.

"What were you thinking coming in here like that?" she demanded. "Don't you ever threaten Blaser again!"

Gary fell onto his back, blinking tears from his bloodshot eyes. "Who the fuck was that guy?" he wheezed.

"He is Blaser's new best friend," Bri said. "Bear that in mind the next time you come over to ruin our evening." Standing up, she nudged his ribs with her foot. "Why are you out of jail?"

"New lawyer." Gary coughed and managed to sit up, rubbing his throat. "Cut me a deal."

Blaser appeared in the hallway.

She jumped over her brother to run into his arms. "Love, I'm sorry, are you okay?"

"Dax took care of business," Blaser said, embracing her. "Dude just came in and dropped to the ground. He assessed the situation in a second, did this sweeping move and took Gary's legs out, boom, he was on the ground. The gun went off. By the time I realized I wasn't shot, Dax had Gary by the throat."

"I was so scared," Bri said. Burying her face in his still bare chest, she closed her eyes and tightened her embrace. "If he had hurt you… if you'd…. What would I have done without you, Love?"

"This isn't gonna happen."

Gary's snarl brought her around, but she remained in Blaser's arms, using her body as a shield between the men.

"This, what?" Blaser asked.

"You two. I fucking told you, Warner!"

"He has looked after me," Bri said. "While you were going around waving guns and shooting people, Blaser got his life together. He took care of Rafe, and now we're going to be together."

"No, not a chance," Gary said. "I took care of Rafe, me, not this piece of shit!"

"You don't need to take care of anything," Bri said. "It's done. Blaser dealt with it!"

"You can't be with him," Gary spat. "His fucking family—"

"Accept us," Bri said. "They have helped me in ways you can't even imagine. Colt listened. He took the time to listen, unlike you who is more interested in running his mouth, and Colt's fiancée? She's a therapist, she's helped me process what happened last year, she has listened and praised me. We're working together and you know? It's working! Blaser and I made love last night. I am moving on. I am getting better. But you, you're stuck in the past and won't even think about growing as a person or developing any sort of maturity!"

"He's no different," Gary said, climbing to his feet. "He's going to screw you over, he's a prick!"

"He took the rap for all of you," Bri said. "You should be grateful to him. He went to prison and kept his mouth shut about all of you! He took the rap, and could've taken you all with him, you, Marshall, Mattie, all of you! But he didn't. He kept his mouth shut and set me free. He told me to get away from you, from all of you, and he was right! Look how great his life turned out when he cut ties with you and your crew!"

"He's no fucking saint!"

"No, he's not, but he doesn't pretend to be! Don't stand there and act like you're coming after Blase for my benefit. You're not worried he'll hurt me, you're scared I won't be dependent on you anymore! That's what you need, you need the power and when you don't have it, when someone doesn't need you anymore… you can't handle that."

"We're family, I need to look after you."

"And if that's what you were doing maybe I could cut you some slack. But that, what you just did, that wasn't love, that was a power trip. You wanted to take control of me, and of Blaser by taking me away from him… If you were sure I was going to choose you over him, you wouldn't have come in here with the gun… would you?"

Grabbing Blaser's wrists, she pulled his arms further around her. "I love her, Wilcox, all the way. Isn't it time we all grew up?"

Blaser's calm words were the final piece she needed, exhaling the panic, she relaxed.

Some of Gary's anger was gone though she wasn't sure if that was through acceptance or embarrassment.

"You're gonna choose him?" Gary asked her. "All we've got is each other."

Her heart broke a little. Her brother needed her, maybe more than she needed him. "I don't want to choose anyone," she said. "I want both of you in my life. I wouldn't stand by and let Blaser bully and threaten you, I won't do the same for you. I can't let you think it's okay to behave that way anymore."

Gary examined the whole scene. She anticipated his response, hoping he would choose to stand with them instead of against them. But her brother said nothing, he turned around and walked out without saying another word.

Her impulse to follow him was obstructed by Blaser tightening his embrace, holding her in place. "Let him go, Doll," he said. "He's out and we know where to find him. Give him time to think about this. Hopefully, he'll realize we're not kidding around and accept us, but it's not going to happen overnight."

"I guess," she said, listening to a vehicle engine outside.

It flared a couple of times, then sped out of the parking lot and faded into the distance.

Blaser's phone rang. He kissed her head then eased her out of his arms to retreat to the bedroom and answer it. To distract herself, she went into the kitchen and opened the damaged cabinet.

Glass showered down. The bullet had lodged itself in the back of the cabinet. They'd have to pick it out and mend the hole, but time was short. She was due at Risqué for her shift, covering for one of the other waitresses.

Seeking out a clock, she gasped when she read the time. Already behind schedule, she grabbed her purse, ran out and up the stairs to her own apartment to get ready.

Her shower lasted less than three minutes. Freshening up, she ran a brush through her hair and opened the bathroom door intending to dash across the hallway into the bedroom opposite. Except as soon as she opened the door, there was Blaser standing in front of her.

Fully naked and still glistening from the body butter she'd slathered over herself before brushing her hair, she smiled when words fled his lips. His hungry gaze did the talking for him.

"I wasn't running away, I was getting ready for work," she said, easing him aside to pass and enter her bedroom.

"You don't have to work at the club anymore," he said, coming after her. "You can move into my place."

"Yeah," she said, picking out underwear and an outfit. "That was my plan all along, get into your pants so I could move into your place and never work another day in my life."

"We're together, right? Why shouldn't we—"

"I am not going to rush this," she said. He sauntered across to sit on the bed next to the clothes she'd laid out. "Yes, we're together, but I want to keep seeing Lyssa and keep working through this. Just because we've been physically intimate doesn't mean that all my issues are gone."

"I know that," he said, fingering the lace of her bra. "But I want to spend the night with you."

"Case and point why we shouldn't rush into living together," she said, fastening in earrings then heading over to don her underwear. "We haven't actually spent a whole night together yet."

"We will."

"Yeah, we will," she said. "But we have to pace ourselves. Even when we do decide the time is right to move in together, I won't stop working. I will pull my weight. I want to help out here and at the garage. I want to be more involved in the club. I want us to be a team."

"We are."

"Good," she said. "Because I don't want you thinking I need to be looked after and I don't want you doing anything illegal, not even for me."

"Understood."

"I want us to take the time to learn each other again and develop our relationship properly, at a normal pace."

"We've lived together before."

"Yes," she said. "A long time ago. We should enjoy this, maybe you could take me out somewhere."

"Like a date?"

"Yes."

"I can't tonight. That was Crystal on the phone, there's a problem at the club, something about the air conditioning they think I fixed last night."

"But you didn't?" she asked, getting dressed then moving on to makeup.

"I got a guy in to do it this morning."

"Everyone thinks you fixed it once so you can do it again," she said. "You didn't tell Crystal about last night?"

"I didn't tell anyone, except Dax."

"Can it wait five minutes?" she asked. "I could use a ride to the club."

"Sure," he said and pushed up on his hands to bounce back and lie down on her bed.

Flicking her eyes to the reflection of him staring up at the ceiling, she swiped on her mascara. "You're distracted, Love."

"Thinking about what I'm going to say to Ruger."

"When will he be here?"

"Don't know," Blaser said. "Could be in an hour, could be in a day. Everything you told us is just proof we don't really know where he is or what he's up to."

Finishing up with her makeup, she looked at her own reflection for a while. "Do you think that Dax has killed people?"

"Don't know," he replied. "From the way he was today… I'd guess he's more lethal than a lot of guys around here."

The ex-cons Blaser hired tended to be former thieves

or dealers. Somehow Dax had slipped through the net. One of Blaser's requirements for hiring guys and leasing them apartments was that they live legit. No way Dax was a low-level criminal, caught because of his own stupidity like most of the other guys around there.

Ivy was cagey about answering questions. The story her friend had told about how she and Dax had met was shocking, but broad strokes. Dax didn't raise his hands to Ivy, and he'd bailed them out of a jam. She couldn't judge his skills negatively; they might have saved Blaser's life. Giving him a pass seemed like the least they could do.

"We'll worry about that later," he said, springing off the bed to come over and grab her hand. "Let's get to the club. There's nothing else we can do until Ruger gets here. Dax's business is Dax's business, let's just be grateful he's on our side."

That was true. Being on Dax's bad side wasn't a place anyone would want to be. Blaser was right. The best way to tolerate the wait was to stay busy. Until Ruger got back, her love would be tense. No matter how long it took, she'd do everything possible to ease her man's burden.

TWENTY-SEVEN

MESSING AROUND with the AC unit wasn't actually supposed to yield results. Giving it a final thwack, it shuddered into life, and he looked up, triumphant. The girls applauded, all except Bri, who was hiding a smile behind her hand. With a wink at his girl, he sent his audience back to work.

The rest of the night was just like the old days, routine, boring, normal… except his view had improved. Bri's drinks orders got priority because whenever she headed in his direction, he automatically gravitated to her. She didn't seem to notice, but the other girls had and delighted in giving him a hard time. Crystal was the only one without good humor about it.

Bri stayed after all the other girls. Even after the place was back in order, she remained to put away the last of the cleaning supplies. Counting the cash out of the register, he noted the figures in the columns of his accounts book as he went along. Keeping a nightly tally in ink was a habit he'd started on night one.

The only lights left on were behind the bar, so when the front spotlight blasted a white beam onto the stage, it caught his attention. He hadn't expected such a bright flash.

He heard the footsteps before he saw her, the glare of the light shielded her form.

When his girl entered the shining white glow, he stopped counting and watched her stretch her arm to curl her fingers around the streak of metal dozens of his women had thrown themselves around.

Transfixed by her body moving around the pole in a down and up pendulum move, she twisted to lean back, lifting her arm above her head. Coiling a leg around it, she went around again, the thrust of her breasts captivating him.

Putting down the money, he rounded the bar, keeping his eyes on the performing woman causing his jeans to feel tighter. She undulated to inaudible music, rocking her hips left and right. Bending at the waist, her ass rose high as she straightened her legs and tossed back her hair.

Picking up the pace, he leaped onto the stage and gripped her waist, making her gasp. He'd never craved a woman on that stage and there he was up there with one thing on his mind.

"You're hired," he whispered and kissed her neck.

She laughed, resting her weight on him. "Who says I want a job," she asked, rubbing her ass back into his groin. "I wanted to know if I could still do it."

"You can do it, Doll, all night long."

Keeping close contact, she circled around and began to open his jeans. "We're all alone," she whispered.

"We are," he agreed.

"Have you ever had sex on this stage?" she asked.

"No."

"Then tonight's your lucky night."

She took off his tee-shirt to kiss his torso. Bri could get away with anything. There were tasks to take care of like cashing out and locking up. All that was forgotten when she stepped back and took her top off. Her breasts bounced out of the spandex, and he caught the glorious soft flesh, thinking only of her. Gripping and kneading the mounds, he tried to get closer, but she dropped to her knees and pulled off his jeans.

She took his hands and yanked him down on top of

her. "You're not going to fire me for getting kinky with a colleague on your premises, are you?"

"This is the only time you take your clothes off on this stage, or anywhere, when I'm the only one in the room to see you."

"Deal," she said, sliding a hand around to the back of his neck to pull him down for a kiss.

Tracing his fingertips through her cleavage and down her abdomen, she parted her thighs to welcome his digits. Her skirt bunched around her hips, but he kept working his fingers over her panties, rubbing and teasing her clit. Her breathing quickened as the moisture his attention garnered soaked right through her underwear.

"Yes," she exhaled and brought up a knee to plant her foot on his shoulder, pressuring him away.

When he sat up, she shimmied out of her thong and used her feet to clasp his hips, bringing him back toward her.

Kissing her mouth, he tasted her deep, pushing a finger into her. She was wet, ready to accept him, but he wouldn't move too fast. Urging his finger deeper, he curled it and pulled out then slid it in again. His kiss was warmed by the pulse of her breath. Each inhale betrayed her growing arousal and when she reached fever pitch, right on the cusp of her orgasm, he stopped. Everything, fingering her, kissing her, he stopped to gaze down into the devotion she poured into him.

He didn't need to check if she was comfortable or happy, he could tell by the way that her body squirmed under his. The point got a whole lot plainer when she grabbed his dick, pulling, fighting to join their forms. When she raised her hips, he let her keep hold of him and force the bulb of his head between her folds. Pushing down, he slid in deeper. Her hips stayed up, but her hands fell away.

Gliding through her juices was easier. Her body and mind showed no hesitation. Her loose muscles welcomed the bulge of his arousal, no tension or strain, just the woman he loved basking in the thudding bass of their deafening hearts.

"Blase," she called, gritting her teeth and pushing her hips higher, begging him to move faster.

Working harder, he kissed her, holding her head to trace his thumbs up and down in the grooves behind her ears.

Spasm locked their bodies together. Her crescendo squeezed his cock so tight the ferocity of her reaction pitched him to his own summit. Forcing himself deep, his spunk pumped out in an erratic stream. Even after he'd gone soft, he didn't want to leave the heat of his favorite cocoon.

Her broad smile grew as she sagged onto the solid floor. "Oh, Love, we did it."

They'd already had sex, so either she meant him on top or at Risqué.

"We can do it again," he said, kissing her throat and cheek.

"Let's get dressed and finish up," she said. "You'll need your sleep now you have another job to take care of every day."

"Every day?" he said, taking her hand to pull her to her feet when she gave him a nudge.

"You never know when I'll need satisfaction," she said, swiping up their clothes from the stage.

"So I'm on call now twenty-four seven?" he asked, taking his tee-shirt when she handed it over.

"You can have weekends off," she said, covering her breasts.

He groaned. "Don't need time off, page me whenever you need me, Doll."

The fizz of her static energy bounced off him making him hyper-aware of her proximity. Overcoming her fears infused her with such a powerful delight it was contagious. There was still a long way to go, and he wouldn't be pushing any boundaries for a while, but it was nice to see her playful.

It was banter. Flirting. Teasing. She wasn't capable of throwing out her hang-ups. But they'd get there, to that time they could be on each other every minute of the day. He'd be there for her, provide whatever she needed, whatever she asked for.

Together, they completed the last of the tasks at Risqué. The novelty of having a companion with him during his routine was strange and fun. Now when he spoke, someone spoke back. Someone laughed with him, gave him opinions and advice, and cut the work in half. They left the club, everything done, earlier than he ever had before. They locked up and were in the truck on the way home in record time.

Pulling on the parking brake, he turned off the engine. She leaned over to kiss his cheek, then was out of the truck, running upstairs toward her own apartment. His wish of spending the night with her seemed to have faded.

Not giving up without at least asking, he followed her and reached her door at the same time she stuck her key in it.

"Are you going to invite me in?" he asked.

She spun to reply, but Suzette's door opened in time with Ivy's. "I called Gus!" Suzette announced to the sheet-wrapped Ivy. "He's going to throw you out!"

"I don't think so," Ivy declared. "Maybe you better invest in some earplugs… or just ask a surgeon to remove that stick from your butt!"

"What's going on?" Blaser asked, approaching the feuding women.

"That… that pair of Neanderthals! That's what!" Suzette shouted. "They're always at it! It's stupid o'clock in the morning and all I can hear is them panting and grunting!"

Suzette's red-faced fury was nothing to smile at, so he cleared his throat and switched his focus to Ivy, but she was no calmer.

"Someone needs to chill out!" Ivy said. "We're consenting adults! He's my husband! He can fuck me any way he likes anytime! We don't live by your schedule! If you don't like it: fuck off!"

"I don't think so," Suzette said. The women moved toward each other. "I'm family! You're a troublemaker!"

Rushing over, Blaser got himself between them to prevent it getting physical. No doubt Ivy was naked under that sheet, not that it would slow her down if her huffing rage was any indication.

"You're the one banging on walls and cussing us out!" Ivy said, trying to swipe his arm out of the way.

Gus bounded up the stairs. Doors were opening

along the walkway. The only person not watching events unfold was Dax. The women continued trying to get around him. Gus came over to help extricate him from the flailing limbs swatting at their opponent.

His cousin grabbed Suzette, yanking her back toward her apartment. He got her through the door, though she tried to sneak around him when he looked back.

"Take her in there and calm her down," Blaser said to his cousin, pinning Ivy's arms down at her sides.

Gus nodded and did just that, closing the door to cut off Suzette's screeching.

"She is so uptight," Ivy said as Blaser directed her toward her own apartment. She noticed the many gawkers and stared right back without shame. "What the fuck are you looking at?"

"It's over," Blaser said to the other tenants. "Go back inside."

Most of the men were not long back from their shifts at Risqué. For those who worked in the garage, they'd be expected at work bright and early. So there were no objections, just some smirks and snickers as the men returned to their abodes.

Worried about what he'd see, he took Ivy inside her apartment, but saw no sign of Dax. "You were making the racket alone?"

If Dax was there, Blaser couldn't see why he'd leave his wife to deal with the complaining neighbor alone.

"He's in the bedroom," Ivy said, lifting her arm then tugging it down to free it from his grip.

"He let you out there alone?"

"She can handle herself!" Dax called from the bedroom.

He might not have made an appearance, but he'd obviously heard everything that went on.

"There were ten guys out there," Blaser said, exaggerating only slightly. "She's naked."

"Every one of them has met me," Dax said. The blurred outline of his figure came into the hallway but remained next to the bedroom. "Do you think any of them would take the chance of touching my wife?"

Dax made a good point and loyalty was a big deal around there. Still, Blaser wouldn't have liked Bri to be on show for a group of slobbering men.

"He has a deep end philosophy," Ivy said, tucking in her sheet.

"What does that mean?" Blaser asked.

"I like to watch her jump in and give it her best shot before I dive in to bail her out."

"I swim just fine, thank you," Ivy said, directing her scowl into the darkness. "Your family made sure of that."

"Always pissed about something," Dax muttered and disappeared back into the bedroom.

"Are you spending the night at Bri's place?" Ivy asked him.

"Uh… I don't know yet."

"You should. Then that wench will get it in surround sound. There's no way we're going without sex just because her panties are full of cobwebs."

"She's had a rough time," Blaser said. "Cut her some slack."

"Fair enough," Ivy said and shrugged. "Since you asked so nicely and all. Goodnight."

Dismissing him, she sauntered back to the bedroom without seeing him out. The apartments were his and he was a friend. He also wouldn't stand there all night listening to the couple enjoy each other, so he guessed he was supposed to kick himself out.

Leaving, he closed Ivy's apartment door just as headlights swept the length of the building. A car drove into the space next to his truck. Going to the railing to see who was getting in so late, the headlights went off, the engine died, and a door opened.

It took his eyes a moment to recover from the dazzle of the headlights. When they did, he picked out the features of his cousin Mattie, standing next to the car looking up at him.

"This a bad time?" Mattie asked without raising his voice too much in the quiet night.

"What do you want?" Blaser asked him.

"A word."

These days, crossing paths with Mattie was rare. Sometimes he heard whispers at the club or from the guys at the garage about what his cousin was up to, but this recent spike of contact had him intrigued.

Glancing back, Bri's door was closed and there were no lights on. So she'd gone to bed alone. Everything was quiet again, as it should be at close to four in the morning. Other than his own niggling need for sleep, he had no reason to say no to Mattie.

"My place," Blaser said, going to descend the stairs.

Digging his keys from his pocket, he unlocked his apartment and led his cousin inside. Mattie went to the kitchen table and sat down, choosing function over comfort, heightening his intrigue.

"I'm amazed you're still living here," Mattie said, spreading his hands on the table.

Blaser flicked on lamps and retrieved a couple of beers from the fridge though he wasn't surprised when Mattie turned up his nose at the offer. Slipping the second beer back into the fridge, he opened his own and propped himself on the kitchen counter crossing his ankles as he took a long slug from the frosty bottle.

"It's convenient," Blaser said. "And you wanted me here to look after the place. It was one of your conditions for selling me the garage."

"Five years ago," Mattie said. "You're still happy here?"

"Like I said, it's convenient. I've got an early day tomorrow, so why don't you cut to the chase?"

"I heard about what went down in Risqué."

"What went down?"

"The fight night."

Lowering his bottle, he slid it onto the counter, keeping his eyes trained on his cousin. "What about it?"

"You haven't lost your touch; you can still sniff out a winner."

"It wasn't my idea," Blaser said. "I did it for a reason,

it was a one off."

Denying it would be ridiculous. Mattie hadn't factored into his decision to hold the fight night in Risqué, but it shouldn't have been a real surprise he knew. Mattie had his ear to the ground, at least his men did. There was little that went on in the neighborhood that Mattie didn't know about, especially related to his own family and illegality.

"I didn't care when I heard," Mattie said. "I wasn't surprised. If Bri's back in your life, I guessed your old ways wouldn't be far behind."

"She's got nothing to do with it," he snapped, pushing away from the counter. "Don't bring her—"

"Does she know?"

"Yeah. She knows everything, Colt too, so if you're here to blackmail me—"

"Blackmail you?" Mattie said, smiling. "I think it's incredible… When I heard you had the Ravager—"

"This is about Dax?" Blaser asked, recognizing the name he fought under.

"We could make a fortune."

"We?"

"You have to get him on board. We can keep using Risqué—"

"You have plenty of your own buildings."

"My facilities aren't suitable."

"Because they're too upmarket?" Blaser asked. "Or because you'd prefer not to get burned when we all get caught?"

"Dax is your friend," Mattie said. "Bring him to a meeting—"

"He lives right upstairs. Why don't you knock and ask him yourself?"

"He doesn't like to be approached. The way I understand it, he has a scout who makes his connections for him."

"Then what use am I?"

"You already have his ear," Mattie said.

"Dax isn't interested in making a habit of fighting in my club. I think his wife would have something to say about him getting beat up every night just to satisfy your buddies."

"You don't know much about his reputation if you assume he'll be beaten," Mattie said. "And his wife can be persuaded."

Blaser didn't like that sinister edge. "Did you just threaten his wife? If he gets a whiff you even suggested—"

"Hurting his wife would be stupid," Mattie said. "I'm not interested in being his enemy. Women are easily swayed by promises of diamonds or cash. There's something she wants, if we make her happy, Dax will follow."

"I don't think Ivy is the sort. I can tell Dax you're interested, but I wouldn't hold my breath."

"You're open to it? If we get Dax on board—"

"No," Blaser said. "I'm not getting involved."

"Why not? It will be lucrative."

Shaking his head, Blaser went back to his beer. "Not everyone is motivated by money."

"What does motivate you, cousin? That sexy number upstairs?"

"Why?" Blaser asked, twisting to peer over his shoulder. "You thinking about making another play? She's not interested in you."

"I got that message loud and clear," Mattie said, defeated but not dismayed. "How long is she going to stay interested in you if you're working every hour God sends? Think about it before you turn me down flat." Rising from the table, he tipped his chin toward Blaser. "She won't want to live here forever. She'll want a house, a decent car, a life... She's not going to be interested in running around after you while you work, unless you're looking for a glorified slave to fuck. She'll put up with that for a while I'd guess, but eventually she'll want your attention. Women are all the same. They tell you it's okay, and they play the game. But unless you can hand over the dough and show her who's boss, eventually she'll want you to hand over your balls. You want to provide for her, right? To look after her?"

"Sure," Blaser said and shrugged.

His fingers were growing numb around the glistening bottle sliding through his digits. Increasing his hold, he balanced his grip so as not to break the glass, but he'd lost his taste for the liquid.

"This is the best way. Think of the money you could earn literally overnight. You wouldn't need to work all night every night. We could do this once or twice a month. That would earn you enough to support Bri, to look after her in the way she deserves."

"Dax won't be interested."

"I think he will," Mattie said, coming around the table. "Even if he's not, he's not the only fighter around. You've got a name now, everyone knows Risqué. This can happen… It's late. I know you're up early every single morning, so I should let you sleep. It's a shame you've got such a sexy girl right above your head. You're just too busy to spend the night with her… How long will she put up with that? How many mornings will she wake up alone because you have to get to work?"

Mattie patted his shoulder, shaking him from his daze. "She understands."

"But should she have to?" Mattie asked. With another pat, he headed for the exit. "Think about it and I'll be in touch." He opened the door. "It would be great to get the family working together again, don't you think?"

Mattie left, closing the door behind him. After a pause, he went to the sink to pour out the rest of his beer. Watching the fizzing liquid foam and slide away down the drain, he couldn't work out if a door had just opened for him, or if he was about to get one slammed in his face.

TWENTY-EIGHT

"YOU'VE BEEN A MILLION miles away tonight, boss," Crystal said, strutting up to his side in Risqué the following night.

His meeting with Mattie had played in his mind for most of the day. Something about the offer niggled at him.

"Come here," he said.

Snatching Crystal's hand, he took her from behind the bar, across the room and up into his office. Closing the door, he released her hand and strode over to the desk.

"What's going on?" she asked.

"Mattie came to see me last night."

"Ah, the great achiever," she said, striding over to the pool table that was usually concealed behind a curtain that cut his office in half. It was open because he'd played a few frames himself that afternoon while trying to straighten out his thoughts. "What did he want?"

"He made me an offer."

"What kind of offer?" she asked, hooking her hands on the table and thrusting herself up to sit on it, crossing her long, smooth legs, leaning back, keeping her focus on him.

"He wants to use this place."

"Use this place for what?" She frowned. "You're not thinking about… are we talking something off the books?"

"Way off the books," he said, moving toward her.

"And you're thinking about it," she stated.

Crystal had been a staple in his life since he left prison. She had never broken his confidence, not that he knew anyway.

"I shouldn't be. I know I shouldn't but… I could pay off this place, pay back Colt and Ruger. I could upgrade the garage; get all the new equipment the guys have been raving about."

"Those are good points."

"I could use the money, Cryst, you know? I could really pamper Bri. I could take her out to fancy places and away for vacations, not like I can now. I'm working all the time, how long will she put up with that?"

"I don't know her very well," Crystal said. "We went to high school together, but I haven't seen her for years. Does she need all those things?"

Crystal had moved from Texas with her family when she was a teenager.

"What woman doesn't?" he asked, stopping a few feet from her and folding his arms. "I mean if some guy came and offered to take you away from all the bullshit of life and pamper you on some beach somewhere, wouldn't you jump at the chance?"

"It would depend on the guy," she said, pointing her toe she nudged his knee. "Lots of money in little time means illegal and with your history…"

"I could go away again," he said. "I know." Groaning, he scrubbed his hands over his face and turned his back on her. "I shouldn't be thinking about this at all."

"Have you spoken to Bri about it?"

"No, we didn't spend the night together and I've been at the garage all day."

"She's working tonight."

"Yeah, but I've sort of been keeping my distance."

That afternoon, Bri had visited Lyssa's again. When he called Colt to check if he'd heard from Ruger, his girl had been over there. The help was getting her back to her old self, she was confident again, smiling more, and engaging customers in conversation.

"If she's smart, she'll have noticed. A woman doesn't like to be ignored, Blasé. I don't care how much money you have, or how many vacations you take, you have to pay her attention."

"Exactly," he said, swiping her ankle to move her leg aside. "How many mornings will she have to wake up alone, huh? And I'm in here almost every night, how long will she put up with that?"

"She'll be alone a lot more if you're in prison," Crystal said. She sat up and reached for his shirt, taking hold of it, she pulled him close. "Look, you've worked really hard for everything that you've got. It's not always fun and yes sometimes you're a tired old grumpus…"

"Thanks," he grumbled.

"But you've done so much. You have to be proud. If she's the type of girl that wants diamonds and your undivided attention, she's not the girl for you. I'm sorry to say it, but if you can't talk to her about this then one of two things is going on. Either you're worried she'll say yes you should do it and you actually don't want to, or…"

"Or?"

"You're worried she'll say no, that she doesn't want you to do it."

"And if she says no?"

"Do you think you'll lose her if you don't shower her with time and money?"

"Bri won't care about the money," he said. "She's not like that."

"So it's the time you're worried about?" Crystal asked. "She's dependent on you and needs you there with her constantly?"

"Not constantly," he said. "But how many dates have you seen me go on these last few years? Maybe I don't have the time to dedicate myself to a full-time relationship."

"Hmm…" Crystal said, pressing her hands to him. "Are we talking about Mattie's offer, or are we talking about you being scared to commit?"

"I want to be with her, I love her."

"And you have no trouble with commitment, you own two businesses for chrissakes… Talk to her, it's all you can do. If she tells you to do it, then I say dump her, 'cause the rest of us wouldn't know what to do with ourselves if you didn't keep this place together."

Crystal did have a way of cutting through the crap. He was more grateful for her than he'd ever expressed. She'd managed to get him laughing again and his mind was much clearer. The office door opened, and he turned to see Dax coming in.

"What's the—"

"Give us a minute, darlin'," Dax said to Crystal, who shrugged and sashayed toward Dax, each of her slow, measured steps got her that little bit closer to the exit but without any hurry.

She trailed a finger the width of Dax's chest as she walked out. Blaser could only laugh at her gall. It had been years since she'd been the slutty party girl, but it was an act she remembered well.

He headed toward the desk. "What's up?" Blaser asked when Dax closed the door.

"You want to get home, now."

He sat down. "What? Why? The club is open for hours yet."

"Ivy just called," Dax said, marching to the desk. "There are cops all over the place."

"Cops?" he asked, springing to his feet. "What do they want?"

"They have a warrant."

"A warrant for what?" Blaser wasn't sure he wanted the answer.

The aloof fighter wasn't giving much away, but cops swarming around the building would be enough to creep out all the residents.

"They're in your place, that's all I know."

"You think they know about the other night?"

"If they did, they'd be here," Dax said. "And no one

has knocked on my door yet."

"So what else—"

"I don't know what shit you're mixed up in, but you better get back there and get it straightened out, and if there's anything you need to tell your girl…"

"She knows," Blaser said. "She knows about the other night, she was pissed, but she got over it."

"That's something," Dax said. "Maybe I should've asked you about other enterprises you had going on before I got involved. Everyone seems to think you're whiter than white these days, are they wrong?"

"I don't know what the cops are looking for," he said, heading for the hat stand by the door where his jacket hung. "But they're not going to find anything at my place or on any of my premises if they want to look further."

"Okay."

"Are you coming?" Blaser asked, swooping his jacket around his shoulders.

"Not a chance," Dax said. "I was taught to run away from cops, never toward them."

"Ivy's over there. If trouble is looking for you—"

"Ivy really is whiter than white," he said then a smile quirked his lips. "As far as the law is concerned anyway."

"Yeah, I don't think there's any doubt what she is behind your bedroom door."

"You calling my wife a slut?"

"No! I meant 'cause of what happened with Suzette, who got the full live-action audio."

Now Dax really did smile. "That really pissed Ivy off."

"Yeah, the whole building knows."

They left the office together. "Go find out what the pigs want, having them sniffing around isn't what we need now."

Blaser didn't need to be told that. For five years, he'd stayed out of trouble, and he'd had no contact with the police, they certainly hadn't come looking for him. The raid a few weeks ago was inconvenient, but it didn't bother him because he knew that there was nothing to find.

Now that the police were at his home, he was concerned. With the fight night and his run-ins with Gary and Rafe, this wasn't the time to blip on police radar. He would have to go home, get rid of them, and then keep his head down until this passed.

TWENTY-NINE

POLICE CARS ANGLED toward his apartment in the parking lot had their flashing lights on, showing no discretion. Various uniformed officers stood in a haphazard perimeter to stop snooping eyes and nosey neighbors from getting too close.

When he pulled up at the curb, Ivy was standing on the top balcony with Suzette beside her. It seemed his misfortune brought the women together, at least for tonight. If Suzette was witness to what was going on, she'd have called Lyssa, which probably meant Colt was on his way.

Colt still had friends down at the precinct, it could be useful to have him around. His twin usually got more information than those actually involved in the crime. Not that he'd been involved in anything criminal, not at the apartment building anyway.

Killing the engine, he wasted no time in getting out and crossing to see what was going on. A uniformed officer stopped him before he could reach his apartment.

"That's my apartment," Blaser said. "I have a right to know what the hell is going on."

"It's okay."

He recognized Detective Hoburn's voice, a homicide detective and former colleague of Colt's. Hoburn appeared from a car a few feet behind the officer, the door had been open, but he hadn't been looking for any occupants.

Hoburn came over and nodded to the side. They moved together to the front of the building but didn't get near his apartment so he couldn't see what they were doing in there.

"You're in some trouble, Warner," Hoburn said. "Where were you day before yesterday?"

Although he didn't know the exact time, he knew it was the early hours of the morning. Yesterday, he'd spent the day at the garage then gone straight to the club. The previous day was Bri's therapy session and all the revelations that came with that.

"I was at Lyssa's, then I saw Colt at the club," Blaser said. "I brought my girlfriend back and we were here until we went to work at Risqué."

All of that was true, he'd just omitted what happened with Gary while he and Bri were there.

"Who is your girlfriend?"

"Brianna Wilcox," he said. "What is this about?"

"And they'll all corroborate your story?"

"It's not a story, it's the truth," he said, trying to look beyond the cop. "You can't just show up unannounced and start emptying my apartment."

"We can," Hoburn said. "We have a warrant."

"How did you get a warrant for—"

"We got an anonymous tip."

"You've had them before," he said. "On the back of that, you managed to convince a judge—"

"Didn't have to rely on that," Hoburn said. "We followed up and found two witnesses who saw you threaten the deceased on the day he died."

"The deceased?"

"Guy you know as Rafe."

A chill went through him. "Rafe is dead?"

"Yeah."

"And he died…"

He didn't have to ask. Rafe died on the same day he and Dax had gone to visit him. He'd bet any money the two weasels sitting in Rafe's living room were witnesses.

Another car came into the parking lot. The distraction gave him time to think.

"Would you come down to the precinct and answer a few questions?" Hoburn asked.

"Uh, sure," Blaser said. Someone got out of the new car. His brother. Damn, he'd never been so relieved to see Colt in his life. "Let me talk to my brother."

"Okay," Hoburn said and turned to make his way into Blaser's apartment.

Typical that strangers could rifle through his things, but he wasn't even allowed to set foot in his own home.

"What's going on?" Colt asked when he reached him.

Some of his own confusion lifted when he read Colt's cop face. This was all business, and this kind of business was where his twin excelled. He took Colt's arm to pull him away from the bodies moving around, in and out of his apartment with purpose.

"Rafe's dead," Blaser said. The slow way Colt lifted his head wasn't good. "It happened day before yesterday."

"How?"

"I don't know," Blaser said. "Didn't ask. They want me to go to the precinct for questioning."

"You're going to be honest, right?"

Scanning around to make sure they weren't overheard, Blaser lowered his voice. "If I tell them everything, about how I got that money to Rafe, they'll put me away again. And it means ratting out Dax and his contacts, they're not the kind of guys you fuck around with. They'd gut a guy and sell the dismembered pieces to the highest bidder."

"Maybe you should've thought about that before—"

"Yeah. Yeah. There's the self-righteous Colt we all know and love," he said. "I didn't kill him. Why would I bother getting that money together if I was just going to slit the guy open?"

"Day before yesterday?"

"Yeah."

"Can you account for the full day?"

"I got up, went to the club. Dax and I paid Rafe a visit, gave him his money and left. That was it. He was alive when we left."

"Then what?" Colt asked, angling his back to the corner wall of the apartment building.

"I went to the garage for a while, came home to shower and then I took Bri to Lyssa's. They had a session. From there, I came to you at the club."

"Lys and I can back you up on that and Bri will—"

"Yeah, Bri will tell Hoburn that, but after we came back here... Gary came to visit, he threatened me, and Dax took him out."

"Took him out?" Colt asked. "What does that mean?"

"Not murdered him if that's what you think. Gary was pointing a gun at me, Dax made him drop it."

"A gun?" Colt asked.

Activity near the apartment door drew both of their attention. Something was carried out of the building and taken to a vehicle. Hoburn came out and split away from the group to come to them.

"You ready?" Hoburn asked Blaser. "I can give you a ride down there."

"Are you arresting him?" Colt asked.

"Not yet," Hoburn said. "But unless what we just found checks out..."

"What did you find?

"Did you petition for the right to own firearms?" Hoburn asked Blaser. "Despite your convictions being non-violent—"

"You have a gun?" Colt asked. "What the hell do you need a gun for?"

"I don't... Shit."

He did have a gun in his apartment, but it wasn't his. The gun in his apartment was left by Gary.

"I'm pretty sure what we found in your bedroom was a firearm. And the slug in the kitchen...?"

Rubbing his mouth, the prickle of foreboding sent

adrenaline to his heart. "I've never fired that gun, you can test my hands, my clothes, there's no residue—"

"Is this where you took the bullet you claim didn't exist?" Hoburn asked.

Blaser had been shot weeks ago, before Gary was taken into custody, and it happened nowhere near there. But letting the cop believe he had been shot was better than letting him think he'd been the one to do the shooting.

"No one was shot here," Blaser said. "The gun went off by accident. I took it away from a friend so he wouldn't hurt anyone."

"What friend?" Hoburn asked.

Blaser sealed his lips. The hope in the cop's eyes became suspicion. If he gave Gary up, there was a chance Gary would go back to jail. Bri might never forgive him for that.

"Maybe I should talk to a lawyer," Blaser said.

"Maybe you should," Hoburn agreed. "If I check the ballistics of that weapon against the bullet taken from the victim, what am I going to find?"

Gary was out of prison because of Mattie's hotshot lawyer. He knew nothing about his movements before he appeared waving that gun around. Since then, Gary had stayed away, from him at least. He'd been so preoccupied with his own issues he hadn't checked in with Bri. It was possible she'd heard from her brother.

"I have to get back to the club," Blaser said and took a step toward his truck, but Colt's arm came up to block his chest preventing him from going anywhere.

"You have to come to the precinct to answer my questions," Hoburn said.

"You said you weren't arresting him," Colt said. "He has the right to an attorney either way and it's unlikely his attorney will be available at this time of the morning."

"It doesn't look good if he refuses to come to the precinct and talk," Hoburn said.

"We know how it looks," Colt said. "But you know he's not a flight risk. You're not arresting him because you want to wait until the ballistics are back. After that, if they match you can get an arrest warrant without a hitch. Right now, you have nothing except circumstantial evidence."

"We have the word of two witnesses."

"Witnesses with little credibility," Colt said, moving to put himself between Blaser and the detective.

"How do you know—"

"Because if they were upstanding members of society, you wouldn't have bothered with the search warrant until after you obtained the arrest warrant… You don't trust the witnesses, but you do know my family. Blaser was with Lyssa the day before yesterday, and he was with me. You'll also be able to check out the club cameras to see that he was there."

"You're saying he's innocent," Hoburn said.

"Yeah, I am."

"As a brother or a former detective?"

"Both. My brother isn't going to fuck up everything he worked for just to wipe out some street scum. It doesn't make sense, and you don't think so either."

"I know he's been framed before," Hoburn said. "I know the raid on the club was bogus and that there's a history of people trying to get him into trouble."

"Which this could be another example of," Colt said. "If Blase was going to start murdering people, he wouldn't start with that piece of shit. He's never been violent, check his rap sheet."

"I have."

"Then you know he's been straight since he got out of prison. You've worked with him. You know he's not the type to go around shooting people."

"And in your experience at the precinct, does every criminal seem like the type?"

Colt drew in a breath. "He'll come to the precinct, tomorrow morning, with a lawyer. He'll answer your questions… gives you time to gather more facts."

Blaser knew that Colt was using a favor for him. Hoburn and Colt had history and it wasn't all positive. They'd reached a tentative truce recently. After this, Colt would owe the detective in charge.

"Fine," Hoburn said. "But stay in touch. I'll be asking questions."

Hoburn left the brothers.

Colt wasted no time in turning to Blaser. "Get back to the club, tell Bri what is going on and talk to Dax. We have to know if he's with us or not."

"Okay."

"I'm going to do some digging on my own."

Colt turned to leave, but Blaser caught his shoulder. "Thanks."

"You're my brother," Colt said. "Where else would I be?"

"You could be warm in bed with your sexy as sin fiancée right now instead of out here in the cold cleaning up my mess."

"Don't worry about it," Colt said, offering a smile. "She's ovulating next weekend. If you get yourself in trouble then, you'll be on your own."

Despite the drama, Blaser smiled at his brother. Yes, Colt was concerned for the outcome with the cops, but the happiness he exuded just talking about Lyssa lightened the load for a few seconds. Too soon he had to shake off that contentment and the envy he had toward Colt's security with Lyssa. He vowed as soon as this was cleared up, he'd find that same stability with his girl.

THIRTY

THE BOUNCERS WERE THROWING out the last of the patrons when he got back to the club. Going in the back, he passed the dancers at the rear exit, without speaking to them even when they called out.

When he stuck his head into the locker room, Crystal and Destiny were the only two people present.

"Where have you been?" Crystal asked him.

"Where's Bri?" he asked, ignoring her question.

"Out front, but—"

He walked out. There was no time for explanations, he had to get to Bri. Hoburn or another detective could come for him at any minute. With the witnesses and a gun showing up on his property, they had enough probable cause.

The only reason Hoburn was decent in letting him go was because of his history with Colt and Lyssa too. But even he wouldn't be able to stop the arrest if a judge felt his alibi was insufficient. The witnesses said they saw Blaser threaten Rafe, not kill him, that's what Hoburn had said. The detective would be wise enough to know that was flimsy, circumstantial evidence. Not enough for a conviction if they ended up at trial. Especially if the ballistics of the gun found on his property didn't match the murder weapon.

Waitresses took on the role of cleaners at the end of their shifts. With all the lights on, they were sweeping up and clearing glasses. Interrupting the collegial banter, he took the brush from Bri, propped it on the bar and threaded his fingers through hers to pull her away from her work.

"What's going on?" she asked as they went through the backstage door. "You were here, then you disappeared with Crystal. She came back, but you didn't. Where have you been?" Storming into the office, he closed the door then held her against it. "Blase—"

Bending his knees, he stole her mouth. Her plump lips gasped in a breath of surprise giving him the chance to dip his tongue inside her, licking and tasting every crevice of what he could be stolen from.

If he needed further confirmation he didn't want to go back to jail, tonight was it. This kiss was his incentive, this woman his reward for being good. With his eyes still closed, he forced himself to release her mouth but couldn't separate his body from hers.

"Rafe's dead," he said. Her pliable body tensed. "The cops searched my place and found Gary's gun."

"Oh my God," she said. Although she increased pressure on his chest, he didn't give her more than a couple of inches of room. "You're a felon, you shouldn't have a gun at all, should you? Did you tell them it wasn't yours?"

"I said it belonged to a friend. The detective in charge of Rafe's case is checking the ballistics."

"Rafe," she said. Her gaze flitted around his chest. "How did he die?"

"I guess he was shot," Blaser said. "Colt will get more information."

"Will he be awake now? Won't he be pissed if—"

"The cops took my place apart, Suzette called Lyssa. Colt got to my place not long after I did. He's on the case, he'll see what Chavez can glean from others."

Chavez was a cop and another of the Warner cousins, Colt still had plenty of sway.

"What will he find out?" she asked. "I mean, what

does it matter? He knows you didn't do it, doesn't he?"

"Yeah, it helps that he and Lys can provide an alibi, except…"

"What?" she asked, curling her fingers into his tee-shirt.

"There are witnesses who saw Dax and me there on the morning Rafe died. He was alive when we left. I figure the witnesses said that or I would be behind bars right now."

"So they're looking for Dax too?"

"Hoburn didn't ask me about him. Either the witnesses didn't name him, or the cops think he can't be responsible, maybe they just can't find him. I don't know. I guess that will come up when I go to the precinct to answer their questions. Colt told Hoburn I'd go tomorrow with a lawyer. I think Hoburn wants more time for the ballistics evidence to come back. After that, he'll know if he's got the murder weapon or not."

"You went over there, to Rafe's, with Dax?" she asked. "To give him the money from the fight night?"

"What he was owed, yeah."

Her head dropped. Resisting the urge to shake her or force her to look at him wasn't easy. Absorbing events still consumed him and the novelty of it had worn off. She needed to take in this information herself; he had to give her time to process it.

"You could go back to prison," she whispered.

"I didn't do it. Why would I go to the trouble of having the fight night if I was just going to shoot the guy?"

"It doesn't matter," she said. "They could pin it on you. The only way you can argue what really happened is to admit the fight night took place. You'll go back to prison."

"I went to Rafe's to give him money. They don't need to know where that money came from. I won't rat out Dax."

"And Gary?" she asked. "You'll have to tell the police what happened that afternoon in your apartment. It's the only way to explain the gun." Her hands drifted to his abs. "Tell them it's mine."

"Yours?"

"Gary is my brother. I would've taken the gun away

from him to protect him. People will probably have noticed you and I have been spending time together.”

“I’m not putting any guilt on you. None of this was your fault.”

“It wasn’t yours either and I’m not suggesting I take the blame for the murder. There’s no way that gun is the murder weapon.”

“You don’t know where Gary got it from. It could be stolen. Maybe it was used in other crimes. You don’t take ownership of a weapon you know nothing about.”

“I’m not saying it’s mine. I’m saying I took it from Gary and left it at my boyfriend’s home. That’s plausible.”

“Plausible, yes, but the slug in the kitchen? Will you tell them Gary was waving it around and Dax took it away from him?”

Not knowing what was going through her head put his into overtime. She eased him aside and wandered deeper into his office. Giving her time, he stayed by the door but had to put his hands into his jeans pockets to prevent himself reaching for her.

She slid her pinkie through the fingers of the other hand then used it to draw around them then go back. When indecision fled, she dropped her hands and went for the door.

“Where are you going?”

“I’m glad that we…” she said, “that we got the chance to be together again.”

“I don’t like the sound of that,” he said, intercepting her hand on its journey to the doorhandle.

“I’m not saying goodbye. I just… I needed to let you know. Anything could break any minute and if they took you from me before I got the chance to…” Smoothing her hands around his waist, she pressed her form against the cocoon of his, holding him. “I love you, Blaser.”

“Will you wait for me?”

Startled, her attention jumped to his. “What?”

“If they put me away… If this all goes wrong and I end up doing time again…, will you wait for me?”

“You didn’t ask me that last time.”

“There wasn’t time, and I was a different person back

then. This time I'm asking."

"You won't call me into visiting and dump me again, will you?"

"I don't want any other man to have you. I couldn't stand to have you out here, on the market, for any guy to lay his hands on. You're my girl, Bri… I need to know."

"I'll wait," she said.

Some of the uncertainty cleared, her features relaxed. It was enough and maybe all he could offer her.

Cupping her face, he guided their mouths together again. "What do you say we leave the grunt work to the lackey's tonight?"

She wasn't tempted and left his embrace with a pat on his chest. "Another night," she said. "I have to get this straightened out. I'll wait for you if I have to, but I'd rather not have to."

"What does that mean?" he asked, snatching her hand again to pull her back. "I won't let you go alone."

"You don't have a choice. You'll make things worse where I'm going."

"Make things worse? Where are you…?"

"I'm going to Gary's."

"He'll convince you not to be with me," Blaser said.

An ache of panic clambered up his spine and fumbled its way through his ribs. They were all a little lost, sure, one fact he knew with absolute certainty? Gary didn't want Bri anywhere near him.

"He will try, just like he always does," she said. "But tonight's visit isn't about us."

"It's three in the morning, he'll be asleep."

Dropping the door handle, she came back to him. "Every minute we waste is another minute the police are investigating. The police might end up at Gary's place. I have to talk to my brother while there's time."

"If he had anything to do with this, he'll run."

"You don't… do you think that he did this?"

"No, I… I don't know. You saw how desperate he was at my apartment."

"Oh God." She paled. "He made a comment about

taking care of Rafe and I corrected him.”

“I’m sure he wouldn’t—”

“I don’t even know my own brother anymore. All those years I stayed away I only talked to him a handful of times and he never came to visit. Is it…? Is it possible that he…?” Avoiding eye contact, she went to the door and pressed both palms to the wood.

“Gary’s a lot of things, but a murderer?” Blaser asked unable to believe his old friend would go that far. Though his erratic behavior could be a symptom of a larger instability Gary hadn’t faced in himself.

“What if it was an accident?” she asked. “Like with you, you said he shot you by mistake, maybe he was threatening Rafe and—”

“Maybe,” Blaser said. “He could try to explain that to the cops.”

The cops wouldn’t believe it, not with Gary’s rap sheet in front of them.

“Our father was violent with my mom. He’s in jail for murder… do you think…?”

“I don’t know,” Blaser said. “On purpose or an accident, it’s a possibility, so I don’t want you going over there alone. Take Dax if you won’t let me be there.”

“He’s not our personal bodyguard. When I was outside your place with Ivy and the gun went off… I was terrified something had happened to you, but Dax was in there because of us. If he had been shot… if Ivy lost her husband…”

“Lys is family, she patched me up great.”

Trying to lighten her burden wasn’t appreciated, she completely ignored his reassurance.

“If he had been hit, Ivy would’ve been alone because of us. Gary has to know his behavior is damaging, or one day he will kill someone… if he hasn’t already.”

Blaser wanted to stop her, but Gary had never threatened her harm. If he went, a confrontation would ensue, it always did. So as she left the office, he stayed put, listening to her footsteps recede. Inhaling, he told himself to go back to his routine and he would… right after he called Colt for an update.

THIRTY-ONE

GARY HAD LIVED in the same shithole one-bed apartment for a couple of years, she knew because she sent him a Christmas card every year, not that she ever got one back.

Only after moving in with Erika did she visit her brother. The damp-stained walls and cracked windows didn't entice her to repeat that experience. After that first and only visit to his place, she never came back. When they wanted to get together, Gary came over to Erika's.

But in that moment, she embraced being there. That was the day she was going to do what she should have done years ago: stand up to her brother and have him face facts. At Gary's door, she didn't waste any time waiting to knock.

At this time in the morning, he should have been fast asleep. But he didn't take long to answer, as if he was expecting something or someone to come over. Whatever he was waiting for, it wasn't her. His surprise at her presence was palpable. He tensed and tried to come into the hall, but she wouldn't be blocked out and crowded close to keep him on his side of the threshold.

"What are you doing here?"

"You told me I could come stay with you and now

I'm not welcome? Aren't you going to ask me in for coffee?" She could already tell he didn't want her to come inside. Why? And why should she care? "Are you alone?"

"Yeah," he said. "I'm alone."

"Great," she said. "Just cream for me."

In the long delay that followed, he was probably trying to come up with excuses why she couldn't come in. He must have come up short, because he grumbled and stepped back, holding open the door. She went into the living room ready to lecture him about the mess, but when she locked on to the real reason he didn't want her there, she stopped.

On the coffee table was a glass tube with a spherical end and beside it was a rock she couldn't mistake.

"What the hell do you think you're doing?" she exhaled and whipped around to glare at her brother.

"What? I'm just chilling."

"No," she said. "No, you're not."

He passed her to saunter deeper into the living room, taking a seat at the head of the table.

"It's not that bad, come here, you might enjoy it."

She couldn't speak, couldn't even think. She wanted to run over there and beat him around the head. She wanted to scream and cry and ask him how he could do this.

"You're asking me to take drugs," she whispered. "Gar, how could you…? After everything that we went through with mom and dad, you promised you would never, that neither of us would ever—"

"What did you think I was going to do when you disappeared on me?" he shouted and pounced to his feet. "You just fucked off to suit yourself and left me here alone!"

"You had friends, you were… you were always more social than I was and Blaser—"

"Yeah," he snarled, snapping his growling eyes on her. "You just locked yourself up with that fucking bastard. When he was gone, away in prison, you didn't have any reason to hang around, did you? After all I did for you—"

"For me?" she said, unwilling to accept him pinning his troubles on her. "You loved it! You loved the attention. Every time you brought in a new stolen car, you'd gloat, never once thinking about the person you'd taken it from or what it would mean to them. Then you sold off the parts and got rich quick, but the money never lasted, did it? You bought clothes and treated your numerous girlfriends. Was that for me, was it? Did you do that for my benefit?"

"I was getting us by! I was looking after you!"

"No," she said, clenching her fingers around the strap of her purse. "In the early days, sure, you and Blase took over my life and didn't give a thought to what would happen if you were caught! It was the money you loved and the credibility you had among the idiots and ingrates that hung around you. At least Blaser came home to me every night, you would fuck off for weeks at a time!"

"We're family," he said, marching over to her. "We stick together! You fucked off, not me! I might have taken a vacation, but you, you left me alone here for six years! What did you think would happen to me?"

"I thought you would get yourself straightened out. You never needed me to look after you, and you didn't need Blaser either. You were the king, you looked out for you, you should have realized we were moving on and you should've got yourself together."

"Oh, like your fucking saint boyfriend, huh?" Spreading his arms, he kicked the end of the couch. "Let me tell you about that prick, you know he had an illegal fight night in that club of his, he—"

"I know all about it, and I know why he did it. He was trying to help me. He was trying to make sure Rafe would leave me alone so we could finally put that life behind us and move on."

"I took care of Rafe! I fucking told you—"

"What does that mean?" she asked, calming her voice. "You said it to me before in Blaser's, but what do you mean you took care of—"

"What the fuck do you think it means?"

She couldn't remember her brother being such an angry person. Maybe it was just easy to ignore that aspect of his character in the early days because everyone was getting along, and life was good as far as Gary was concerned. His lowered chin and narrowed eyes gave her chills, but it was the long blank stare that gave her the truth.

"You… you did it, didn't you?"

A wry smile took time to build on his face. "Yeah," he exhaled. "Are you proud of me?"

"No," she said, shaking her head. "How could you think I would…? Who the hell have you turned into?" The sad answer was Gary had turned into their father, cold and uncaring, only reacting when he was provoked, overreacting every time. "You can't expect… you left the gun at Blaser's, you didn't even ask for it back."

"Don't need it back," he said. "He can take the rap. We're leaving in the morning."

"We?"

"Yeah, Marshall was gonna come and pick you up, but if you're here now, I guess—"

"I'm not going anywhere with you," she said, backing toward the door.

"You're my sister and I look after you. I got out that shitty jail and Marshall gave me an update. Soon as I heard what was going on with Rafe, I went over there and took him out. I came to Blaser's place to get you, to keep you safe, and you stabbed me in the back. You chose him when it's me who has always been there for you. I've always looked after you, even when you were a bitch, I was the one there for you."

"A bitch?"

"Yeah, screwing around with my best buddy in high school. Fuck you, Bri, you started all this shit! Then dancing in that club and setting Blase on me. I let you get away with all that shit. I loved you and I looked after you."

"You didn't do any of it for me. Blaser at least faces up to what he did, he paid his debt and what did you do? Nothing! You're here now, exactly the same as when we were kids, only now, you're buzzing! You're taking the drugs we promised would never be a part of our lives!"

"You need to grow up, Bri," he said, turning his back on her. "This is life. This is who we are." Facing her, he pointed to the drugs on the table. "People like us need this shit just to make life bearable!"

"No," she said. "I don't need it and neither does Blase. I can't believe you… you murdered a man! You took a life, Gar!" Hot tears cascaded over her lashes, grazing her cheekbones and slithering to her chin. Her brother, her only family, was unrecognizable. Maybe this was who he always had been, and she'd been too busy idolizing him to notice.

"When we found out Rafe was gonna come for you, I had to do something."

"We?"

"Yeah, Marshall knows one of Rafe's guys," Gary said. "I was desperate to get out of that jail, I knew what I had to do."

"You didn't have to… murder wasn't an option; it shouldn't have entered your mind!"

"Don't be immature, Bri. The guy was bad news. I took care of the problem you caused."

"I didn't cause any problem! Would you rather I'd worked off the debt with Rafe? Is that what you wanted me to do?"

"You've never been able to look after yourself," he sneered. "You shouldn't have gotten involved at all, but you just walked right into it."

"Easy to think that, isn't it?" she said. "You don't know anything, you just… you got involved in something that wasn't your business. Blaser—"

"It's not my business but it's his? Don't you see how fucked up that is?"

"We are living our lives, moving on. Blaser dealt with Rafe, and we were putting it all behind us."

"Guess you don't know what he's cooking up with Mattie Warner then?" he said. "You're still so fucking naïve."

"And you are clueless. The Rafe problem was solved."

Gary shrugged. "Don't care what Warner told you. All I know is I got out of prison and the first thing I did was take care of the bastard hurting my family, I didn't need anyone's say so. Rafe was going down and I was going to make damn fucking sure of it."

"It was done," she said. "Blaser—"

"He can't take care of you! He's a schmuck who pays his taxes and only crosses at the green, that's not the kinda life you want!"

"Yes, it is."

"No…"

Her back met the front door. Ignoring her impulse to flee, she scrutinized her brother and the small apartment with no flooring and barely any furniture. He was just like Erika; he hadn't changed at all. If he had changed, it was for the worse. Anything of value had been sold, after witnessing the rocks on the table, she knew why. He was throwing his life away, just like their parents. She wanted to help him, to tell him they'd get him help, except he saw nothing wrong with the way he lived.

He could have straightened himself out and kept his promise to her. Instead of wanting out of this oppressive life, he was trying to entice her into it. Gary offering her drugs was an alien concept. He wasn't the brother who'd protected her from their father. This was a stranger.

"I love you, Gary," she said. The stinging sensation inside her skull wanted her to cry, but she kept her eyes on her brother. "This wasn't the life either of us was supposed to have. Going on the run, that's forever, you can't… You can't live your life that way, neither of us can."

"You're going to stay here? With him?"

"Blaser loves me. We can have a life together, a family. I want you to be a part of that, but you can't be unless… you can't run away from what you've done wrong."

"The cops already want to throw me in jail," Gary said. "I'm bailed until the trial and then—"

"You have to do what's right," she pleaded, wishing he would show some sign of remorse.

"I do what's right for me."

"You want to leave, you're going to run away, where are you going to go?"

"Marshall's got family who run a hotel in Cancun, says we can go there. Sun and sand, it'll be like a vacation twenty-four seven."

"You can't… you would never be able to come

home."

"Why would I need to if I've got all my family with me?" he said, approaching her. She tensed with every step nearer he got. "Come with me, you'll find a new life there, away from all the bullshit here, away from all the crap you went through. We can be whoever we want to be down there."

Some of his anger had receded and he was nodding, like he really believed every word he was saying.

"I don't know if—"

"I can look after you. I've always looked after you, Bri," he said, picking her fingers off her purse, when it slipped to her wrist, he took hold of her hand. "I took care of that Rafe prick, didn't I?"

She didn't want her brother to throw his life away. Murdering for her? The thought made her nauseous. But she couldn't ignore what had happened. Gary could be past the point of redemption, but until she made him face what he had done and pay his own debt, she couldn't be sure of that.

"You can't pick me up at the apartments, Blaser will never—"

"I don't give a fuck about what that bastard will—"

"If you wait," she said. "If you can wait until he's at the club or the garage, then you could pick me up."

His eyes lit. "If you stay here right now and—"

"No, I want to go back and pick up my things," she said. "And I want to say goodbye to him, even if he can't know that it's goodbye. Please, Gary, what's a few more hours?"

Neglecting to tell him the police had been searching Blaser's apartment was risky. He might find out. Though if he planned to stay in his apartment getting high until they left, he wouldn't be talking to many people.

"Two o'clock," he said. "We'll leave at two. Bring your passport and don't say a word to anyone."

She nodded and lunged into his arms. He squeezed her so tight she had to hold her breath to dam her tears.

When he relaxed, she looked up to see a smile the full width of his face. "We've got this," he said. "We're going to be a family again, you and me."

"Yeah," she said, swallowing to moisten her mouth.

"We are."

Slipping out of the apartment, she left the building on autopilot. On this quiet street there was no chance of a cab, she had to walk to the end of the block to grab one, now, quickly, before she could rethink her intention.

Adrenaline kept her going through the cab ride. When she eventually got to her destination, heat was permeating her pores. She wasn't going to back out, and she wasn't going to sleep on it. It didn't matter that it was the middle of the night, almost daybreak in fact, sleep wasn't going to slow her down.

Running up the stairs into the building the cab had delivered her to, she went straight to the front desk and waited for attention.

"Can I help you?" the desk attendant asked.

"I'm Brianna Wilcox," she said. "I need to speak with Detective Hoburn."

THIRTY-TWO

AS IF BLASER didn't have enough on his mind, when he got back to his apartment after closing up Risqué, Mattie was sitting in his car in the parking lot waiting for him. For years, he hadn't seen anything of his cousin and now he was becoming a regular feature. Mattie hadn't been around with this kind of frequency since before he did time in prison.

"What do you want now?" Blaser asked, unlocking his apartment and going inside without waiting for his cousin.

"I heard the cops were here," Mattie said. "As soon as I heard I got in the car."

The place was still a mess, but he retrieved a bourbon bottle from the kitchen unit and two glasses. If Mattie was there anyway, there was no point being rude. He poured two measures and slid one across the kitchen table to Mattie, though both men remained standing.

"Looks like I'll be going away for a while again."

Blaser emptied his glass in one gulp and resisted the urge to pour another measure. Until Bri was back, he was staying on alert.

"I'll get you a lawyer, a decent one, not like last time, and this time you won't be pleading guilty. You're going to fight this."

"What's the point?" Blaser asked. "If they're going to get me for it anyway, I might as well try to cut a deal. All I have to give them is a guilty plea."

"Self-pity is what you're going with?" Mattie asked, swirling the liquid in his glass. "What does Bri say?"

"We haven't had time to talk about it. But she knows there's a chance... they could come for me anytime, it all rests on the ballistics. If that gun is the one that killed him..."

"She won't let you take the fall," Mattie said. "I've got a few cops on the take, we might be able to—"

"What? Get me in deeper? Get me on bribery charges too?"

Sucking oxygen through his teeth, he tipped his head back and lifted the glass, ready to pitch it across the room, except he couldn't let Bri come home to that mess. This could be their last opportunity to spend a night together and he didn't want to spend it fighting.

"You're family," Mattie said, sliding his glass onto the table though the alcohol remained untouched. "You know I've always had a soft spot for you, why do you think I was so eager to have you on my side back in the day? You're smart and you're loyal, two things a guy like me needs on his side."

Mattie wasn't there out of the goodness of his heart. His words were kind enough, but Blaser knew his cousin too well.

"What are you saying?" he asked.

"I'm saying I can make this go away."

"How would you do that?"

Shrugging, Mattie displayed a humble smile that wasn't quite convincing. "All it takes is a few witnesses."

"We've got those, witnesses who say I had beef with Rafe, and they were right. I did."

"No one needs to know that, and it's easy to shut guys like them up. Then all we're left with is the gun and that can be explained as a plant, or we make it disappear from evidence. What I'm saying is, there are ways around these things, how do you think a guy like me has stayed out of jail for this long?"

"Why would you do that? Why would you use your money and influence to help me?"

"We're family," Mattie said. He must have known that wasn't believable because he carried on. "You know Marshall?"

"Gary's friend Marshall?"

"Yeah, he's been in my employ for a while. He's a sort of informant for me, an ear to the ground with the underclasses. I heard about Bri's trouble with Rafe, thought for sure you'd come to me."

"Is that why you asked her out?"

"I asked her out because she's hot," he said. "Yeah, I thought she might ask for help. I didn't know you two were back on."

"You wanted to win her over because she never really warmed to you. You knew she was the reason I didn't accept your offer to join your crew. You wanted to know if she'd changed? If she was open to your kind of business now?"

"Something like that maybe," Mattie said and took a deep breath. "I asked her out because I needed to spur you into action. I knew another guy making a move on her would force you to counter and make your own move. Yeah, I thought I might have gotten some sex out of it first, but what I really wanted was you two back together."

"Why would you care about that?"

"Because when you're with her, you're willing to consider anything. You'll do whatever it takes to look after her. I already knew Rafe was giving her trouble. If you two were together, well, I thought you'd be open to working with me."

"All of that effort just to get me onto your crew?"

"What effort?" Mattie asked. "Going on a date with a beautiful woman? I didn't even need the date, just asking her out was enough to piss you off, and you moved in on her, just like I wanted you to. My work was done."

"Congratulations," Blaser muttered.

He'd walked right into that one. Mattie was known for being conniving in order to get what he wanted. Blaser had acted exactly as Mattie knew he would when someone tried to annex Brianna from him.

"I was right about you doing anything to protect her. When I heard about the fight night, I really couldn't believe it… That was… it was something, Blase. You showed you still had the same spirit, the same smarts you've always had. I sent Marshall along to keep an eye on it, even he was impressed."

"Well, that's why I did it, cuz, I just wanted to make you proud."

"You did," Mattie said, ignoring Blaser's sarcasm. "And now it's my turn. I will get this murder charge off your shoulders, I can make it disappear. You can have the girl and the freedom."

"Just like that?"

"Maybe not just like that. All I want from you is the club, just like we talked about."

"You want me to sign Risqué over to—"

"Not sign it over, she's yours, that club is your baby. But talk to Dax, get the fight night set up as a regular feature—"

"Not a chance," Blaser said, shoving his empty glass onto the kitchen counter.

"It's a small price," Mattie said.

"You want the fight nights happening in a club that's under my name so the liability lands on me when the cops hear about it."

"I've proven I can take care of you."

"For your own gain, you want to protect your lifestyle. You'd throw me to the wolves if it protected you."

"It's human nature to protect ourselves and those we love," Mattie said. "Isn't that what you were thinking when you took care of Rafe?"

"I didn't kill him."

"No," Mattie said, his certainty didn't waver. "Gary did."

His thoughts cleared. For a few stunned moments, he said nothing. "You don't know that."

"I do, Gary told Marshall everything, and Marshall brought it to me. I know Gary killed Rafe with the gun the cops found in your bedroom tonight. How long before the ballistics are confirmed? You're right, you will do time, you will go away because without my help there's no way to explain why that weapon was here. You would be lucky if the cops listened to your denial of ownership. Are you going to drop Bri's brother into the mess? He'll go down for life. Will she forgive you for putting her brother behind bars?"

Processing the revelation, it wasn't easy to maintain his cool. Throughout the night, he'd tried to calm himself by convincing his subconscious the gun wasn't the murder weapon. If the gun the cops found here, in his place, wasn't the gun used to kill Rafe, he'd get a slap on the wrist, if the cops even bothered to take it that far. He'd petitioned the court for the right to have a gun at the club, but he'd never used it and never planned to.

"How can you be so sure about this? Maybe Gary—"

"Marshall has never lied to me," Mattie said. "Gary told him everything, including his plan for the future. He's going on the run tomorrow, down Mexico way to stay with some relatives of Marshall's…and his sister is going with him."

"No," he said. "She's not going anywhere."

"She's over there right now making plans."

"She doesn't know anything about this," Blaser said, rounding the table. "She doesn't know anything about the murder or what Gary did… We don't even know that he did it, the prick mouths off about—"

"About things he did," Mattie said, unintimidated by Blaser's proximity. "Gary's not smart enough to lie, he told that cop the truth. It was you who lied about the shooting to cover his ass. Just like you always did. You went to jail for stealing a car that you didn't steal! You could've dropped a dime on Gary, but you kept your mouth shut, you took the heat… We're all grateful for that."

"Yeah, as long as your secrets are safe, right?"

Passing his cousin, he went into the living room and collapsed on the couch. Resting his head against the back, he closed his eyes and contemplated how his life had turned to shit so quickly.

The gun tied him to the murder and unless he ratted Gary out to the cops, there was no way to get out of the charge. With the history he and Gary had, it would be one word against another. Gary would call his statement lies in a bid for revenge. Gary was an idiot, he never thought things through, and his impulsive actions were usually predicated around someone disrespecting him. Maybe that was why Gary felt the need to assert his masculinity by putting a bullet in Rafe.

"I run this town," Mattie said from the kitchen. "Rafe was a bastard who stepped out of line, you took care of it, took care of your woman in an admirable way."

Claiming Bri as his own, declaring to Gus he was going to protect her, sent a shockwave through the family. Mattie would've been one of the first to hear. Finding out Bri's troubles wouldn't have been a stretch given his contacts.

His cousin expected him to come begging for help, except he hadn't. Somehow, by taking care of things in his own way, he'd piqued Mattie's respect again. This was just a repeat of all those years ago when Mattie tried tempting him onto his crew.

Blaser couldn't figure it out. He didn't want to be that guy anymore, didn't want to be scared of the law because he operated outside of it. Yet, he wanted to be free, out in the world with Bri, building a life and starting a family. If he was in jail that wasn't going to be possible, and Mattie was offering him a way to avoid incarceration. Except his cousin was just through telling him Bri was riding off into the sunset with Gary, leaving him in the dust.

"The fight night changed everything," Blaser muttered.

He could never have gone to the cops about Rafe hassling Bri, it wasn't in his nature, in fact, it went against it. They had no evidence of any trouble anyway. Dropping Rafe in the shit would also have meant dropping Bri's friends in it as well. He'd tried so hard to protect Bri from the messes that followed her around that he didn't see himself getting dirty in the process, not until it was too late.

"You're an entrepreneur, I should have seen it

before," Mattie said, sauntering into the living room to stand in the center. "Now with your connection to Dax and his associates—"

"He won't do it," he said, lifting his head. "Dax won't get involved."

"Arrange a sit down for me, I think I can persuade him if you provide the introductions. After that, all we need is the club. It's the perfect place and provides excellent cover. The cops raided it and found it clean, they're not coming back, not for a long time. They're still living down the humiliation of believing a low-level criminal like Gary. A guy that low in the pecking order is always looking for ways to break through… I guess now, after Rafe's murder, he's going to think he's made it."

"Except he can't enjoy it because he's going to run."

"Yeah, and while he's sunning himself, the cops will be knocking down your door. How long will Risqué last if you're serving a life term for murder? Do you think Bri will wait twenty-five to life?"

"It wasn't premeditated, if—"

"You don't know what it was, or what they'll pin on you. You had motive and opportunity, that's all the prosecution need. They already have the murder weapon and the body. This is an open and shut case. You're a felon, how much time will they spend listening to your stories?"

Having committed murder, Gary would have an over-inflated sense of his own importance, he probably felt invincible right about now. But if he got away, if he left the country tomorrow, he'd be long gone before Blaser tried to pin the murder on the rightful perpetrator. The cops wanted someone behind bars. He would be the only one left behind to take responsibility.

"I'll have to think about it."

His body was too tired and his mind too fried to make sense of what was going on. Other than discussing it with Bri, the other name that kept coming to mind was Colt. He had to wait and see what his brother could find out from the cops tomorrow. Except if he waited until tomorrow, he'd have to go to the precinct for questioning, just like he'd promised

Hoburn.

"You know this makes sense," Mattie said, coming closer. "I can make this go away, isn't that tempting?"

"Yeah," he said, dropping his hands to his lap. "It's damn tempting, but I'm not sure I want to pay the price."

"I'm not threatening you with jail time and that's the only other offer you have on the table."

"I don't know that, not yet. I have to exhaust my other options before I decide to give up on everything I've built. If I go into business with you, there's the chance I could lose everything. I could lose the club and the garage. I could lose my girl—"

"Think of what you could gain," Mattie said, crouching beside him. "You'd never have to worry about money. You could spend time with your girl instead of working every hour of the day. This is a great offer, and it will solve your problems. On my crew you'll be protected, I'm offering you family within the family. You've always been made for the big leagues."

Mattie was good at the sales pitch, Blaser had to give him that. Mattie didn't blink, his confidence was unwavering. "It sounds like a great offer—"

"What's going on?"

Both he and Mattie turned around to see Bri standing just inside his apartment, the door handle still in her grasp.

Leaving the couch, Blaser rounded Mattie to get to her. "Thank fuck you're back," he said. "Where have you been?"

"What is going on here?" she asked, a frown etched into her features. "What are you two talking about at this time of night?"

Though it was actually closer to morning than night.

"Mattie heard about the search," Blaser said. "He came to offer his help."

"I won't disturb you guys anymore," Mattie said, moving to the door where he locked eyes with his cousin. "Think about my offer."

Blaser wasn't going to say any more about it. Mattie nodded at Bri then slipped out. She didn't close the door, so he took it from her hand to do it for her.

"Thank God you're here," he said and cupped her face.

Before he could kiss her, she spoke, "What's his offer?"

"Can we talk about it in the morning?" he asked. "I'm beat."

"No, I want to know what you were talking about. What is Mattie offering you?"

"What does it matter?" he asked. "Mattie came over to talk, he said what he had to say and now he's gone, nothing has changed."

"Maybe it has," she said. "I want to know what you're getting involved in."

"I'm not involved in anything." The scowl hadn't left her face. In the name of honest, he released a breath and confessed all. "He wants to use Risqué again, on a regular basis, to hold more fight nights."

"He what?" she said, grabbing his wrists to pull his hands from her face. "And you agreed with that?"

"I didn't agree to anything. He put it to me before. Now that the cops are going to pin murder on me, Mattie thought he'd try it again."

"The cops?"

"Mattie said that Gary did it," he said, hooking his fingers through hers. "I'm sorry, babe, but Marshall has been feeding Mattie information. He says they're going on the run tomorrow."

"They're not," she said.

"That's not what Mattie says, and once Gary is gone, the cops will pin Rafe's murder on me. They have witnesses and the murder weapon. I have a criminal record so I'm not the most credible person to begin with. They're never going to listen—"

"Blaser," she said, taking his other hand so both of them were joined and she closed in to rest her body on his. "I need you to promise me you will never do anything illegal again. I need to know, one hundred percent, that all of that is behind you. I don't care how you try to rationalize it. I have a zero-tolerance policy. If I find out you've so much as used your cellphone while driving, I'll leave you."

So sure, her expression so clear, her wide eyes were determined. How she managed it while he was so messed up, he couldn't figure out.

"Why would you want to—"

"Blase, please, promise me you won't join Mattie."

"If it's going to keep me out of jail, I have to consider it. He has the money for great lawyers and enough pull with the cops that—"

"No!" Throwing his hands out of hers, she marched past him toward the hallway then whipped around. The determination tinged with anger. That intensity of emotion raised her finger to point as she chastised him. "I had to make a choice. It's a choice I should've made fifteen years ago, but tonight, I made that choice. For the first time ever, I am taking control. I'm taking control of my life and of yours… and of Gary's too."

"What are you—"

"You and Gary messed everything up when you tried to be in control, so I'm taking over now. The first part is done and there's nothing I can do to retract it. I will not let you mess up my life and our future. I want us to be together. I want to get married, and I want to have your children, but I have to take care of me and mine as well."

"Oh, yeah? Mattie told me you were running off with your brother. Is that what this is about? You're giving up on us to run away with Gary?"

"You would really judge me for that?" she asked. "Think about your own brothers and what you would do for them."

"Neither of them has killed anyone!"

"Don't be too sure about that," she mumbled.

His instinct was to argue his brothers' innocence, but he couldn't. Ruger was supposed to be on his way. A part of him still wanted to think it was some big misunderstanding. Except what Bri had gone through was no delusion. She'd felt every second of the torture while being held captive by the monsters who wanted to sell her. Just thinking about that truth diverted his attention from this fiasco onto Bri's past. If she needed to get away, away from what she'd been through then he should accept that… except he couldn't give her up.

"Gary didn't have to do what he did."

"And Ruger did?" she asked. "I know what happened to me wasn't his fault, but let's not pretend we live in a black and white world. Gary thought he was doing something right; he was trying to protect me."

"And coming over here, waving the gun at me, what was that? I'm going to go down for this, Bri. I'm going back to that goddamn place and all because… because…"

"Because what? Because my brother left his gun here?"

"No, because I'm keeping my mouth shut to protect him! Again! I shouldn't have clammed up when the cops found that gun here. I should've told them exactly who it belonged to and how it ended up here. I should've told them about Gary shooting me the first time! I should've made Colt take me to the goddamn emergency room instead of making him risk his relationship with Lyssa by asking her to patch me up! But I didn't do that! I kept my mouth shut to protect Gary. Not because he's some great hero or friend, but because I love you!"

"You don't sound happy about that."

"I'm happy that I love you. I'm happy that I have you back, but… I'm not happy I'm going to lose you again. When we broke up, when I asked you to come to visiting, I saw how you tried not to cry. I was so tired of making you cry. I really hated myself. I promised I would never do it again."

She began to walk toward him. "Then promise me now that you will never break the law again."

"If I go to prison—"

"You're not going to prison," she said. "You have to trust me. Don't make a deal with Mattie. Don't risk everything because you think it's the only way to insulate me."

"If going to prison is what it takes to—"

"You're not going to prison," she insisted, her body wilted. "Please, Love, promise me."

"You can't be sure that—"

"I can."

"No, you can't," he said. "How could you possibly—"

"Because I made a deal with Hoburn," she said and immediately sealed her lips.

The flare of her nostrils and the wobble of her chin betrayed the conflict of guilt she held. Just like before, with Mattie, he almost couldn't process what she'd said.

"You made a deal with the cops? When?"

Creeping over, she slumped against him. He happily held her in his arms. "I went to see Gary and you're right, he did do it. He told me he wanted me to go away with him and I agreed. Then I left and went to the police. I told Hoburn what I knew about it and the gun, then I told him about Gary's escape plan."

"They'll arrest him."

"Yes."

"He'll go to jail."

"Yes," she whispered, pressing her face to his chest. "He's using drugs. If he runs, he'll never be able to come back."

"You could've gone with him."

"I don't want that life, you know that," she said, tipping her head back. "I want you. I want us to be together without any drama. I want the normal, boring life you promised me. I want it with you. I can't watch you doing more time and losing everything because of something my brother did. Gary has to face up to his actions."

"He'll be pissed when he finds out you set him up."

"He'll be in prison," she said. "I hope he takes the time to get clean in there, but… at least he'll be safe and won't be on the run. It will take a long time, but I hope he'll accept I am trying to help him."

Holding her, he was awed by what she had done. Choosing him over Gary was something she'd always claimed she wouldn't be able to do. But push had come to shove, and she'd done it, she'd chosen him. Tightening his embrace, he closed his eyes. She had told the truth. Gary may never forgive her, but she did what was right in spite of that, saving him in the process.

"I should go upstairs to bed," she said. "It's been a long night for both of us and you'll be up early in the morning, so—"

"Stay the night with me," he said.

She eased out of his arms, not a promising indication of her response.

"I handed my only brother to the cops tonight," she said. "You had them tearing your apartment to pieces trying to find evidence you murdered a man."

Seizing her hand, he pressed it to his chest. "I spent all night thinking this could be the last night we had together, don't ask me to give it up."

"I truly believe that making Gary face what he's done is the right thing. I think getting him away from his friends and the easy to find street drugs will be what's best for him. He spent years making decisions based on what he thought was best for me, now I'm returning the favor… But a selfish part of me was at work too, I want a future with you, and I knew you were innocent, I wasn't going to watch you…"

"You did the right thing, I support you," he said. "I'm grateful."

Leaning down he joined their mouths, but she withdrew. "Was I selfish?"

"Rafe was a crook and a sleaze, but he didn't deserve to die. Gary got out of jail, got high and went on a rampage. How would you live with yourself if he did that again? You did the right thing."

Her shoulders slackened and her lips raised in a tired, appreciative smile. "Thank you."

When she came back into his arms, he held her for a moment then began to move toward the bedroom, but she pulled away again. "Are you staying?"

"No," she said. "I'm tired and…"

With a finger, he elevated her chin. "You never have to give me a reason. From now on, I take your orders and make no decisions for myself."

Exhaling a laugh, she kissed him. "Just run things by me before you do anything drastic," she said. "We'll make decisions together.”

"Okay," he said. "I can live with that. Now let me walk you upstairs to your apartment. We both need some rest."

"We could go out for dinner, tomorrow night. After that we could come back here," she said, hope and exhaustion warred in her gaze. "Unless you have to be at Risqué?"

"The club can wait a day," he said, sliding an arm around her and directing her to the door. "Let's get you tucked up in bed."

THIRTY-THREE

BRI BARELY SLEPT. Tossing and turning, she dreaded the new day. Talking to Hoburn seemed like the right thing to do at the time. All through the night while staring at the ceiling, she played out a dozen different scenarios. The knowledge that Blaser wouldn't pay for Gary's crime kept her going.

Her apartment was spotless. She'd been ready for almost an hour when there was a knock on her door. Hurrying over, she opened it and beckoned in Hoburn and the two men with him. After taking the time to scan the parking lot, she closed the door.

Leaning back on the door, she watched Hoburn's cohorts move around her apartment checking surfaces and vents.

"Did you have to come as a trio?" she asked. "I don't need three cops at my door in broad daylight."

"I'd have been coming to talk to you today either way," Hoburn said, sitting on the couch while pointing at the armchair opposite, but she had no interest in sitting down to have a cozy chat with him. "Relax, Miss Wilcox, you've done the right thing and I am not going to jeopardize what we've started. I am on your side."

"Don't," she said, going to the seat he'd pointed at. "Please don't start the police talk, that 'we're all in this together' bullshit. You have to set up your equipment? Fine, do it, then get the hell out of here… I told you I wasn't comfortable with this. I don't like plotting against him. He's my brother!"

"I believe what you've told me," Hoburn said. "So does the judge that gave us the arrest warrant this morning, but we need the confession to guarantee a prosecution."

"I came to you because I believe my brother has started down a dark path and I don't want him to hurt anyone else. And I don't want Blaser to be punished for something he didn't do."

"He won't be," Hoburn said. "I'll be looking out for you today. My guys are putting the listening devices in, and we'll park around the corner. We can be inside this apartment within four minutes, so if you feel threatened and need help—"

"This is my brother. Gary would never hurt me."

"A few days ago, you would have promised me Gary would never kill."

"A few days ago, he was in jail. I don't care how messed up he is, he loves me and would never hurt me. If he wanted that he could've done it last night at his place, and he didn't."

"Because he believes you're going with him."

"And he'll keep believing that. I've packed a bag, so as far as he knows, I'm ready to leave."

Talking about betraying her only family was sickening. It was bad enough her plan was to set her brother up, she hated the conniving.

"How long until he gets here?" Hoburn asked, glancing at his watch.

"About an hour."

"Good, that gives us the chance to get everything ready."

Hoburn rose and the tech guys went to the door with their kit, indicating that they were done.

Bri followed him to the exit. "I never thought I'd be

in this position, doing something like this."

"Look at Blaser, bet he never thought he'd be the respectable business owner he is now. Things change. Eventually we all have to grow up."

His attempts to make her feel better weren't doing their job. "Thanks," she said.

"In a few hours," he said, "this will all be done."

"And Gary will be back in jail."

"Where he'll have a chance to get clean and won't be able to hurt anyone else."

That kind of optimism kept her moving forward, kept her believing this was right. Gary would thank her for it one day… wouldn't he?

THIRTY-FOUR

HIS ALARM HADN'T GONE OFF. The first Blaser knew of the new day was the pounding on his door. Exhaling his exhaustion, he groaned and coughed as he sat up to stretch.

"Blase!"

His twin's voice rattled his skull as he reached to the other side of his bed. Vacant. Bri wasn't there. He hadn't woken up beside her for years, yet his subconscious still sought her out. He was ready to get on with their future together. Pacing himself was tough, if he was overeager, he'd wreck it. Bri still had issues. Whatever happened, he'd be right by her side to work through them.

Stretching again, he turned to plant his feet on the floor and yawned again, fumbling for the clock on his bedside. Keys rattled in his front door. What the hell? Screw the time.

He got to the living room just as Colt closed his front door. To his left was another man, his six-foot five little brother. Just the sight of Ruger shed all remnants of sleep. Storming past the couch, he grabbed his brother's shirt and thrust him against the wall, nudging the TV in the process.

Ruger's open hands came up in surrender and Colt was on Blaser's back, pulling on his shoulders.

"No, Blase, come on!" Colt said.

"I'm sorry," Ruger called out.

Colt hauled him away.

"I told him everything we know," Colt said, putting himself between the brothers.

"I'm sorry," Ruger said again.

The usually smiling, joking guy was solemn. Yeah, wasn't so funny anymore. Pale and contrite, Ruger wasn't himself, but that didn't lessen his anger.

"It's true?" he asked.

All doubt was gone. Not that he'd doubted Bri, but he didn't think it was beyond the people holding her captive to lie, adding psychological torture to the physical ordeal.

"I told him everything you told me and what Lyssa filled me in on. I know you're pissed, but like I fucking told you, you're going to hear him out just like I heard you. If after that you still want to kick the shit out of him, you can go ahead."

Blaser pinned Ruger under his glare, struggling to accept what Colt was saying. Somehow the anger and hate that should be aimed at Bri's attacker rippled through him. Didn't matter he was only in boxers, he was ready to fight like they were in the ring.

Respect for Colt, and that alone, made him back away until he sat on the couch. "You want to talk? Then talk," Blaser said. "You explain to me how the woman I love was stolen from the street because of shit you are mixed up in."

"I don't know," Ruger said, sinking into the chair near the front window. He leaned forward, and with an elbow on his knee rasped his fingers over his stubble.

"Not good enough," Blaser snapped.

Colt held up a hand. "Give him a minute."

"I know Victor and I know the fucks he was working with," Ruger said, wrapping his fingers around his opposite knuckles. "What Bri said about me… about what I do…"

"All these years, you let me believe I was the fuck up. Colt would lecture and—"

"I should've done more to stick up for you, I'm sorry, but… it's been irrelevant since you got out of the joint. You've done good and… I thought if you found out I was mixed up in illegal shit it might give you the excuse to get mixed up in it again yourself," Ruger said. "I didn't want that to happen."

"You were protecting me?" Blaser said, unable to feel gratitude. "You think 'cause you fucked up that I might fuck up too?"

"I'm sorry. I was worried when I heard you were kicking around with Bri again, but I did tell Colt to keep his nose out of your business… I had no idea about… that anything like… had happened to her in Jersey."

"We were meeting up to go out on a date," Blaser explained. "I didn't tell any of you guys we were getting together, I knew you'd judge me, and I wanted to be sure that… that Bri and I were going to be together for real… You guys weren't a big part of my life before prison because you didn't agree with my lifestyle…" Blaser threw his words at Ruger. "Least that's what I thought."

"I know and I'm sorry. The jobs started out small. I started in college. I could make a fortune, I worked with my roommate back then, he got me into it, now I work alone. After college it sorta snowballed, people called me when they wanted things or had things, they wanted rid of. I kept it away from here, from family, because I didn't want anyone hurt."

"Too late," Blaser said, maintaining laser focus on his younger brother.

Ruger may not have noticed though, as it was Colt his attention stayed on. "I'm sorry," their little brother said. "I promise you, I'll find out what happened."

"What happened is my girlfriend went on the street to call me and your buddies grabbed her and held her hostage for a week! During that some dirty ass motherfucker knocked her out and raped her!"

"Why were you late?" Colt asked, calm… calmer than him anyway. "You didn't tell me why you were late to the restaurant."

"It doesn't matter," he said. "It's stupid, I…" Just to move things along he got the confession out the way. "I was at the florist picking up a dumb corsage thing I got her, the same as the one I got her for prom… The guy fucked up the order and I had to wait around while he fixed it."

"What did you do when you got to the restaurant and she was gone?" Ruger asked.

"Waited. She left her coat, so I figured she'd be back. When she wasn't, I tried to call. I figured she left angry and forgot her coat … I called her and called her for two days straight. When I called the cops, they pretty much said she was a grown-up allowed to duck my calls and disappear if she wanted to. I really just thought she was angry, so I kept calling. Two weeks later, she answered and told me to go to hell… about a month later I got an email… she told me what had happened."

"When I found out what Victor and his benefactor were doing, I left," Ruger said. "I told them they were sick fucks and there was no chance of me working with them. I split."

"Which I suppose is when they hatched the plan to take Bri," Colt said.

"Yeah," Ruger agreed. "I didn't hear about it again until a guy I met on that job got in touch about something else. I tried to tell him where to get off and that's when I found out Victor and his crew were dead, that was… months later."

"Rushe?" Colt asked and Ruger nodded.

Deflated, Blaser couldn't be angry because his brother had done the right thing, as Bri had said. His sibling hadn't intended for Bri to be sucked into the sick bastard's game.

"How is she?" Ruger asked, glancing in the bedroom's direction.

"She slept upstairs. She's still working through things."

"Oh, Colt said that you were—"

"We are and we're together, but something else happened last night and—"

"The cops tore your place apart," Ruger said. "That's a battle that—"

"Bri took care of it," Blaser said. Both his brothers reacted with surprise. "It doesn't matter, it's done. What I give a shit about is how our holy saint little brother is actually a criminal deviant."

"It's not like that," Ruger said. "I don't steal, and I don't hurt anyone. I'm just the fence, the middleman. I'm a guy who knows how to get stuff."

"What kind of stuff?" Blaser asked. "People? Weapons?"

"I've hooked people up with guns before," Ruger said. "It's something we were all raised to know well. Mostly it's tech, security or surveillance stuff, how do you think I know a guy like Pinch so well? Sometimes it's boring stuff like furniture, premises, antiques, or vehicles."

"What did Victor want?"

"At first it was men, thugs for hire, you know? He needed vehicles and an indoor water pool… then he needed cuffs and other restraints, so I started to ask questions… When I got the answers, I bailed, I thought that was it."

Everyone who had harmed Bri was dead so he couldn't get his hands on them.

One person remained alive who he needed to talk to. "The cop who got her out, do you know him?"

"Jansen," Ruger nodded. "Knew him on the job. Rushe filled me in after about his real identity. He was an undercover cop. When Victor found out who Jansen was, he took Jansen's girl, forced him to lie to his colleagues, it really fucked him up."

"I know how he feels," Blaser said.

"How could you have lied to us about this, Ruge?" Colt asked. "I thought you had a sales gig. I knew you got hard to find items, I had no idea it was crooked."

"I've never been involved in anything as shady as Victor's deal. I try to work on the side of the good guys, like Rushe."

At first glance, Rushe didn't look like he was on anyone's good side. But he'd proved himself to the Warners by saving Lyssa from her stalker.

"It's still illegal," Colt said.

"Yeah, and I knew you'd give me shit for that. I'm sorry, really, okay? Blase was getting himself straightened out, it didn't seem relevant after that."

"And me going to prison didn't scare you into straightening out?" Blaser asked.

"I don't actually do anything illegal myself, it's the people I acquire from and sell to that are breaking the law."

"Dealing in stolen or illegal merchandise is against the law, genius," Colt said.

"Yeah, but how many cops care about the middleman unless they can squeeze him? They're into the big fish, not minnows like me. Any time I've come across a cop looking for information, I give it to him."

"And how many times has that happened?" Colt asked.

"I don't give a fuck about that," Blaser said, holding a hand up to each of his brothers. "Yeah, you're a fuck for letting me take the heat when some of it should've been yours. What I care about is Bri. You're gonna go up there and apologize to her. If she doesn't accept your apology, you can stay the fuck away from me."

"Wait a minute," Ruger said, shooting out of his seat. "You can't disown me because…"

"Yeah, I can," Blaser said.

From the way Ruger's words trailed off, he got just how bad it was.

Ruger considered this, Colt too. The three of them said nothing, just existed in silence for a good few minutes.

"I'm gonna go one better than that," Ruger said, retrieving his cellphone from his back pocket.

"What are you going to do?" Colt asked.

"We're gonna talk to Rushe."

"About what?" Blaser asked. "Bri said all the fuckwits who were involved are dead."

"All the bad guys, yeah," Ruger said. "Not all the good guys."

"The good guys?" Colt asked. "What do you think they're going to do?"

"Rushe will tell us how to get in touch with Jansen, he's not a cop anymore."

"Like someone else I know," Blaser said, looking at Colt. "Do you all become disillusioned eventually?"

"Most cops, yeah," Colt said. "Those of us who don't quit just go through the motions until they collect their pensions."

"As soon as he gets back to me, I'll track Jansen down," Ruger said. "He'll tell us how those bastards died."

"What about Jansen's girlfriend?" Blaser asked. "Did she get out alive?"

"We'll find out."

"How long does it usually take Rushe to…?" Colt's words faded out.

How could he repay the debt he owed to this Jansen guy? His brothers conversation carried on, but he was too distracted to concentrate on that.

"What is that banging?"

He'd heard it too. A low thud, three times like… his head came up, then he was on his feet. "Shit."

"What?" Colt asked.

Instinct took him toward the door, but damnit, he wasn't dressed. Rushing to the bedroom, he pulled on his jeans. "It's Bri, upstairs. She's in trouble."

THIRTY-FIVE

GARY HAD COME UPSTAIRS and into her apartment without any hesitation. His sense of propriety was no doubt bloated by his latest criminal act. He'd have fun telling Blaser they were leaving the country to let him take the heat if the two came across each other. So he had nothing to fear in striding into her apartment.

Marshall was an unexpected addition to the visitor list. If she'd worried Gary would clam up in front of an audience, she would have been wrong. Gary had already told Marshall what was going on, so when she started to ask questions, he didn't hesitate to recount every detail of what had happened in Rafe's apartment leading up to and including the murder.

Tears dampened her cheeks. To see a man so animated while talking about the death of another was disturbing. The fact that the storyteller was her brother overwhelmed her. This was the same man who'd refused to let her work in that seedy club, who had started his illegal activities just to support her. He reveled in being bad. How had she never seen that? Blaser said he wasn't turned on by being bad anymore. Her brother had gone in the other direction, languishing in pure pleasure watching the life slip out of another human being.

When Marshall came to hug her, she was too upset to be surprised by his compassion. The comfort he offered was nowhere near what she'd get from Blaser's arms. Now knowing what her brother was capable of, she didn't want him to ever be in the same space as Blaser again.

In her living room, in Marshall's arms, she tried to calm herself. The point wasn't to get emotional; it was to ensure her brother couldn't harm anyone again. Unfortunately, that meant taking his freedom.

"God, Bri, quit your bawling for chrissakes," Gary said. "I get it, you're not into it. You don't have to be, I take care of our business."

"She's upset," Marshall said. "You're talking about killing a guy. Why the fuck would you do that with your sister in the room?"

"She needs to know I can do it. I can look after her when we're away from here. I'm the only guy she'll ever need in her life. When we get to Mexico—"

"You're not going to Mexico," Marshall said, still holding her in his arms.

Her body stiffened when he spoke.

Gary's prolonged silence increased her stress level. "What the fuck you talking about, man?" he said, following it with an awkward grunt of a laugh. "We're leaving now, today, getting the fuck outta dodge."

"We're not," Marshall said, flipping her around to pull her back against his chest, exposing her to Gary in the kitchen.

"What's…?"

Her question died on her lips when she heard the hammer of a gun, then felt metal tangle in her hair.

"What the fuck!" Gary hollered and started to come toward them.

Marshall shook his head, his stubble dragged in her hair. "Stay there!" he said. "I'll put a bullet in her, I swear I will."

"You won't fucking dare, you bastard! You hurt her

and I'll—"

"I'm not gonna hurt her, not if you do what I tell you."

"You fucking asshole! What the fuck is this! You're a bastard! I swear to fucking God…"

Gary's rant went on and on, he began to pace then put his fist through the drywall. Losing it, caught in his own ego, he wasn't going to be rational enough to help her. There she was, being held hostage by one of Gary's oldest friends.

"Is this because of Rafe?" she asked, trying to help herself while Gary fumed.

"Rafe? No, who gives a fuck about his shit? This is because of your boyfriend."

"Blaser?" she asked, trying to fathom how Marshall would be connected to her love.

"My boss wants your boyfriend out of jail. If your brother fucks off out the country, that's not gonna happen, is it?"

"Your boss?" Gary screamed. "You're my boy! How the fuck could you go Judas on my ass! You fucking mother fucking—"

"Blaser won't go to jail," she said.

Talking kept Marshall from shooting, but there was one other way she could get help. The cops would be on their way but wouldn't get there in time. Lifting her foot, she pushed back in a deliberate stumble, except when she brought her foot back onto the rug, she slammed it down. Stamping on the floor, she prayed Blaser was in his apartment.

"Yeah, he will," Marshall said. "The cops turned over his place last night. Gary's gun was there, the gun that killed Rafe, Blaser will go down unless your brother turns himself in."

Gary sent out another stream of curses, giving her the cover to stamp again.

Wriggling in Marshall's arms, she tried to get free. "You want him to turn himself in," she said.

His arm around her shoulders kept her pinned to his torso and with the gun so embedded in her locks, she didn't want to take the risk of startling him. Using their argument as cover, she stamped again, closing her eyes to send out psychic messages to Blaser.

Just as hope he was home began to dwindle, the door burst open. Marshall spun toward it and there was Ruger aiming his own gun. She didn't know he was in town, or that he had a gun. His height made him seem almost superhuman, he filled her doorframe, silhouetted by the gleam of dazzling daylight emanating from behind him.

"Let her go," Ruger demanded, both hands on the pistol he aimed at Marshall... well, her too.

"I'm helping you," Marshall insisted. "We get Gary to turn himself in and your brother won't—"

"Let Bri go, and I don't give a fuck what you boys do to each other," Ruger said. "Let her walk."

"I can't," Marshall spat out. "I have to get Gary back where he belongs. Getting him out was a mistake, he's fucked up royally and we can't let Blaser take the fall."

"He won't," Colt said, coming up behind Ruger. Inching his little brother forward, he edged around him, staying out of the line of fire. "We'll get him a lawyer, a good one, and we all know the truth. We know he didn't do anything wrong. You better put that gun down before Blaser gets up here or he will be going to jail for murder: yours."

"Bri!"

Blaser! He barged through his brothers without thought for where the guns were or the danger he was walking into.

"Put the fucking gun down, Marshall or I'll rip your fucking lungs out."

"It's Gary! We need to get him to confess to the cops," Marshall said. "We need to, or you'll be charged!"

"Protecting me," Blaser snarled. "Sweet, but unnecessary. I doubt your motives are noble."

She hadn't seen Blaser so angry, his raw, primal rage was visceral. His clenched jaw and tapered eyes were focused on one thing, the man holding her hostage.

"Blase," she sobbed out. "Blase, I'm sorry, I love you."

His vision shifted around the room in a swift,

calculated assessment of the situation. Two long strides later, he landed a punch on Gary that sent him to the floor. While her brother was dazed, Blaser rolled him onto his front. Colt appeared and the two Warners tied him up with a length of electrical wire.

Gary was swearing again. Of course. That didn't slow the twins, they shared a look before her love got up, leaving Colt to hold Gary down.

Ruger hadn't let his gun waver from Marshall. "There, you got what you wanted," he said. "Put the gun away and let her go."

Marshall hesitated. As much as she wanted to be free, she couldn't blame him for being reluctant in the face of this rage around him. The three Warners weren't a force anyone would want to mess with.

"I… I was trying to help you out," Marshall said.

"Help me?" Blaser asked, coming closer.

Blaser snatched Marshall's gun hand and twisted his wrist back until the gun fell away. Marshall hadn't put up any fight or made any more threats. He had to know that the game was over. But she didn't care, she fell into Blaser and as she sobbed, he stroked her hair and turned her away from Marshall.

Someone threw a punch and a body fell to the ground, she peeked to see Ruger at their side and Marshall on the floor. "He thinks he can help you by threatening a Warner?" Ruger said to Blaser. "Wish we had some time to teach him a lesson."

Sirens wailed into the parking lot, but Hoburn was already up and in the doorway with what she assumed was his surveillance crew behind him. His gun was out, but overdue. The threat had been dealt with. Colt still sat on Gary and Ruger got ahold of Marshall to haul him to his feet.

"Plenty of trash for you to pick up today," Ruger said, handing Marshall over to Hoburn's men who pinned him to the wall and patted him down before cuffing him.

"How did you get here so fast?" Blaser asked him. "How could you possibly have known that—"

"We're just that good," Hoburn said. "We know

where the party is."

"Bri!"

She twisted out of Blaser's arms to see her brother, freed from the makeshift restraints to be cuffed by police. He kept calling for her, but her mouth was sealed. She couldn't reassure him because his confession was on tape. It had been heard by Hoburn and his men. Everything had. She was grateful Hoburn didn't advertise her compliance. Gary would find out she had betrayed him, there was no way to conceal it. But she would at least like the chance to tell him herself, in private.

Her apartment was swarming with cops. It would take time for everyone to give their statements; though it was all on tape so there was no way to spin what had gone down. What the hell just happened? Marshall…? Who was his boss? Where had that come from?

THIRTY-SIX

ALL THE TENANTS loitered around outside still gawking as the cops pulled out of the parking lot. Anyone who'd heard anything gave a statement. Risqué should have been open by now, but Blaser hadn't brought it up. The three brothers and Dax were together at the bottom of the stairs talking while everyone else shared their experiences with each other. Bri was slightly away from that group unable to focus on another intense discussion.

"Are you okay?" Ivy asked, coming over.

Bri sighed. "Yeah," she said. "I mean I'll have to talk to Gary, and he might never forgive me for…"

"You let the cops into your place?"

"He wanted me to leave with him," Bri said. "He thought we could have a new life in Mexico, but Blaser would have been blamed for Rafe's murder. I could never have lived with myself if I knew the truth and an innocent man was convicted."

"Especially since that man is your lover," Ivy said.

"Yeah," Bri exhaled.

The last cops left, and people began to drift back inside. With the drama over, it was time to get to work, which anyone present would be late for by now.

A long shining limo swung into the parking lot and stopped. Those still around froze and after a beat, swung back to gawk again. Such a glamorous car wasn't the norm, everyone wanted to see who would exit. All except the group of four men still huddled behind her and Ivy, ensconced in their discussion.

The driver got out to go to the back of the car and open the door. Several seconds passed before anyone emerged. The man must like to make an entrance, he got out and stood tall. Wearing wraparound shades and a tailored suit, he was just as out of place as the car.

Whispers started again. The man scanned the gang of people staring back. If no one recognized him, why was he there? Lost? Car trouble?

Ivy's frozen form barely moved as her arm swept around to fumble for Dax. When her palm came into contact with his abs, she patted him, without taking her eyes from the man next to the limo.

"Who is that?" Bri asked.

From the way Ivy fixated on her husband, she wasn't sure her friend heard the question.

Dax stared at the stranger. All signs of emotion left his expression to be gripped by solemn resignation. That tell vanished too, his eyes cooled, and his form became solid.

Ivy's hand brushed his, but Dax didn't acknowledge it. He moved through the two women with the suited man in his sights.

"Who is that?" Bri asked again.

"That…" Ivy said, watching her husband traverse the parking lot. "Is his brother."

"Doll?"

Dax's brother left Bri's thoughts when Blaser called on her. With an arm around her shoulder, he guided her to him.

"Where are we going?" she asked.

"Inside."

By the time they got inside, Colt and Ruger were already there. Blaser closed the door behind them.

"Thank you," she said to the men. "For upstairs and… everything."

"You talked to Hoburn last night," Colt said.

Given his connection to the cops, it was no surprise he knew what happened.

"Yes," she said. "I told Blase, I made a deal with them. After I left the club, I went to Gary's, he told me what happened with Rafe. The murder weapon was here… he left it here. I wouldn't let Blaser go down for a murder he didn't commit. So I went to Hoburn and told him everything. Gary thought I was going on the run with him, he was coming here to pick me up. Except Hoburn came to my place this morning with his guys to set up recording equipment. Everything that happened was caught on tape. Gary doesn't know, I'll have to… I'll have to talk to him… if he'll see me."

Blaser guided her to the couch and sat down with her as Colt retrieved beer from the fridge. Before he could hand it out, the front door opened.

Mattie came in with complete entitlement, he did own the building. "That is not how I expected that to go down."

His network was astounding. How could he know what happened already?

"How do you know about it?" Ruger asked.

"Who do you think Marshall was working for?" Mattie asked, swinging the door closed.

"You told him to threaten Bri?" Blaser snarled.

Blaser shifted to get up, but she put a hand on his thigh to stall him. "I appreciate you protecting Blaser," Bri said. "How long has Marshall been working for you?"

"I paid him to keep an eye on you," Mattie said. "He bribed Rafe's man to keep me in the loop too. How do you think I knew how much cash you were handing to Rafe?"

"Is that why they were together at the fight night?" Blaser asked.

Mattie nodded. "I'm sorry this played out like it did, Bri," he said. "Marshall's instruction was to get Gary's confession to the cops, to force him to hand himself in. I couldn't let him leave the country or have Blaser in jail for Rafe's murder."

"Why show up now?" Colt asked. "What do you want?"

"Blaser and I have business to discuss," he said, pinning him with a stare. "Should we take a walk?"

"No," Blaser said. Bri's hand slid from his leg as he rose to his feet. "I'm not keeping secrets from Bri or my brothers, you can take your offer and shove it. My club is legit and it's going to stay that way. Coming home to Bri every night is what I care about. I never want her worrying about living without me again. The best way to support her and look after her is to be here for her."

"Are you sure?" Mattie asked. "I've proven I can take care of misunderstandings."

Getting Gary in jail and saving Blaser's ass wasn't Marshall's idea, it was Mattie's way of tempting Blaser into working for him.

Mattie Warner couldn't understand the strength of loyalty that Blaser showed for her. She understood that Mattie was in the highest echelons of organized crime now. Being away for all these years, she hadn't comprehended just how the pieces had shifted on the board. Mattie ran the town, nothing happened in criminal circles that Mattie didn't know about or have some influence over. But he couldn't influence this, he couldn't break the bond between those in love or between steadfast brothers.

"Thank you for the offer," she said, leaving the couch and tucking herself in at Blaser's side. "But I think we'll be staying straight, all of us."

Mattie observed their group, as unamused as he appeared, he eventually sighed and turned to leave.

Only after the door clicked shut did the rest of them relax.

"It always goes to shit when I leave you guys watching the shop," Ruger said.

Now that Mattie and Gary were dealt with, the subject changed.

Blaser whipped around to glare at his brother. "I haven't heard you apologize to Bri yet."

"Hey," she said, stepping in front of Blaser. "Ruger

wasn't to blame. How many times do I have to say it?" Bringing her attention to Ruger, she bolstered herself to look him in the eye. "I suppose Blaser told you everything."

"Bri, I am so sorry," he said. Traversing to her, he lifted her hand from her side. "I had no idea that… I should've realized Victor wouldn't let it go… I didn't know about what happened to you until Colt told me and—"

"I know, it's okay. You did the right thing walking away from that gang. I'm proud of you for doing that. Today I've seen how sometimes it is hard to do the right thing, but that doesn't make it any less necessary. The only thing you could've done to help me was go back to help the traffickers complete their work. How many other women would've been tortured if you'd done that? And none of them were trustworthy, once they had me, I don't believe they would've let me go."

"Can you forgive me?"

"I have," she said, managing a smile. "We're going to be family, right?"

Blaser slid an arm around her.

Colt came over to join their group. "That doesn't mean it's over," he said. "Ruger's trying to get in touch with the cop who saved you. We're going to find a way to repay what he did for you."

"Jansen," she breathed, remembering the night he'd saved her and the other women from their fate.

"If any of the fuckers are still alive," Ruger said. "I'll find out."

"I don't want more bloodshed because of me, and I don't want you getting yourself into more trouble," she said, pinching his arm.

"You want me to… to give it up?" Ruger asked.

"Sounds like a good idea to me," Colt said.

"We should at least thank Jansen," Blaser said. "I'd like to meet the guy who saved my future."

"You did that yourself," she said, turning her body to his when he encircled her in his arms. "You don't have to take risks to keep me happy. The status quo is sexy. Speaking of which, shouldn't you be at work?"

"Work can wait," he said, bringing his mouth down to hers.

The sweet taste of his tongue had never been so potent. All she wanted to do was be swept into the moment of them safe and together. When she heard a door close, she broke the kiss, expecting to see a new visitor. Instead, they were alone.

"Where did they go?"

"Away," Blaser said. Linking their fingers, he led her through to the bedroom and began undressing her. "The drama is over, it's just us now. I want to show you how thankful I am for that and what you did today with Gary. It couldn't have been easy to make the decision."

"It was much easier than I thought," she said, pulling his tee-shirt off over his head. "Being where he is now is the best thing for Gary. Out in the world he would've hurt more people, which would only have made things worse for him… And seeing him with drugs…"

"I'm sorry," he said, rubbing her bare arms. "I'm sorry that he broke the promise you made to each other."

"You'll never do that, will you?" she asked. "You promised me you were going to be good from now on, will you stay clean?"

"In every sense but one," he said, shoving his jeans down to the floor.

Grabbing her hips, he lifted her up and threw her onto the bed. She was still laughing when he landed above her.

His deep kiss filled her with an arousal that definitely wasn't funny. "Help me forget," she said. "When I'm with you, all I want to think about is the future."

"And it's a future I don't plan to risk."
Curving a hand to the back of her head, he cradled her skull and brought their mouths together again.

TO BE CONTINUED...

Thank you for reading this tale!
If you can, please take the time to review.

~

Ask your local library for more Scarlett Finn
novels!

~

For all things Scarlett Finn
check out:

www.scarlettfinn.com